❑

"Marshall's novels feature seemingly supernatural events that turn out to have logical, if not precisely rational, origins. He has savage fun with police procedure."

—*TIME*

❑

"Among the best police procedural series on the market."

—*Detroit Free Press*

❑

"Nobody rivals Marshall's ability to expose the links between comic hysteria and the most mundane human foibles, from greed to cowardice to simple funk. It's great to see him still crazy after all these years."

—*Kirkus Reviews* (starred review)

❑

"An audacious mixing of near-slapstick comedy with mass murder, realism with pulp-style fantasy ... wholly original and utterly addictive."

—*20th Century Crime & Mystery Writers*

❑

"Outrageously imaginative. . . . Marshall's breathless, twisted tale teeters between madness and melodrama and leaves the reader tottering as if he's just stepped out of a roller-coaster car."

—*Alfred Hitchcock's Mystery Magazine*

❑

INCHES

WILLIAM MARSHALL

THE MYSTERIOUS PRESS

Published by Warner Books

A Time Warner Company

MYSTERIOUS PRESS EDITION

Copyright © 1994 by William Marshall
All rights reserved.

Cover design by Diane Luger
Cover illustration by John Patrick

The Mysterious Press name and logo are registered trademarks of Warner Books, Inc.

 Mysterious Press books are published by
Warner Books, Inc.
1271 Avenue of the Americas
New York, NY 10020

W A Time Warner Company

Printed in the United States of America

Originally published in hardcover by The Mysterious Press.
First Printed in Paperback: August, 1995
10 9 8 7 6 5 4 3 2 1

This one is for Hilary and Ian Knights

The Hong Bay district of Hong Kong is fictitious, as are the people who, for one reason or another, inhabit it.

An inch ahead, all is darkness . . .
The Kan-ying-p'ien
(The Book of Rewards and Punishments)

INCHES

HIGH-RISK ENTRY

In only his second time out with a rapid-response team, Inspector James Arthur Winter had shown himself to be just the sort of material the Police Emergency Unit was looking for by staying cool on the fifth floor of a darkened apartment building as a suspected armed perp ran towards him and waiting until the absolute last minute before deciding whether to open fire with his shotgun.

The armed perp turned out to be a seven-year-old deaf girl who had not heard any of the warnings in English and Chinese to stop from all the other members of the team, and Winter, holding his fire until the last moment, had gathered her up, instantly earned a reputation for coolness and professionalism, won a gallantry medal, and, at twenty-three, the youngest ever in the history of the Hong Kong Police Department or probably anywhere in the world, been given the command of an Emergency Unit rapid-response team of his own.

What no one knew, and he did not have the courage to say, was that he had forgotten to shuck a live round into the breech of his pump-action Ithaca Deerslayer shotgun, and when he pulled the trigger on the girl, first as a shadow at the top of the stairs, then again halfway down the stairs, and then for a third time when he had even seen who it was, nothing

1

happened and he had dropped his gun and only gathered her up by accident as she crashed into him as he turned to flee in terror.

Now, it was all happening again.

Hunched down beside Sergeant Tack outside the closed and curtained Asia–America–Hong Kong Bank against the railing of the third floor of the Lotus Flower Shopping Mall on Wyang Street, Winter asked, wanting an answer quickly, "Well, what's happening in there? Is there anyone in there or not?"

It was a little after eight o'clock at night—the busiest time for the mall. Sergeant Tack, bent down over his radio with a look of concentration on his face, said, starting to sound desperate, "I don't know! I can't tell!"

There was sound everywhere. In the earphones he held pressed hard against his ears with both hands there was the sound of buzzing from all of the thousands of fluorescent lights on all of the eight circular galleries of the place, the hissing and whirring of hundreds of air-conditioning units, the sound of the six automatic escalators going up and down continuously in the central atrium of the place, and, from where the uniformed police had evacuated them to the first floor and packed them in like sardines, all the sounds and movement and motion of thousands of people, talking, shuffling, waiting to see what was going to happen.

He had an electronic-surveillance line plugged up against the center window of the bank with an eighty-percent extraneous-sound dampener rubber suction cup, but it damped out nothing and all he could hear were the sounds from the mall. Hunkered down with Winter against the railing, Tack said, shaking his head to tell the man it was no good, "I can't tell if there's anyone in there or not!" He reached down to the radio and tightened the surveillance-line connection and then turned the volume in his headphones up full to make sure, "I can't make out anything over all that background sound!"

"Try again." The rapid-response team four-man frontal-assault squad was in position at the main door of the place, dressed for maximum first-sight shock value in black, military-style coveralls and hoods and gas masks that covered their faces. They had their pistols out, held muzzle-up and ready, and—in a quick-grasp supply line—their military-style carry bags of explosives and backup gear: stun grenades, tear-gas guns and cannisters, night-vision goggles, handcuffs, lines, grapples, and emergency first-aid equipment. Winter said, "Try again. Take your time and—"

He heard something. Tack said suddenly, "Intermittent voices! At least two! Two voices! Intermittent speech!"

"Hostages or perps?" The frontal-assault team had a shaped charge wired up to the main door, ready to blast it down the moment he gave the command. Winter asked, "Can you ID them?"

"And clickings! Intermittent clickings." He shook his head to try to clear them away, but his ears were full of the noises of the machines and the lights and the whirring of the air conditioners. Tack said, "I can't even hear the voices anymore! There's too much background!"

"All right." Winter stood up. Dressed like all the others in black with his fifteen-shot Sig-Sauer nine-millimeter automatic in a low open-top special-forces holster on his hip, micro radios and command microphones held onto his uniform by Velcro bindings, he towered over Tack like a study in sudden death. He had a voice-activated microcassette tape recorder clipped inside his top pocket with a wire running to a microphone attached to his right-hand collar and then back again to the command microphone on his uniform, and Winter said into it, not only for the frontal-assault team fifteen feet away from him at the door and the telephone-negotiating team three floors below in the security office, but also for the taped record of the incident, "Situation still unclear. All teams: hold your positions."

He heard instantly back on his radio in response: "Frontal-assault team copies *hold position,* and from the telephone-negotiating team downstairs: "Negotiating team copies *hold position,*" and it calmed him. It gave him time to think. Squatting back down again next to Tack, Winter said, to review the situation, "Okay. Intermittent voice contact. Possibly two. Intermittent clickings. But so far, no indication of gunshots or threats. Right?"

"No, nothing!"

"Good." He patted him on the shoulder with his gloved

hand and leant in to him to hold his eyes for a moment. Winter said, "Okay. There's no hurry. Everyone's holding their positions and there's no immediate threat, so what we'll do is take it from the top again to give you more time to listen." Winter said, trying to be intimate, "It's going to have to be your call. It's up to you to try to make out what's happening in there and then give me your best evaluation so I can decide what sort of action to take." He managed a cheerless grin, "But so far we haven't heard any gunfire—that's right, isn't it?"

Tack said, "That's right!"

"—or any demands or—"

Tack said eagerly, "No. Nothing."

"Okay. Take it easy now and just listen." He touched at the microphone on his collar, "All teams: we're going down again from the top. Telephone-negotiating team?"

He heard on his radio, "Telephone team ready."

"Stand by to attempt contact following situation review." He was talking, from the angle of his head, not so much into the radio link, but into the steadily turning tape in the microrecorder. Winter said for all three teams to hear, "By the book. One: *secure location.*" It was secured. With his eyes closed, concentrating on it, he nodded. Winter said, "Location secured. Gallery cleared. Frontal-entry team in position with charges set. Telephone-negotiating team in position—."

In his earphones, Tack could hear nothing. He could hear only Winter's voice next to him. From inside the curtained bank on the third-floor gallery, he could hear no sound at all.

Winter said, "Time: twenty-thirteen hours."

The manual that laid out the steps for a high-risk entry read at the top of every page in big capital letters, CHECK THESE STEPS! EVEN IF YOU THINK YOU KNOW THEM BY HEART, CHECK THESE STEPS! YOUR OVERCONFIDENCE COULD COST A LIFE! CHECK THESE STEPS!

Steps, after securing location:

1. *Ascertain exact situation.*

Winter said in a voice that sounded so close Tack pressed the earphone harder against his head to drown it out or bring it up—he didn't know which, "Possible hostage situation on bank premises. Alert reported by private security company when vault and alarm systems not shown activated by closing time on their monitoring board and staff failed to respond to attempted telephone contact. Bank appearance from the outside normal. Bank appears locked and secured. Preliminary attempted contact by telephone team with staff also unsuccessful. Unidentified voices and sounds heard inside bank by Electronic Surveillance. Electronic Surveillance continuing to listen."

Because he had forgotten to chamber a round into the breech of the shotgun the weapon had stayed uncocked, and when he had pulled the trigger on the little deaf girl three times, one after the other, there hadn't even been a click to give him away, and he was a hero.

When he had originally volunteered for the Emergency Unit, he had thought that all he would have to do was follow orders.

2. *Locate owner or landlord or lessee of premises.*

Winter, his voice hard and tight, desperate for orders to follow now, said into the tape recorder, "Premises are the Hong Bay Lotus Flower Mall premises of the Asia–America–Hong Kong Bank. Corporate ownership. No individual owner or landlord or lessee available."

3. *Get key or other nondestructive means of entry.*

Winter said into the microphone, "High-security premises. No key in possession of mall staff or cleaners. Sole key in possession of bank manager. Security company and local police advise that manager has not returned home. Other staff, where names are known, have not returned home."

Tack said suddenly—not even listening for it, but suddenly hearing it—"Voices! Two!"

It was working. All he needed was a plan, orders to follow. Winter, not stopping, not even looking down at the man, said, unflappably growing in confidence, "Now running final operational checklist." He glanced at his watch. "Time now: twenty-eighteen hours."

Tack said in a rush, "Intermittent voice contact! At least two! One calm and authorative, the other nervous and high-pitched!" He heard them, felt them through the line running from his earphones to the black heavy-duty suction cap on the shutter, "Cantonese speakers! Two!"

"Continuing steps checklist: previous attempt at telephone contact with interior unsuccessful. No visual contact. Sounds of intermittent Chinese-language conversations taking place. No judgement available on emotional state of speakers. May or may not evince state of alarm. Intermittent clicking sounds reported." He knew the figure from the security company, "Number of innocent personnel possibly at risk, nine. Number of possible perps—unknown."

Tack said in a rush, "Female voice! Cantonese speaker! Saying"—he translated the words into English without pausing, " '*Depends . . .*' I've lost it again! '*Desperate.*' '*. . . anxious.*' I'm only getting the higher register words: . . . '*anxiety—*' " Tack said, "A clicking sound!"

4. *Identify, if possible, types and firepower of hostile weaponry.*

Winter said with his eyes closed, "Not known."

Tack said suddenly, straining to hear, "Now something—a sound! The sound of a door closing!"

5. *Institute immediate voice, bullhorn, or telephone contact to defuse any immediate risk of panic reaction from perps. Get perps' short-term demands and ascertain number of perps and location inside premises and transfer to premises' master layout plan.*

There was no master layout plan of the premises. When they went in, they were going to go in blind. Winter, tapping Tack on the shoulder and motioning for him to take one of his earphones off so he could hear him, said tightly, "What I'm going to do is try to make contact with the bullhorn. I'm going to tell them to pick up one of the telephones in there so the negotiating team downstairs can talk to them. I'm going to tell them that if they don't know how to work the telephones, to get one of the bank staff in there to show them. I'm going to speak first in Cantonese and then in English with long gaps between the words so you'll have time to hear if there's any sort of reaction, and, if there is, what sort of reaction it is. If anyone picks up the phone, the telephone team will begin negotiating with them by phone and we'll transfer the entire incident command to them and wait for their judgement call as to whether we have to go in. If no one picks up, I want you to try to work out from any movements where the people in the bank are. I want you to see if you can ascertain a single location where there might be a group of people gathered. Okay?"

"Yes, sir."

"Is your equipment still working?"

"Yes, sir."

6. *Finally, apprise all members of teams involved in your plan of the specific details of your plan and verify that they understand them and are capable of executing them.*

Winter said into the microphone, "All teams acknowledge that you copied plan of operation."

Touching at the metal detonator pencil stuck in the center of the shaped charge of Semtex fixed to the front door, the lead man at the head of the frontal-assault team gave Winter a thumbs-up. He bent down to his collar microphone, "Frontal-assault team—acknowledged."

On the radio, the lead negotiator of the telephone-negotiating team said tightly and efficiently, "Telephone team acknowledges."

Winter said, more to himself than to the radio links, "Acknowledgements copied." He nodded to himself. Under his black coveralls, he wore a bulletproof vest. He tapped at it with his knuckles to check whether it was still there. Winter, taking a bullhorn from the materiel bag next to Tack's radio and carrying it over behind the last man on the assault team at the door, said deafeningly in Chinese as he tapped at his microphone three times to start the telephone team downstairs calling all the numbers listed for the bank in series, "You in there! This is Senior Inspector Winter of the Hong Kong Police Emergency Response Unit! All we want to do is talk to you! You are in no immediate danger and there is no need for you to react to any threat from us! All we want to do at this stage is talk!"

He glanced across to Tack and saw him nod and shake an imaginary telephone receiver with his fist to show that in the bank all the phones were buzzing with calls, "We only wish to talk to you by telephone. Answer any of the telephones you can hear ringing in the bank by lifting the receiver and then pressing the appropriate button beside the flashing light. If you do not know which button to press, ask one of the bank staff to show you. I will take no action against you while you do this. I will wait five minutes while you decide calmly and clearly in your own best interests to pick up one of the phones and talk."

He lowered the bullhorn for a moment and glanced down at his watch. Winter said through the bullhorn, "It is now 8:21 P.M. I will allow the phones to ring for exactly five minutes while you decide."

He glanced over at Tack and saw the man hunched down on his knees with his hands clasped hard against his earphones with a look of concentration on his face.

Drawing a breath, Winter repeated the message in English.

Winter said through the bullhorn, calmly and unhurriedly, just the way the manuals said to do it, first in Cantonese and then in English, "The phones will continue to ring for another four and a half minutes."

In his earphones, above the ringing of the phones, all Tack could hear was the humming of the air conditioners and the sound of the elevators and escalators. Bent down, pressing the earphones as hard against his ears as he could, he heard only—

He heard a click.

Then he heard a woman's voice say in Cantonese, "Who would have—"

Then he heard a door close.

Then another click.

He heard everywhere in his ears, in his head, hummings, buzzings—background noise.

Winter said through the bullhorn, first in Cantonese and then in English, "The telephones will continue to ring for another four minutes. Pick up any one of them and we can work this all out together."

Inside the bank, there was no audible movement at all. All Tack could hear from in there through his headphones was the ringing of the phones with no audible movement towards them at all.

He listened, but he could hear nothing.

Winter said through the bullhorn, much sooner than Tack would have thought, "Three and a half minutes—!"

He heard nothing.

Then, suddenly, abruptly, he heard a single click.

Then he heard nothing.

Then, suddenly, he heard the woman's voice again. He heard her say, *"Who would have thought—"* He heard her say it for the second time, surprised.

He turned and saw Winter watching him, waiting.

Winter said through the bullhorn, "Three minutes! Pick up one of the telephones and talk to us!"

He heard a click.

He heard the woman's voice say again in Cantonese with her voice not terrified but only surprised, *"Who would have thought—?"* and on his knees, hunched down, Tack screamed inside his head, "What are you saying? Who are you? *What are you saying?*"

He saw Winter look hard at him, waiting.

"Nothing!" On his knees, straining to hear, Tack, shaking his head, his face tight with the strain, mouthed, "Nothing! *Nothing!*"

With the bullhorn still in his hand, Winter, going forward to the door to check the placement of the Semtex charge to make sure it was ready to go on his command, said nervously to the hooded squad leader holding the firing box ready in his black-gloved hand, "This isn't good, Sergeant." He reached out gingerly to the two-ounce charge of explosive with his gloved hand and put his fingertip on the protruding end of the detonator to make sure it was pushed down deep into the explosive and anchored there. "I don't know how many there are in there, I don't know how many hostages they've got, I don't know what sort of weapons they might be armed with, and I don't know—" He turned to glance hard into the hooded eyes. Winter said, "The electronic-surveillance man, Tack, doesn't seem to be able to get anything solid, and I don't want to go in until we know exactly what might be in there facing us. What do you think yourself?"

The hooded man was ice calm. The hooded man was a fifteen-year veteran of the Emergency Unit named Tan. All he and his team had to do was follow orders. Tan said tonelessly to show he knew who was in charge, "I think whatever you say, Inspector, we'll do."

Winter said with an attempt at a smile, taking in all the hooded faces of the team at once, "Okay. If we have to, we'll give them more time to see what happens." Winter said in a tone that convinced no one, "Just like training, aye, boys? Nothing to it."

He tried to swallow, but could not.

He touched his bulletproof vest under his coveralls to check whether it was still there and hoped that they did not notice.

He heard it. It was a man's voice. *"We are at the end of—"*

Tack, snapping his fingers hard to get Winter's attention at the door, mouthed, *"Voice!"*

"—we cannot survive!"

Tack said quickly into his tactical collar microphone to everyone on the net, "Man's voice! Cantonese speaker! Distressed!" He heard another sound. "A clicking! A long click!" He saw Winter make a movement in the air of cocking a bolt on a submachine gun. He saw him mouth word, *"Weapon?"* and Tack, shaking his head, said into the microphone, not just to Winter, but to all of them, at the door and downstairs on the phones, "I don't know! Just a single click! I don't know what it is!" He heard another sound. Tack said, "Now the woman again—!"

Winter, with Tack not thirty feet away, said with his head bent down to his collar microphone as if he was out of sight three floors away, "Panicking?"

"Yes!" Tack pressed the earphones so hard against his head he had to shut his eyes with the pain, "She says—in Cantonese, 'We are— We are full of anxiety—desperate!' " Tack said, "She says—now there's a man's voice! The man says—" Tack said, "A click! Now the woman again, but I can't—" Tack said desperately, "Now nothing! No sound at all except for the phones—nothing!"

At the door, Winter said in a whisper to the assault team leader, "Tan, what do you think?"

He was ice calm. Tan said evenly, shaking his head, "I

don't know." He had heard what Winter had done in the apartment building on only his second time out with the unit and, compared to a man like him, his own opinion didn't count.

Tan, glancing only at the charge on the door to check whether it was still in place, said with no other comment to offer, "Whatever you say, Mr. Winter, we'll do."

Winter's hands under his black gloves were wet with perspiration, and he could not stop sweating.

"Who would have thought—?"

Tack said, "The woman again!" Bent down almost double on the floor to shut out everything except her voice, Tack said in a prayer to whoever it was he could hear, *"Say something more! Tell me where you are in there!"*

At the door, Winter pressed his hands hard together to wipe away the sweat with the inside of the gloves, but the gloves also were wringing wet.

He was twenty-three years old, a proven hero.

4. *Identify, if possible, types and firepower of hostile weaponry.*

Winter said in desperation, "I don't know who's in there! I don't know if they're armed or not!"

He heard it in his earphones. He heard the sound of a scream. Tack shrieked across the gallery, "A scream! The sound of a scream!" It was the woman. He heard her shriek, *"Aiiiya!"*

Tan glanced at his watch. With his hand ready on the firing button for the explosive, his team behind him coiled and ready to go with Winter ahead of them in the lead, Tan said urgently, "Well, Boss, go or not? What do we do?"

At his radio across the gallery, Tack yelled, "Rapid human movements!" He heard the woman shriek. Tack yelled, "Another scream!"

At the door, Tan demanded, "Senior Inspector, give the order! Tell us what to do!"

He heard it. He heard the woman scream in terror, *"Aiiiya!"* Tack yelled, "The woman's screaming and I hear rapid movements in there and—"

Reaching out and grasping him hard by the shoulder, Tan

yelled into Winter's face, "Senior Inspector! I need a command call! I need a command call now!"

He was a coward. He had been a coward all his life. He had been a coward when he had pulled the trigger of the shotgun on the little girl and then tried to run away, and he was a coward now.

Tan, shaking the man like a dog, yelled, "Give an order! *Give an order!*"

"I can't! I *can't!*" Everyone on the net heard him say it. His hands were shaking out of control, and, squatting down only inches from death and darkness and the unknown, all the strength went suddenly from his legs and he could not stop himself from falling. Winter, reaching out to catch himself and almost dislodging the explosive charge from the door, shrieked, *"No, I can't face it! I can't face it again!"*

From his radio, Tack yelled in a panic, "Rapid human movements! Rapid human movements!"

At the door, wrenching Winter out of the way and hurling him to one side, Tan yelled into his microphone, "I'm taking over command! We're hitting the door for entry now!"

In Tack's earphones there was another scream. He heard the woman shriek again, *"Aaiiiya!"* and then Sergeant Tan, on his feet with his team at the door, yelled, "Firing entry charge now!" and instantaneously there was an explosion at the door that sent splinters of wood and metal of the door blasting and spinning inward, and then the door was off and then Tan roared to his team at the top of his voice, *"Go! Go! Go!"* and everything turned brilliantly white with the instantaneous detonation of flash and stun grenades inside the bank itself.

The woman's voice said in Tack's earphones so loudly he heard every word, *"Who would have thought it would be so easy?"*

The man's voice said in reply to her, *"Our future is now certain!"*

They both said together, *"Thank you Asia–America–Hong Kong Bank!"* and it was a tape. Transfixed, his eyes burning with the smoke pouring out from the blasted-down door of the bank, Tack shrieked at the top of his voice, laughing, almost crying in relief, "It's just a tape! It's just an advertising tape for the bank running over and over on an endless spool! It's just a tape! There's no one in there at all—it's just a *tape!*" He saw Winter picking himself up from the ground like a child with tears running down his face, and Tack, going to him, said, as if he was a child who needed comfort, "It was just a videotape advertising loans from the bank. All it was—the woman saying "Aiiya" was just—the rapid movements were just—it was probably the sound of the—It was just a *tape! There was never anyone in there at all!*"

He saw, through the smoke, the interior of the bank.

He saw, everywhere he looked in there, the bodies of dead people.

He saw everywhere on the floor—in knots, in lines, in rows, with their arms flung out—dead men and women.

He saw inside there, Sergeant Tan and all the members of the assault team standing in a silent circle, staring at them.

He saw, everywhere in the bank, the dead.

He thought the assault team had killed everyone in there with their explosives and grenades. Tack said, beyond comprehending it, "Oh, no—!"

Getting to his feet at the door of the bank, gasping and coughing, Winter, seeing what was in there, yelled, "No! No! *Not again!*" He had no idea what the hell had happened, but he knew who had done it.

At the open, blasted-down door, fighting desperately for air in the swirling thick smoke, wanting to lay the blame fair and square, Winter screamed, "You dirty bastard, Tack! You dirty bastard, you did this! You! You! You're responsible for this! You— *You did this to me!*"

1.

An hour and a half after the assault, Winter's teeth began chattering and he could not control it, even though he clamped his jaw tight with the strength he had in all the muscles of his jaw and neck. It was only on the left side, at the back, but he could not stop it happening and he thought everybody in the bank could hear it.

He had taken off his bulletproof vest, and his black coveralls were open to the chest, but even though the air conditioning in the bank was on he had still not stopped sweating, and he had to keep wiping his forehead with his hand.

In the bank the tape was still running on each of the six twenty-one-inch old-style box television sets set on the counters and walls of the otherwise stark and functional main customer area of the place, playing over and over the thirty-second color film of the ease with which a personal loan could be obtained from the good and avuncular and kind personnel of the Asia–America–Hong Kong Bank, Hong Bay.

Titled in Cantonese, "Lending Hope to Life," it began with two worried, clearly good people—a young married Chinese couple of slightly above coolie status, on the brink of financial despair through the machinations of usurers and their own innocent lack of planning—huddled together in a

14

bank manager's office awaiting news of their application for a loan.

Tearfully, their faces heavy with television makeup, they reviewed their situation:

Husband: We are at the end of our hope! We cannot survive! (*There is a clicking sound as the young man, his eyes full of tears, raps at the surface of the manager's desk with his fingernails.*)

Wife: We are full of anxiety. Everything depends on this loan! (*She is young, no more than twenty or twenty-one, clumsily padded to look pregnant, too pretty even under all the heavy careworn makeup to look like anything but an actress.*)

    ... a pause, and then the office door opens to one side of them and in strides, with a benign but inscrutable smile, a balding, concerned-looking man holding a sheaf of loan-application papers and official-looking documents in his hand ...

    He pauses but a moment, then closes the door behind him and looks down at the poor struggling pair, the wretched and ill-used, but yet to the trained eye of the all-knowing Asia–America–Hong Kong bank, the salt of the earth and hope for the future ...

    With a little smile, he nods. He says a single word. The word is ...

Manager: Hai! Yes!

    The couple emote with a fury not seen since the days of Pola Negri. Hands fly to brows. Long gasps are gasped. The young man throws his hands up to his throat in thanksgiving.

The good wife regains her composure first, but yet with tears of joy still flowing down her cheeks and her hands still clasped in amazement to her breasts not only to the kindly saviour of the manager, but also, through the camera eye, to her husband, her family, her yet-to-be-born children, and to the entire population of the world at large.

Wife: Who would have thought— (She looks heaven-ward.) Who would have thought it could be so simple?

Humbly, happily, a little overcome himself, the manager clears his throat and smiles. Smiling is clearly something he does at least a dozen times a day.

Manager: We are here to help.

Wife: Aaaiiya! (She shrieks again and again in joy and relief.) Aaaiiiya! Aiiya!! Our future is now certain! Thank you, Asia–America–Hong Kong Bank!

All: (with swelling music) Thank you, Asia–America–Hong Kong Bank!

Then *darkness,* then from all the sets on all the counters and walls, a click on the endless spool as, from the top, it all began again—and in the air-conditioned bank Winter, try as he might, could not stop his teeth chattering and had, again, to wipe at his forehead with his hand.

There were nine of them altogether, five men and four women, lying dead in every part of the bank, the men all dressed identically in dark suits and ties and the women in knee-length brown skirts and modest long-sleeved white blouses. In the main customer area there were five of them, three men and two women, together in a knot on the gray-carpeted floor lying on their backs.

They lay dead and unmarked and pristine, like mannequins, with no marks or signs of violence on them at all.

In the corridor leading to the staff washroom behind the counter there were another two men, and, in the washroom itself, two more women lying dead at the foot of the water cooler.

The two women in the washroom both still wore glasses. They were both young, junior bank tellers: they lay like discarded dolls, with their eyes open, staring up at the ceiling with the lenses and silver-metal frames of their glasses shining in the light.

Kneeling in the center of the five dead in the main customer area of the bank, Detective Chief Inspector Harry Feiffer, taking an ID card from the coat pocket of the older man, said for the tape recorder the Government Medical Examiner Dr. Macarthur had running on the floor beside his medical bag, "Body number one: Lee, T. M., male, age fifty-one." The dead man was a slight, pockmarked southern Chinese wearing rimless glasses and a brown sweater under his buttoned-up chain-store brown suit coat. Feiffer said, "Probably the manager." He was no more than five foot two, unremarkable, nothing like the actor's portrayal on the television ad of what an Asia–America–Hong Kong Bank manager should look like at all. "Home address: Western Light Apartments, Causeway Bay, Apartment 8D."

He moved on to the next body, one of the women. Uniformed had collected three brown imitation-leather handbags and a single brocaded shoulder bag from the washroom lockers and laid them all out in a line around the bodies in the front with the ID cards from them placed neatly on top of them. Feiffer, glancing at one of the women near the manager and matching it to the card on one of the bags, said for the record, "Body number two, main customer area: L. S. Chiang, aka Louise Chiang"—it was the Western version of her Chinese given names—"Age twenty-five." He looked at her hand and noted she wore no wedding ring. The Cartier watch she had on her wrist was a copy made in Taiwan and bought for a few dollars at a street stall. "Home address:

Apartment 2, Third Floor, Sun Lai Apartments, Empress of India Street, Hong Bay."

The eyes of the other girl out there were closed as if she was sleeping. She wore the identical bank teller's uniform of brown skirt and long-sleeved white blouse, but she was so unlined and young, lying there unprotected and without female artifice, it looked at if the clothes were too big for her and she was only a child dressed up to look like a woman. She wore a thin gold chain around her neck that, unlike her friend's Cartier watch, was real gold and had probably been a gift. At the end of the chain there was what looked like a tiny gold lucky elephant: it had probably been given to her by her parents to celebrate her graduation from school, or for a special birthday.

Feiffer, matching the ID with the face, said softly, "Body number three: Mary Sun. Age 20. Home address: 2/567 Peking Road." The girl still had baby fat on her face, and her hands, clenched hard into fists, were smooth and pudgy, like a child's.

He was a tall, fairhaired man wearing a slightly stained white suit, a giant bending down to examine the bodies of a race of insignificant, miniature people. The air conditioning was on, hissing chemically pure zephyrs of refreshing cool air everywhere throughout the bank; but, as if he had just run hard and fast, bending down over the dead, Feiffer could not quite catch his breath, and so that the crime scene would not be compromised by the perspiration forming on his brow and neck, he had to keep wiping at his face with the back of his hand.

There were two more dead men near the two dead girls and he looked at their ID cards and read the names: *Wing, L. L., aka Louis Wing, age thirty, 9/87 North Canton Street,* and *Chan, T. W., aka George Chan, twenty-nine, 13/482 Ice House Street.* The others—the two men dead in the corridor to the washroom and the two women in the washroom itself—were *Lin, C. F., aka Henry Lin, age thirty; Mok, M. T., aka Martin Mok, age thirty-one; Fan, J. K., aka Jessie Fan, age twenty-four;* and *Wong, S. L., aka Jennifer Wong, age twenty-five.*

He glanced at his watch. It was a little after ten at night, and behind him, seen through the open door of the bank outside in the mall, all the shoppers and mall staff had been questioned and cleared out and the entire eight stories of the huge place shut down and night darkened. All the elevators and escalators had been turned off and the only people left in all of the enormous place were a few uniformed mall security men moving like ghosts on their rounds and the police crime-scene photographers, fingerprint men, and coronial undertaking staff standing at the top of the frozen escalators waiting for when they were wanted.

The rapid-response team had cleared all their gear from the gallery area immediately outside the blasted door of the bank, and there was only on the wooden gallery floor around the door a ragged line of wood splinters and shards of dully glowing metal from the lock to show they had ever been there at all.

There was no smell of the smoke of the explosive charge they had used to get the door open: the air conditioning had sucked it in, cleaned it, treated it, and then sent it back out again as clean, recycled air.

To assist Macarthur as he bent down to examine her, Feiffer touched the second dead girl on the hand—the girl with baby fat still on her face—to get ready to move her a little to one side.

It was like touching the hand of a child.

There was not a single mark of violence or trauma on any of the bodies anywhere in the bank. They lay, as they had fallen, pristine, buttoned-up, in full, neat bank uniforms and suits, some of them in spectacles, like a collection of dolls in a toy box waiting for their owner to revitalize them.

As Feiffer looked at them there was not one single mark of violence or trauma on any of the bodies—not anywhere.

Behind him, on all the glassed-in counters and walls of the bank, the six television sets with the sound turned down played the tape of the happy couple and their bank manager forging a new life together over and over and over again.

Only Senior Inspector Winter, standing by the counter, continued to watch it as it went around over and over on its endless spool, but bending down over the dead girl, wanting to touch her hand again as Macarthur bent down low to peer into the girl's opened dead eyes through a retinoscope from his bag, Feiffer did not notice him or the look on his face at all.

When Macarthur finally finished with the girl and Feiffer came over to him, Winter, swallowing hard, but determined to answer the question by the book, said in response to Feiffer's inquiry, "It was a standard no-show on vault-lock alarm call from the security company, who then alerted the mall security people, who then came up here and found the bank locked and alerted the local Uniforms who, when they couldn't get entry or raise anyone on the phones or at their home addresses, alerted us. Following standard operating procedure, I then immediately (1) secured the area in case there was a crime in progress, (2) attempted to locate a key holder for the premises or someone with some other form of nonviolent access, and then, (3) when I was unable to ascertain the nature of the situation from the outside or make a nonviolent entry to gain access to the inside, put my team into a low-security containment pattern around the premises, set up a rear-wall diversionary plan in case it became necessary to enter forcibly, and (4) set up an electronic-surveillance line up here to ascertain the nature of the situation inside and a telephone-negotiating team downstairs in case of contact with possible hostage-takers or hostages." He touched, for some reason, at his temple. The tall, drawn-looking man facing him reached inside his coat to offer him a cigarette, but Winter, not a smoker, never having been a smoker, and never intending to be a smoker, shook his head.

Feiffer asked, "What did Electronic Surveillance hear in here?"

"Clickings, and intermittent conversations involving at least two to three persons. My electronic-surveillance officer came to the conclusion that there was at least one conversation going on in here that involved a high degree of emotional stress. Efforts to make contact by telephone and bullhorn with whoever was involved were unsuccessful. So then, according to procedure, the next step was the execution of a high-risk entry by a shooting team through the sole access available—through the front door."

Feiffer said with no tone or judgement, merely following

the progress of events as Winter explained them one by one, "And?"

"And we made entry through the door."

"Once you were in, did you or any member of your team fire any shots in here?"

"No, we did not!"

"Your main charge to gain entry was what—? A heavy concussion explosive wired up directly against the front door?"

"My main and only charge was a shaped entry cutting charge." Technical detail was like orders—something to hang onto. Winter said patronizingly, "If we'd set off a heavy concussion shot against the main door it would have blown half the wall in. The wall's intact. It was just an entry charge to knock the door down and nothing more."

He looked at the man hard and wondered. "What about the stun grenades? Is it possible they could have—?" It was a stupid question. There were two bodies in the corridor a hundred feet away from where the grenades had gone off and two more in a washroom at the end of that corridor, even farther away. "Is it possible the shock could have—?"

"No." He looked away to one of the television sets on the counter endlessly playing the tape, with the sound down, like a silent movie: playing it from the top, endlessly, over and over again. "No, it's not possible." On all the TV sets the tape began playing again and he looked away to see it.

Husband:	We are at the end of our hope! We cannot survive!
Wife:	We are full of anxiety. Everything depends on this loan. *Then:*
Wife:	Who would have thought—who would have thought—? *Then:*
Wife:	Aaaiiya! Thank you Asia–America–Hong Kong—

Feiffer asked, "When you entered the bank with your team—"

Winter said, "I don't know what killed them! I didn't enter the bank until the team had already gone in! They went in prematurely! I don't know what killed all these people! For all I know, they were already dead when we got here!"

"They probably were." He could not understand the man at all. He had heard about the incident in the apartment block on Canton Street—it had been in all the papers—and he had not expected him to be like this. Feiffer said, "Judging by the temperature of the bodies, they could have been dead for several hours before you even got here."

"Well, there you are. I didn't do anything wrong *at all!*"

"I didn't suggest you did." He had met a lot of people, one way or the other, who he thought of as heroes, or brave. He had met people who had been brave in a single instant of violence and terror and triumph, and he had met people who had been brave all their lives merely living out the lives they had been given, but he had never met one before like Winter. Feiffer said, "Okay." He almost reached out to touch the man on the shoulder, but thought in his present state he might suddenly pull away in fear, and did not.

Winter said suddenly, "It was my goddamned electronic-surveillance officer! He made the call too quick! He took it on himself to make the call to go and everyone was so charged up the fucking door was down in one second flat and the entire place was full of stun grenades!" Winter said, "It was the television! It was the fucking television! He couldn't tell the difference between real voices and voices from a fucking television!" He could not stop sweating. He kept moving from one foot to the other. He was twenty-three years old, a proven hero. Winter said, "I was the one in that fucking siege in that apartment building on Canton Street who held his fire and saved the life of some innocent kid! If I'd had my fucking idiot electronic-surveillance man there that day she'd be dead—and then we'd all have been in a lot of trouble! Right?"

Feiffer said soothingly, "I'm just trying to find out what happened in here." He looked hard into the man's eyes, "You've done your job by the book, and now I'm trying to do mine. I'm just trying to find out what it was that killed all these people in here." He held Winter's eyes, looking into them for an answer, "All right?"

We are at the end of our hope!

"Yes!" He nodded. With a look on his face that Feiffer could make no sense of at all, he looked back to the television set on the counter.

We cannot survive! We are full of anxiety. Everything depends on this loan.

Who would have thought—who would have thought—?

Even with the sound off, he knew all the words by heart, but as if he had never seen it before in his life and was riveted by it, Winter turned back to see it, glancing at, first, the screen on the glassed-in counter and then another on the wall and then another and another, to watch the little drama play out over and over again to its conclusion.

Midway through the second running of the tape, making Winter and Feiffer turn, Dr. Macarthur said abruptly as his announcement of the preliminary on-site determination of cause of death, "Asphyxia. The cause of death in every case was the same: asphyxiation brought on by a sudden withdrawal of oxygen to the brain, followed by a mechanically induced chemically progressive oxygen starvation of the entire tissue structure of the body."

He was a hawk-nosed, gaunt man in his early forties wearing a well-used white dust coat with a thirty-pack of French Gauloise Disque Bleu cigarettes and long plastic Briquette lighter sticking out of the torn top pocket.

He waited for a moment. He knew, from someone using nothing more than a retinoscope and what looked like a cursory physical examination, the finding sounded like a piece of pure magic. Macarthur, savoring the looks on Feiffer's and Winter's faces, said in the direction of the tape recorder still running on the floor, "The classical gross sign of asphyxia—a dusky countenance—is marginally noticeable in all of the victims, but of insufficient definition at a preliminary on-site examination to postulate with exclusive certainty. This is due to the southern Chinese complexion and coloring being slightly darker than the European models forensic texts are predicated on. However—" He drew a breath and permitted himself a small acknowledging nod to his own brilliance and glanced down at the dead twenty-year-old girl with the lucky elephant around her neck and the baby fat still on her face, "—However, one of the nine victims examined, a Miss—" He looked at Feiffer.

Feiffer said softly, "Mary Sun."

"Miss Mary Sun, being of considerably lighter skin coloring than the rest, shows this postmortem dusky shading of the skin very clearly." Macarthur said, looking not at her, but at the tape recorder, "I have also examined the pupils of the eyes of this particular victim and, there, the staining that accompanies the dusky skin appearance in cases of death by asphyxiation is markedly present and pronounced."

He thought he was one hell of a forensic pathologist. Macarthur said for the tape, "The discovery of several of the dead in the vicinity of the water cooler in the washroom is also consistent with asphyxia. One of the symptoms of the onset of asphyxiation is a burning sensation in the throat and a desire for water to cool it." He answered Feiffer's question before he even asked it, "Because both of the dead in there are of slightly heavier body weight than the other victims, the asphyxiating agent would have taken more time to penetrate their tissues and they would have had more time to try to get to water before they collapsed." He reached into his pocket and lit up a Gauloise in a fug of acrid blue smoke, "Autopsies will place the time more exactly, but my preliminary examination suggests that death took place in all nine cases approximately four to five hours ago." He looked at his watch, "Between the hours, approximately, of 5:00 to 6:00 P.M. this date."

Macarthur said as the final word on it, "Death was caused in all cases by the oral ingestion of a chemical solution of sufficient toxicity to almost immediately deprive the brain and tissues of oxygen by altering the bodily cellular mechanism and preventing the absorption of oxygen from the blood." He took a puff on his cigarette. Standing a little back from the dead, pudgy, twenty-year-old girl, looking at her not at all, Macarthur said confidently, "The toxic agent used was cyanide. A concentration of potassium cyanide in oral, probably liquid form—*poison.*"

Macarthur said softly, with no tone in his voice at all, "And, judging by the positions of the bodies and the lack of any signs of attempts at resuscitation or aid, probably—*undoubtedly*—all nine of them drank it together at exactly the same moment."

Winter said from behind Feiffer, relieved beyond description, "It was just some sort of suicide thing!" He had survived again. He almost couldn't believe his luck. There would be no inquiry. No one in the Colony, especially not the European cops, ever got a big inquiry started where Chinese religion was involved. Winter said, "So we give the whole thing to some sort of Chinese priest or necromancer or fucking witch-doctor or something and just keep well out of it, and keep our fucking mouths shut about the whole—Isn't that what happens now?" He looked at Feiffer, "Right, Chief Inspector? Isn't that what happens? Just shut up about every little bit of it as if none of it ever happened and just keep the entire stupid story under wraps and just sit on it as one of those Tales from the Exotic East to bore our grandchildren to—to fucking death with—right? Is that right?"

His teeth stopped chattering and suddenly he was no longer sweating, and he had made it. He had made it twice. He looked at Macarthur's face and saw only a tightness as if there was more, but he did not want to hear more. Winter said, going to him and reaching out like a child to pluck him on the shoulder to get his attention, "Isn't that right, Doctor?" Everywhere in the bank there were the dead. Everywhere, in the main room of the bank, in the corridor, in the washroom, they lay young and snuffed out, like discarded mannequins. Winter, moving past Feiffer and then turning to face him, demanded, "That's right, isn't it? They never have an official inquiry into something like this because it's too delicate—*that's right, isn't it?*"

Feiffer said to Macarthur, "Then where are the cups?" He saw in front of him, not Winter, but the poor dead little girl with the lucky elephant chain around her neck. Feiffer said with barely controlled anger in his voice to Macarthur, "Tony, if they drank the poison together and died *then where are the cups?*"

Winter said, "What fucking cups?" He was out of his league. He had been out of his league for a long, long time. Winter, like a small unimportant child suddenly excluded from a conversation between grown-ups, demanded, "What fucking cups? I don't even know what anyone's talking about anymore!"

Macarthur said evenly, "They're in the washroom near the water cooler, washed and dried in a row on the sink."

Feiffer, holding Macarthur's eyes, asked in a voice suddenly as cold as ice, "And how long would it have taken the poison to work, Tony? Approximately?"

"Depending on the dosage—which would seem to have been massive—five to, maybe, at most, forty-five seconds."

Winter said in protest, "I thought you just said we could shelve all of this away forever under the heading of—"

Feiffer roared at the man, "Shut up!" He knew now just what sort of hero Winter was, and for an instant he wanted in the name of all the real heroes he had known over a lifetime to draw his fist back and smash the man to the floor. "Shut up! Just stand there and keep your mouth *shut!*"

Feiffer said tightly to Macarthur, "Someone did this, didn't they? Someone else?"

"Judging by the fact that two of the victims tried to get away to the washroom to save themselves, yes."

"And they were the ones who took the longest to die."

Macarthur said softly, "Yes."

And whoever it was, he had watched them. After he had given the nine of them the poison—five men and four women, one of them little more than a child—whoever had done it had stood a little to one side and watched. There was no staining or spillage anywhere on the carpet of the main area of the bank or on any of the clothes of any of the dead: they had taken their little porcelain tea cups of cyanide and drunk them dry and, like good little boys and girls, not spilled a drop.

Four of them, heavier than the rest or with a slower metabolism, writhing in agony, had tried to crawl away to the washroom for water, and he had watched them too, not interfering with them, knowing they would never make it, following maybe, a few steps behind them all the way down the corridor, until, one by one, the last two women almost making it, finally, all of them were dead.

And then, after it was over, he had collected all the cups, taken them down to the washroom in maybe two trips, and washed and dried them at the sink.

In the main customer area of the bank, and in the corridor, and in the washroom, everywhere there were the dead.

Feiffer said in a whisper, shaking his head at the enormity, at the pure, calculated cruelty of it all, "Jesus Christ! *What sort of person could have done something like this?*"

He felt Winter, like a child, pluck at his sleeve to get his attention to tell him something, and Feiffer, full of a sudden uncomprehending anger, roared at him as an order in the silent, terrible place, "You! I want to know from you, in detail, everything you saw and heard, everything you did, everything that happened here tonight! I want to know everything, in detail, from the moment you got here! *Everything that happened!*"

2.

The Horror! The Horror!

Well, at least, the Revolting Seediness of it all. (People crossed the street to get away from it.)

At first light, after happy, hiding, concealing night had fled, it came down the steps of the Yellowthread Street Police Station and paused for a moment and blinked at the daylight as if it mulled over somewhere inside its maddened mind whether to (a) mosey merrily out into the metropolis, (b) maneuver back into the massive, mansard-roofed monument, or (c) merely melt into a mound of mulch where it stood.

It decided to mosey out into the metropolis. (For eight blocks around, although they were not quite sure why they did it or what had alarmed them, people got onto buses and into cabs to go somewhere else.)

It was horrible.

It was a ragged, bent-over figure wearing a torn and flapping heavy winter topcoat and exploded army boots, carrying a coat hanger in its hand, a big stick of yellow chalk behind its right ear, that, because of the twenty-five feet of half-inch chain it wore wrapped around his entire body under the rags under the coat, clanked as he walked.

It was sad. Once, it had been somebody. Once, it had been

Detective Senior Inspector Christopher Kwan O'Yee, mild-mannered man about town, married man and father of three, person of importance, defender of justice, and altogether an all-round good egg.

And it all wasn't so long ago either. About twenty minutes.

Now, muttering and mumbling as it meandered, what he was was your Average Street Lunatic.

And what did your Average Street Lunatic think about as he mooched miserably down the main throughfare in the direction of Market Lane?

Your Average Street Lunatic thought that somewhere deep in the bowels of Headquarters where all the orders came from *someone was out to get him.*

Your Average Street Lunatic examined that thought to see just how lunatic it was.

It wasn't lunatic at all.

Your Average Street Lunatic, going on apace, because of the irrefutable logic of the first premise, let a second mad thought creep into his mind.

The second mad thought, based on the first, was that in Headquarters, somewhere behind a desk surrounded by a big barricade of filing cabinets and defended by a massive moat of stacked wooden In and Out trays and wire baskets full of files—*with the nameplate on his desk buried in the mess so you could never find out in there who he really was!*—there was someone who hated him.

Yep, that was how your Average Street Lunatic thought.

Or was it?

He asked himself, "Is it?" (A few people still on the street around him either too poor or tardy to have found buses or taxis crossed away from him and began shouting for rickshaws.) He stopped and swung his coat hanger on his hand to think. O'Yee said, "Nah!"

The motion of the coat hanger soothed him. (It didn't soothe one last blind and deaf person tapping along the street with his cane: he felt the motion in the air and ducked as O'Yee went past him.)

O'Yee said, "No, it's ridiculous. It's just paranoid. It's not someone in Headquarters who hates me—— It's just someone too busy with other more important matters to think what effect his orders might have *on a good, decent person who's worked like a dog all his life to make something of himself!"*

Yeah, that was it. Right. He settled on the thought. Who hated him? No one. Everyone loved him.

He nodded happily.

Then why the sealed orders delivered secretly to the station in the middle of the night and left on his desk when there was no one there to see who delivered them and left them on his desk—what about that? And why wasn't the job passed down the normal channels of communication until it reached his boss, Detective Chief Inspector Harry Feiffer, who was a nice person and his best friend and who always smiled comfortingly when he gave you a job that wasn't very nice? O'Yee demanded from the coat hanger in a voice that made the blind man hit the dirt and go crawling away at top speed for the corner like a terrified crab, *"Well?* How do you explain *that?"*

He stopped, didn't notice that by now the entire street was as completely and utterly deserted as if it had been the set in an end-of-the-world movie, and chewed on the end of his coat hanger to think it over.

He chewed out the answer. *Because the case the person in Headquarters who hated him had sent him out on wasn't a normal case. It was undercover.*

Of course.

Right.

Natch.

Of course! So obvious.

Somewhere deep in Headquarters there was another decent, respectable, hardworking family man like himself fighting a desperate rearguard action against all the forces and ignorance and dumbness and criminality in the world and he had picked O'Yee for the job and sent around the orders to do it in the middle of the night when no one saw *because he knew it was too advanced for the average, through-channels, run-of-the-mill cop mind and only he and O'Yee could see the shining beauty and planning and nobly self-effacing importance and cleverness of it all!*

In the street, O'Yee said to himself, "Right!" He thought

that sounded like an extremely convincing thought. (The rider to the extremely convincing thought was that the decent man working away at Headquarters was the secret friend who, over the years, had gotten him all the best jobs right from the start and who, once he made commissioner, was going to reveal himself and make O'Yee chief of detectives.)

That was not a convincing thought. That thought, as thoughts went, was insane.

O'Yee, stopping in the street, shouted to the little shit wherever he was at Headquarters, "No! You can't fool me! I know! *You hate me!*"

The secret orders said he was to dress in rags and various appropriate lunatic accoutrements and act like a mad person.

He was dressed in rags, with a coat hanger in his hand, a stick of yellow chalk behind his ear, and twenty-five feet of half-inch chain wrapped around his body.

The rags had come from the Police Evidence Room at the station. The chain and chalk and coat hanger had been left on his desk in an airline bag together with his sealed orders.

They were very heavy chains.

They hurt like hell.

It was all part of a diabolically clever, brilliant undercover plan to get a spectacular, resounding result.

The only problem, as he clanked and muttered and mumbled to the far end of the street and turned onto Market Lane and cleared it in an instant, was that O'Yee had absolutely no idea on earth what that plan was . . .

Even by the next morning there was still the smell of violent death in the bank and the smells of all the things that attended it. It was the smell of the chemicals and powders Forensic and the fingerprint team had used to dust down the place, the faint burned smell of flashbulbs, and the smell of rubber and plastic from the body bags the coronatorial undertakers had used to take away the dead.

There were the smells of something gone, extinct, no longer living, like the musty, abandoned smells in a museum.

It was a little after 9:00 A.M., the beginning of a new work day, and as Mr. A. S. Mansor, the auditor for the Asia–America–Hong Kong Bank Corporation, dressed in a buttoned-

up blue suit and striped tie, moved through each of the
teller's cages checking the tills and tapping at his calculator
to check the amounts in there, he smelled of shower-fresh
talc and sandalwood after-shave. He was a short, slight Pakistani in his mid-thirties. His thick black hair, as he bent
down to examine the tills and their contents, was plastered
down with some sort of hair oil that had the fragrance of in-
cense about it.

Like all Pakistanis and Indians, he lived for titles and
badges of rank. On his lapel, he had a little plastic card bearing the name of the bank and his own name and title, MR. A.
S. MANSOR, AUDITOR, and the legend, MY AIM IS TO GIVE YOU
EXCELLENT SERVICE.

In the main customer area of the bank, all the television
sets had been turned off, and with the entire third floor of the
mall closed and cordoned off by police crime-scene tapes,
the only sound anywhere as Feiffer watched him work was
the clicking of his calculator.

He had his notebook out. Feiffer asked the man, "Mr.
Mansor, are you the auditor for the bank on a full-time
basis?"

He looked up as if he had been shot. He almost sprang to
attention. When he spoke, he looked Feiffer directly in the
eye and spoke clearly and distinctly so he would understand
every word, "No, sir, Mr. Feiffer"—part of the excellent service was to address each and every customer by name—"I
am employed by the Association of Small Banking Businesses and General Commerce Accountants, 52 Great
Shanghai Street, Suite 2398. That company, which I have the
great fortune and honor to represent in a small capacity, of-
fers complete and full outside auditing services to such banks
as this one." He drew a breath, "The service is very highly
respected. Our audits are accepted without question by all
the banking-control bodies in the Colony and overseas, and
by the government and taxation department for all purposes
of assessment, statement of assets and liabilities, even court
cases and appeals." He drew another breath. He waited to
serve further.

"The reason I ask is that your name was listed on the
bank's last year's balance sheet. And the year before that."

Mr. Mansor said, "Yes, the Asia–America–Hong Kong Bank has been satisfied for several years with my work for them." He touched at his calculator with a manicured fingernail to suggest, with great respect, that it was, perhaps, not an unearned satisfaction. Mr. Mansor said, "It is always my aim to give excellent service. When you make out your report I hope you will mention that."

"Have you any final figures from the vault?" When Mansor had first entered the bank, after the amenities, he had gone straight to the unlocked vault that had first triggered the alarm and spent almost three-quarters of an hour in there clicking away with his calculator checking what was there and what was not.

Mr. Mansor said, "Yes." He wanted to get all the figures for the entire bank together for a final definitive picture, but if a premature answer was what the customer wanted, then a premature answer was what the customer got. Mr. Mansor said with no expression on his face at all, "A thorough examination of the contents of the vault so far reveals all listed currency notes, instruments of exchange, bonds, promissory notes, bank-draft forms, and travellers' checks to be present as well as all other miscellaneous items of value listed in the vault entry and sign-out book." Mr. Mansor said, to explain how he had done it so quickly and thoroughly, "The bank was audited by me only last week. Various items for future use, such as blank cashier's checks counted and sealed by me at that time, are still in the packets I put them in, and still sealed. One package has been opened and three check forms removed and the transactions noted in the check ledger, but the amounts, in total, come to less than one hundred and fifty dollars. The appropriate paperwork for which, no doubt, will be found in one or more of the individual teller's daily transaction record books."

"Is there anything missing from the vault at all? Something you might not have checked?"

"No. Nothing."

"Negotiable instruments of some kind? Bearer bonds, for example, or—"

"No."

"Safety deposit boxes?"

"The bank has none. It is too small."

"Valuables stored as collateral against loans?"

"No. Again, the bank is too small to keep anything in its secure vault area other than its own items of value used in the transaction of its daily business."

"Firearms?"

Mr. Mansor shook his head, then reached into his inside coat pocket and took out a little scrap of paper and inclined his head slightly to apologize for not knowing guns and having to write it down. "In the firearms box, as inventoried, one British Webley and Scott, Mark Four, .38–caliber six-shot revolver with a three-inch barrel." Mr. Mansor said, looking up, not needing anything to remember numbers, "Serial number 897211C. Loaded with six rounds of ammunition, the weapon itself in overall dirty and neglected condition, the ammunition—although I did not attempt to remove it from the chambers, old and heavily corroded."

"What about the tellers' tills?" The smell of the hair oil and talc was starting to get to him and he needed a cigarette. Feiffer asked, "Is there anything missing there—so far as you've got?"

"No. All cash and check balances match, unopened packets of reserve currency are intact, deposit and withdrawal running totals are consistent, foreign bank notes and coins tally with sums paid out in exchange for local currency, drafts and checks are in order, and all petty cash—loose coins and coin rolls—are correct to within an acceptable point of one of one-quarter of one percent margin of error for counter transactions." He was doing it all in his head. The calculator in his hand was only a prop.

"Then what the hell *is* missing?"

"Nothing." Mr. Mansor, holding Feiffer's eyes, said evenly, for the report he hoped would treat him well and land on the desk of his superiors for their approval, "Nothing is missing or unaccounted for. Here, at the Asia–America–Hong Kong Bank, third floor, Lotus Flower Shopping Mall, Hong Bay, everything, following an unannounced spot audit of all transactions, holdings, and records by a representative of the Association of Small Banking Businesses and General Commerce Accountants, 52 Great Shanghai Street, Suite

2398, Hong Bay, everything has been found just, exactly, to the penny, as it should be."

He gave excellent service. His word, with fear or favor to none, was accepted without question by the banking control board, the courts, the government, and by the taxation department.

Mr. Mansor said, "Having now examined the vault and tellers' accounts, I shall now examine any miscellaneous records held in the manager's office."

He nodded, bowed his head a little, and waited respectfully for Feiffer to join him.

The manager's office was a tiny cubbyhole of an office directly behind the tellers' booths, furnished not at all like the big manager's office on the video ad with leather chairs and a warm desk, but instead with only a gray-metal army-style desk with two straight-backed stenographic-style chairs facing it for the customers.

Standing at the open door, looking for any signs of who the man who had worked there had been—photographs, awards, memorabilia—and seeing none, Feiffer asked, "Did you know him well—the manager?"

He was bent down at the side of the desk, opening drawers and speed-scanning the files and papers he found in there. Mr. Mansor said, looking up, "Oh, yes. Mr. T. M. Lee? Oh, yes."

He smiled momentarily and then went back to the files, closed the last drawer at the bottom of the desk, and then pulled both piles of files and documents in the In and Out trays on the desk towards him and began going through them alternately.

"What about the bank staff? The tellers and—"

"Oh, yes, them too." He had formed from the two trays a single pile of documents and papers and folders covering the last day's business. He picked up the pile in both hands and tapped it gently on the desk to align it into a single neat sheaf. Mr. Mansor said, "Oh, yes, very nice people." Mr. Mansor said for the record that he had no doubt was sooner or later going to find its way to the desks of his employers, "The manager, Mr. T. M. Lee, made it a point to create a

happy-family atmosphere among his staff. Even I, as an out-
sider, was always treated with painstaking kindness and respect each time my business brought me here. Mr. Lee never
failed to take me around and introduce me to each and every
one of the staff each time I came, just in case they had forgotten my name since the last time or I might have inadver-
tently forgotten one of theirs. He was a very polite and
considerate and thoughtful man."

"There were only eight of them in the staff? Nine with Mr.
Lee? No one else? No part-time or casual workers or—"

"No, just nine, including Mr. Lee."

That took care of any wild notion that whoever had been
inside the bank with them when they died had poisoned them
then simply gone home and expected to get away with it.
Feiffer asked, "When you made your routine audit last week,
how did they all seem?"

"Oh, efficient and smiling—as always."

"I mean, personally?"

He looked down at the pile of papers and documents and
folders on the desk and skimmed through them, scanning
them at what looked like lightning speed to verify what they
were before handing them over. Mr. Mansor said, "They
seemed fine. Very happy in their employment."

"And Mr. Lee? The manager?"

"Fine. Happy and smiling. As always." He looked up and
smiled to indicate it was a comment merely on the thought-
fulness of the man and not on his mental state or his memory, "He took me around yet again to introduce me to all of
his staff, but, of course, they all knew who I was."

The smell of the shower-fresh talc and sandalwood after-
shave and scented hair oil in the little room was almost overpowering. "Is there anything missing in here that you can
see?"

"No. Nothing."

"Is there anything at all unusual or out of the ordinary—is
there anything *different* that you've noticed? Either in here
or—"

"No." Mr. Mansor said with a touch of pride, "Very regu-
lar audits are done here, and they are always done properly.
At this bank, because of the caliber of the manager and the

staff and, of course, the regularity of auditing, everything is always to the penny exactly as it should be." He touched at his calculator on the desk and made it click to signal his pronouncement, "No, everything in the Asia–America–Hong Kong Bank, third floor, Lotus Flower Shopping Mall, Hong Bay, is, this day, exactly as it should be."

"The Asia–America–Hong Kong Bank on the third floor of the Lotus Flower Shopping Hall is *not* exactly as it should be! *Less than twelve hours ago the coroner took the bodies of nine human beings out of it!*"

Mr. Mansor said in alarm, "I did not mean to give offense by my tone."

"You did not give offense by your tone." Feiffer said tightly, "What gives offense is that there are nine dead people lying on steel trays in the Morgue who were murdered for no apparent reason!" He took a step closer and looked hard into the man's eyes but saw only lines and columns of numbers and a mind like a calculator that reckoned all life only in terms of profit and loss. Feiffer said, to fix it firmly in the man's calculations, "There was at least one other person in this bank when they died. Somehow that person or persons managed to make nine people drink cyanide poison all at the same time, and then, after they had drunk it, that person or persons stood back and watched. Then after they were all dead—out there in the main area of the bank, in the corridor, and the last two in the washrooms—he or they then stood like a good little housewife at the sink in there and washed each of the nine porcelain cups the poison had been in, dried them carefully to remove his fingerprints, and then stacked them neatly in a line and left." He paused to let it sink in, "You know this bank. *Is there any evidence or sign at all of anything out of the ordinary that might give me any idea at all what the hell happened in there and why it happened?*"

Excellent service did not always mean giving the client what the client wanted. It meant being true to the facts. Mr. Mansor, looking hard at the tall, slightly rumpled man in front of him awaiting an answer, then quickly down to the sheaf of papers and files that represented the last things the manager Mr. Lee had written or contemplated or calculated on this earth, said anxiously, always remembering to use the client's name wherever possible, "No, sir, Mr. Feiffer, in my official, expert opinion as auditor, nothing happened in this bank—with the exception of the deaths you mention—out of the ordinary at all . . . Nothing."

"I see."

"—except perhaps for the problem with the telephones. But then, that was merely a personal inconvenience for me and did not directly relate to—"

Feiffer asked, "What problem with the telephones?"

It was nothing. It was subordinate, a minor matter, nothing to do with the bank at all: a momentary irritation from an outside source that had nothing to do with his relationship to the bank and the bank's relationship to him at all. He glanced down at his calculator and tapped his fingers on the buttons one at a time as if to prove to himself, compared to the mathematics of commerce and calculation, just how unimportant it was. Mr. Mansor said cautiously, "Well, it has nothing to do with the bank or the Association of Small Banking Businesses and General Commerce Accountants and is probably rightfully the business of the quality-control department of the Hong Kong Telephone Company, but yesterday, when I attempted on three occasions to telephone the bank to set up a changed audit date for next month, I could not get through."

"What time did you call?"

"I called, altogether, four times, first at exactly five, when the bank closed its doors and I knew the manager and his staff would not be engaged with customers, and then again at five-thirty. Both times all the lines were out of order." He touched at his calculator. He shrugged a little. "I tried again for the third time at exactly two minutes to six when, after finishing their accounts and office work for the day, the staff would be getting ready to go home, but on that occasion, too, the phones still did not seem to work and were still out of order."

He gave excellent service. He was not a man to let things hang.

Mr. Mansor said, "I tried later, one more time, at 7:00 P.M. before I went home myself—I thought I would report the trouble to the telephone company as a service to the bank—but by then—" He looked up from his calculator and saw Feiffer's face, "—by then, by seven when I left the office for my home, all the phones in here were working again, but, of course, by then there was no one there."

He gave excellent service, but he only gave it in his own predictable, rational world and, suddenly touching at the nameplate on his lapel as if to protect himself from something he could neither understand nor deal with at all, Mr. Mansor asked, "Why? Is it important? Does it mean anything?"

He could not read the expression on the tall policeman's face at all. He touched at his little lapel plate and tapped at it nervously with his manicured nails.

Mr. Mansor, for the first time genuinely curious, forgetting to call the client *sir* or use his name, asked, as if it were something suddenly desperately important to him, "Why? What time do your medical people estimate all the people in here . . . What time, approximately, do you estimate they were *killed?*"

All he needed now to make his disguise complete—to be the Compleat Looney, to be everything that bastard in Headquarters who hated him wanted him to be—was to stink.

It was a little after nine-thirty in the morning. It was, as usual at that time of morning at the height of a Hong Kong summer, already a hundred and one degrees Fahrenheit of dripping, humid heat.

Turning onto South Canton Street, O'Yee cried, bootless to heaven, "Why *me*? Why *me*? Why *ME*?"

He muttered.

He mumbled.

He clanked.

He stank.

3.

In the bank, Feiffer didn't hear the sound clearly until Mansor had gone and the bank was at last still and deserted. With all the people in there last night, Scientific and Fingerprints and Photographic, there had been too much noise, and this morning with Mansor clicking away at his calculator—but now, with everyone gone, with even Mansor gone—alone in the bank Feiffer heard it and thought at first that it was the sound of the air conditioning. But it was not. The air conditioning hissed almost silently and at a metered, measured outflow with no sound of the machinery working it, and the sound he heard—a low, muted, buzzing noise—was not coming from that.

It occurred to him the sound could be something buzzing in the bank's telephone system, and he went to the foreign-transfer cage—the one where the girl with the elephant necklace and baby fat had worked—and picked up the phone there to listen.

All he heard there was the steady burr of a dial tone, and he put the phone back down again and tried to work out again where the sound had come from and what it could be.

The main door of the bank was still hanging off its hinges where it had been blown open by Winter's rapid-response team, and, moving across the main floor of the bank to examine it, he thought perhaps it was something in the stressed wooden doorjamb starting to give way.

It was not. The charge set against the door to blow it open had been the scientifically calculated minimum to do the job it was meant to do and there was not a mark on the jamb, and the jamb, like everything else in the bank—cages, the cash tills, the filing cabinets, the furniture in the manager's office—was anodized metal and was not even bent by the blast.

He listened. The buzzing turned into a low humming. Standing a little back from the blasted-open door and looking around, Feiffer cocked his head and tried to work out where it was coming from.

He thought for a moment that maybe it was the hot-water urn in the washroom coming on, but after Fingerprints had dusted it and found nothing—found it wiped clean—they had turned the urn off at the point and drained out the water so Scientific could take it away and test it for poison.

And the sound was not coming from the mall. The entire third-floor gallery up there was still closed and cordoned from the night before, and, except for a few uniformed mall security guards making sure people going to the upper floors on the escalators and elevators kept going, there was no movement or anything up there that could be making the sound at all.

He listened.

Alone in the bank—the last one left before the place was finally boarded up and made secure and, once the cordon tapes were removed, turned into a locked and secure museum piece for the curious—he listened and tried to work out where the sound was coming from and what was making it.

He heard the buzzing, the humming, barely perceptibly, suddenly deepen.

He heard something in the awful, dead, sterile, and deserted place *click*.

Then it was gone. There was what sounded for an instant like the movement of some sort of liquid—a bubbling sound—and then another click, and then the sound of the buzzing and the humming was gone completely.

He listened. In the main area of the bank everything had

been searched, dusted, checked, then searched and checked a second time, and there was nothing anywhere in there that had been missed.

It was not the television system in the bank. All the sets on the counters and on the walls had been turned off and all the lines examined in the vain hope that there might have been some sort of secret surveillance camera linked to them, and when he touched one of the sets just on the off chance, it was cold.

He listened, but all the sounds, the buzzing, and the sound of liquid moving, and the click, had gone and there was only silence.

Then he heard it again.

He heard a *click*. He heard, behind it, just for an instant, as if something reset itself, the faint sound of some sort of liquid moving.

He thought maybe it was the sound of an insect trapped in one of the wastepaper baskets in the bank, but all the wastepaper baskets in the place had been tipped up and emptied and their contents taken away for examination by Scientific, and the baskets all lay on their sides in a row against the back wall behind the tellers' cages, and it could not have been that.

At the broken doorway, reaching out for it with his left hand as he listened, Feiffer touched at the main light switch for the place. The heavy curtains on the main windows were still drawn—fixed in place so they could not be pulled back—and in order to see anything as they worked, the staff would have had to have kept the lights on all day.

He thought maybe the buzzing came from one of the banks of fluorescent tubes on the ceiling, and he touched at the switch to turn them off, plunged everything into a gray dimness, and in that instant saw something there in the bank he had not seen before.

He saw a glow.

It was coming from behind the glassed-in foreign-currency transaction cage, where the girl with the pudgy fingers had sat, radiating up in a yellow half circle against the back wall.

Crossing quickly from the door through the open counter

door to get to it, he saw it light up the gray-metal machine it came from and pick out the brass logo plate on its side. *Canon. High-Speed Copier. Model CXE3.*

The machine, from the day before when everybody in the bank had died, was still on.

He heard it suddenly click, and then, with a burbling sound like liquid moving, click again to try yet again to clear whatever it was that was jammed inside it.

What was jammed inside it was the bottom corner of a sheet of photocopying paper that had been pulled out of the machine too fast and caught in the axles and cogs of the feed rollers.

Lifting the protective plastic cover up from the rollers, Feiffer pulled it free to see what it was.

Crushed and balled up to the size of a pea by the action of the machine trying over and over to clear it, unfolded, it was the torn left-hand corner of a sheet of copying paper in the shape of a ragged triangle about two inches long by an inch wide.

As he closed the lid to hold the paper up to the poor light, there was another *click* and, on the side of the machine, the counter, freed at last, its cycle over, made a single clicking sound and brought up the number *18* on its dial, and then, on the timer dial below the counter brought up first three numbers: *5:45*, and then two letters P.M.

It brought up a time squarely within the time span Macarthur estimated all the people in the bank had begun to die.

It brought up the number of copies it had made of the last document that had been inserted in it before it jammed and no one in the bank either bothered or was still alive to clear it, *18*—for each of the exactly nine staff in the bank, two copies.

The torn section of paper was part of a copy of some sort of form. The corner of the paper read in black type *Form I–797–6–29–88,* but it was not one of the forms from the bank. With Mansor, he had seen all the forms they used at the bank and it was not one of them.

Form I–797–6–29–88. The torn scrap of paper was from the left-hand side of the bottom of a sheet of paper with the words printed in black and, next to them, what looked like part of a stylized engraving—part of a trademark or a logo.

It was not the logo of the bank. Their logo, framed on the rear wall of the bank where everybody could see it and above the name on the windows and door outside in the mall gallery, was a dollar sign entwined by the letters AAHK and the Chinese ideograph for riches and prosperity.

It was not that. It was no dollar sign or part of a Chinese character for riches or prosperity, or anything like it.

Next to the form number, the thing on the logo was part of the wing of a bird, a predator, a raptor.

It was part of a representation, from the way what was present of the wing seemed spread, of a bird of prey at the moment of attack.

Hong Kong is an island of some thirty square miles under British administration in the South China Sea facing Kowloon and the New Territories areas of continental China. Kowloon and the New Territories are also British administered, surrounded by the Communist Chinese province of Kwantung. The climate is generally subtropical, with hot, humid summers and heavy rainfall. The population of Hong Kong and the surrounding areas at any one time, including tourists and visitors, is in excess of six and a half million. The New Territories are leased from the Chinese. The lease is due to expire in 1997, at which time Hong Kong is slated to become a special, semi-independent administrative region of the People's Republic with the promise of a peaceful blending of British parliamentary rule of law and the Chinese Communist People's Army to enforce it—and if you believe that is going to happen peacefully, you will believe almost anything.

Hong Bay is on the southern side of the island, and the tourist brochures advise you not to go there after dark.

With the machine, finally, at last off, in the silence of the still-darkened bank, Feiffer took the little scrap of paper into the bank manager's office and placed it carefully on top of the pile of papers and folders and documents Mansor had put together for him of the manager's last day's business, but, even though he stood there staring down at it for what seemed a very long time, he could not even come close to working out what it was or where, originally, it had even come from.

4.

Halfway out of the open passenger-side door of the car on the ground-floor parking lot of the eighteen-story Hop Sing Wa Investment and Insurance Building on the corner of South Canton Street and Tiger Snake Road, Detective Inspector Auden roared in a voice that echoed like thunder in the cavernous place and made Detective Inspector Spencer, the purveyor of all things underhand, rotten, and lowlifelike cringe, "It's in the what? It's in the Inner *what* Institute on the eighteenth floor? It's in the Inner *Yu* Institute on the eighteenth floor? *You didn't tell me the job was in the Inner Yu Institute on the eighteenth floor! You just told me the job was on one of the floors of the Hop Sing Wa Investment and Insurance Building!*"

It was exactly the same feeling of betrayal and disappointment he had always got when his dear departed mother had lied through her teeth to him and instead of taking him out for a nice walk around the shops had lured him by trickery, low cunning, and pure vile evil maternal machination straight into the dentist's office to have one of his fangs yanked out at the roots. Auden yelled, "You lied to me!"

Standing at the driver's side of the car, keeping the bullet-proof barricade of half a ton of Detroit metal between them by imperceptibly moving back and forth along its length as

Auden—perceptibly—considered how to get to him and kill
him, Detective Inspector Spencer said in a voice he hoped
sounded full of sweet reason, but to Auden's ears *sounded
just like the voice his mother had always used when she lied
to him,* "But, Phil, clearly, the Inner Yu Institute *is* on one of
the floors of the Hop Sing Wa Building." He tried a little
grin. (That was a mistake.) "Clearly, it's on the eighteenth
floor, and, clearly, the eighteenth floor"—his sweet reason,
at the sight of Auden's eyes watching it work, did a convulsion and died—"*Clearly,* if there are eighteen floors in a
building and something is on the eighteenth floor, then the
eighteenth floor . . . is a floor." He tried a little grin, "Right?"

Wrong. Auden said without a little grin, "Give me the car
keys."

Spencer said with another grin, "Now, come on: you know
you don't mean that . . ."

Auden said, still with no grin, "Give me the car keys!"

It was worse than taking a kid to the dentist. Spencer,
brushing the whole silliness of it away like a mother brushing away some minor trivial concern of a child, said, to dismiss it all as a joke, "Now, come on, and don't be so silly.
It's just a little job in some sort of self-help psychiatric foun-
dation that isn't going to hurt in the least, and as a matter of
fact—"

Auden said quietly, "Give me the keys or I'll kill you."

"No, I won't give you the keys! Not for anything!"
Spencer, running out of patience, said sharply to bring the
man to his senses and put things in perspective, "You're just
being silly! Don't you realize that the people who run the
Inner Yu Institute asked for us on this job by *name?* It's a
great honor! They're important people, respected members
of the psychiatric profession. They're apparently so important that when they want something done they go straight to
the commander at Headquarters!" Didn't he realize it was
all for his own good? Spencer said, "The commander himself
called me up in the middle of the night to tell me about it."

"I don't care! *I'm not going up there!*"

"*Why not?*"

"I don't have to tell you why not, but I'm not!" He seemed
to forget about killing people and began doing a little dance

back and forth along the length of the car like a little boy who needed to go to the toilet. The dancing Auden said as an accusation, "What proof have I got that the commander talked to you? None! For all I know this could all be just some private idea of your own to get me to go to the—" He changed his mind in step about where he thought Spencer might be trying to get him to go, "Why didn't the commander call *me* in the middle of the night when he called you?"

"He did call you in the middle of the night! He called you first! You weren't at home!"

Auden said, *"I've got a normal sex life!"*

"No one said you didn't!" He stopped for a moment and looked over at the dancing bear on the other side of the car. Spencer asked, "Did they?"

"Who?"

"Anybody."

"What?"

"—say you didn't have a normal sex life?"

That was it. That was too much. Auden yelled, "I've got a perfectly normal sex life! It's probably a better sex life than the one you've got!" He stopped dancing. He stood like stone. Auden, telling the world, said in a voice that echoed in the cavern of the place, "There's nothing wrong with *me!*"

"Great!" Spencer said happily, "Good. I'm pleased for you. So if everything about you is just the way it should be then let's both go on normally up to the eighteenth floor, meet with the jolly old doctors and see what the problem is, solve it in a mere trice, and then—Bob's-Your-Uncle—we'll trot back down here again feeling good and bright and happy again. Problem solved." Spencer asked, already feeling good and bright and happy, "Okay? How's that?"

Evidently, not too good. Auden, stopping dancing and starting to stare, said in a voice full of darkness, "They can see right through you, you know—people like that. Psychiatrists."

Spencer said, "No, they can't."

"Yes, they can."

"No, they can't."

"Yes, they can."

"No, they can't." He happened to know a little about it.

"That's only in the movies where a psychiatrist takes one look at you and knows all about your—" He tried to think of something simple and basic. "—about, say, your repressed feelings of hatred and loathing for women because of—I don't know—the fact that your mother didn't love you enough or something. In real life, it takes years of analysis and study to even come close to working out what makes someone tick."

"They know what sort of person you are!"

"Good." Spencer said to keep him cheerful, "Well, you're a good person with a normal sex life, so you'll be all right, won't you?"

"I am a good person!" Auden said with his jaw set, "There's nothing wrong with me! I don't have to keep proving how brave I am just so my mother won't be disappointed in me!"

"Good." He looked at his watch. He went around to the other side of the car and patted Auden gently on the back. Auden was six-two, two hundred and thirty pounds, Spencer three inches shorter and forty pounds lighter, but as he patted, smiling at the man, somehow, just for an instant he had the impression he had to lean down to do it. Spencer said, "Let's do it then."

He patted again. Making a little joke of it as he led the shambling silent man gently towards the elevator to go up to the Inner Yu Institute on the eighteenth floor, Spencer, full of hope and anticipation, said brightly, "Well, here we go. Say *"Ah—"*

Sitting on an upturned fish basket at the bottom of South Canton Street, O'Yee said in a snarl as his comment on it all, *"Grrr!"*

He had his sealed orders in his hands and he opened them again and read the communication from He Who Hated Him:

HEADQUARTERS, ROYAL HONG KONG POLICE
Special Assignments Section

By Hand

FROM: RTG–68

TO: Detective Senior Inspector C. K. O'Yee,
            Yellowthread Street Station, Hong Bay.

RE: Undercover Assignment, Environs of Beach Road,
            South Canton Street, Queen's Street, Street of Un-
            dertakers, Cuttlefish Lane et al.

ITEM: 1. *Description of immediate area.*

Oh, thanks. God bless good Cap'n RTG–68 for treating
him so kindly—after all, he'd only been a street cop in the
immediate area for fifteen years!

> *The immediate area of operations consists of a grid
> of from five to fifteen various arteries and capillaries
> of pedestrian and vehicular movement, depending on
> their size, importance, and volume of activities,
> toponymically termed "streets," "roads," "lanes," or
> "alleys." (The last two occasionally used inter-
> changeably and, in several instances, for example
> Ladder Alley—which, having only pedestrian traffic
> for the rear entrances of one or two large busi-
> nesses on Wyang Street should be, in fact, termed
> "Rear of Wyang Street Access" or similar—quite
> incorrectly.)*

> *Architectural and commercial features of this area
> include a number of modern, high-rise skyscrapers,
> multistory apartment dwellings, a wholesale fish-
> market area, various coffin- and casket-making
> businesses, and, built around the recently reclaimed
> shore of the area along Beach Road (which, clearly,
> no longer has any evidence of natural beach), vari-
> ous fishing-boat moorings and a typhoon shelter for
> inclement weather.*

Well, at least he didn't talk down to people. In his last job as the kindly old guide of Bus Tours for the Brain Dead he must have just been a joy to be with.

ITEM: 2. *Disguise.*

> *You will appear to all who come into contact with you to be a hopeless, ill-used and mistreated, unloved bum.*

Yeah. Sure. But what about the disguise?

He knew it: RTG–68 wanted him dead. He didn't just want him bewitched, bothered and bewildered, he wanted him dead. RTG–68 hated him. He had made all this stuff up and he had a contract out on him. The whole thing was some sort of Hitchcockian horror scenario, some sort of Agatha Christie intricate murder plan—*some sort of Nazi Final Solution for the minority races*—and he wanted him dead in rags and humiliation in the gutter. Maybe, in the night, one of his Moriarty-type minions had snuck into his home and unloaded his undercover gun to make sure he died without even a single shot fired in his own self-defense. Maybe even—

Sitting on the fish basket, O'Yee suddenly reached down and pulled out his Walther PPK automatic pistol from under a filthy woollen sock and drew back the slide with a snap to check it was loaded.

There were two obviously olfactorily handicapped people going by, a man and woman in coolie hats, pushing a fruit barrow of rotten fruit.

They pushed very fast.

They pushed faster.

They heard the lunatic shriek in triumph, "Ha! Ha-ha! You missed that one, RTG–68, because I always keep my undercover gun hidden in my underwear drawer! *So I'm still armed!*" and pushing faster than even very fast, they reached V3 on the South Canton Street aerodrome and achieved liftoff.

ITEM: 3. *Nature of Crime or Potential Crime.*

> *This, at your level of involvement, is information
> deemed unnecessary to the successful completion or
> otherwise of the operation. Your sole task, using the
> devices and props as may be supplied to you, plus
> other props not supplied to you but available from
> various sources (Evidence Room, street trash cans,
> private stock, etc.) such as ragged and thick unsea-
> sonable clothing, heavy penitent chains, sticks of
> yellow chalk, a metal coat hanger, and other vari-
> ous inappropriate fashion accessories for the male
> at this time of year as necessary to convincingly
> portray the part of "MR. ETERNITY"—*

He read nineteenth-century character-list bookmarks from
Russian novels. He didn't actually read the novels, he just
read the bookmarks. He sat there in Headquarters by candle-
light reading the bookmarks and dreaming dreams of making
people's lives miserable.

> *—a harmless, twisted little person once touched by
> some terrible experience in his otherwise meaning-
> less life that has set him obsessionally to wandering
> the streets in chains and rags making unintelligible
> grunting noises and writing the single word ETER-
> NITY on the pavements of the Hong Kong Bay area
> in bright yellow chalk.*

ITEM: 4. *Final Instructions.*

> *Whatever may occur, you will take no direct, self-
> motivated action or actions in this matter, unless:*

> *(i) circumstances suddenly and unexpectedly war-
> rant it;*

> *(ii) a situation presents itself;—or*
> *(iii)—in other events.*

On his fish basket, as lunatics oft had wont to do, the lunatic shrieked, bootless to heaven, "Why me? Why always
me? What in the name of all that's holy did I ever do to
you?"

RTG–68: what if . . . what if . . . what if it was a *woman?*

> *(iv) Above all, you will not misplace, vary, or other-
> wise lose physical possession of any of the above
> items aforementioned and listed in Item 3—espe-
> cially, and in particular—the metal coat hanger.*
> *(v) You will continue to operate this case in this
> guise under these instructions until otherwise ad-
> vised.*

He stopped frightening people. Sitting on the upturned fish
basket reading his letter, O'Yee put away his gun and, a
harmless, twisted little person touched by some terrible experience in his otherwise meaningless, normal life, just sat
there staring silently into space.

O'Yee said softly, getting it right, *"Eternity . . ."*

Sometimes—some mornings—it almost seemed like forever.

In the elevator a moment before the doors opened on the
eighteenth floor, Spencer said, full of anticipation, "I've
heard about this place! I'm not quite sure what it is they do,
but whatever it is, it's supposed to be really on the cutting
edge of New Age interpersonal and intrapersonal psycho-
logical development!"

The elevator doors opened into what looked like a shining
white siren song to sterile, autoclaved antisepsis.

Auden said with the horror of a man about to have every
baby tooth in his head torn out by the roots, *"Oh, my God!"*

The Institute of Yu covered the entire top story of the
building. All clinical and white and gleaming, it was not the
size of a dentist's office, it was the size of the spaceship in
The Day the Earth Stood Still, with long, endless corridors
disappearing into the bowels of the place and from all the
windows of the corridors, panoramic views of Hong Kong so

Gort the Robot could get a good shot in from his eye-laser and blast the planet to bits a square mile at a time.

There was no reception area, just a long corridor and doors like dentists' offices. Auden said, "I can smell Novocain!"

He couldn't. There wasn't any.

Auden said, "I can smell human sweat!"

He could. It was his.

Auden said, "I can't hear any sound!"

He couldn't. There wasn't any.

Auden said, "Good-bye." He started back for the elevator button.

There was no button.

Auden said in a strangled voice, "Bill, where's the button?"

There was no Bill. Spencer had disappeared into the mist forming in front of Auden's eyes as into the miasma of the secret mind-numbing gas the aliens used in *Plan X from Outer Space*. Auden said, "Bill! Bill!"

Auden thought he said, "Bill, I want to go home now!"

He didn't say that. What he said was, "Aaawk—!"

He turned back and the mist cleared and he saw, coming down the corridor, two identical alien mutants dressed in white medical coats to drain out his vital bodily fluids and inject him with alien seed.

They were not identical aliens. They were the identical Doctors Yu, Aaron and Douglas. He saw it on their nameplates.

They were brothers, identical twins, young, healthy-looking southern Chinese in their thirties—*the same sort of bland, smiling, harmless-looking types replicants always took on as they transformed themselves from spiders and slugs and dentists in the mire next to the legs of the Saucer!*

Auden said to warn Spencer, going to meet them with his hand outstretched, "Bill! Bill!" but it was too late and Aaron had Spencer by the hand and was about to lead him away to the pod farm and the other one, Douglas, had his gleaming eyes fixed on him, measuring him for the planetary platter, and all Auden got out was, "Hee . . ."

"Ah!" They spoke simultaneously.

"Ah!" the one holding Spencer's hand in his, said, "Ah,

Mr. Spencer." He took a step back and looked at Auden, "And Mr. Auden."

Douglas, following his brother's gaze, said with a nod, "Ah, yes."

If he could have climbed the elevator door and slid in between the crack at the top he would have. Whether the elevator was still there didn't matter in the least.

Aaron said, "Yes." He glanced at his brother and then at Spencer and then at Auden. Aaron said fiercely, "Look. See. How little analysis of the true characters of these two men one would need to do to penetrate their deepest natures."

That was it. Nature. Penetration. Pain. Aliens. He was out of there. He was going to climb the elevator door and get through over the crack into the elevator shaft. Auden said, scrabbling at the elevator door with his fingernails to scratch his way through, "Good-bye!"

Douglas said, "Yes!" He grinned. He looked hard at Spencer.

Aaron said with pride at his little discovery, still holding Spencer by the hand, "Look. See. See it shining from his alert and brightly shining eyes and slightly bent-forward carriage—" He patted Spencer on the hand to identify him— "The Scholar! The Questor Type." He looked hard at Auden, apparently leaning against the elevator door and checking the safe working of its upper door mechanism, "And he—" His voice rang with admiration and pride that such a man should deign to help him in his painful hour of trial, "And there— see how he waits coiled like the finest Swiss spring steel, but yet with the calm and pleasant expression on his face of nothing more than a small child out for a visit with his parents somewhere in the city—the authentic true Man of Sincerity and Iron: the *Hero Type!*"

Auden said—

Auden said, ". . ."

Auden said, "Oh."

He paused a moment, and, one final time, rapped at the door of the elevator to check that it was safe for all the good people who perforce might have to use it in that extremely important medical place of inter- and intrapersonal whatever it was.

He flexed his mighty muscles to soothe the fevered brows of the two good men facing him.

Speaking in his deepest voice as he went forward to gently grasp their hands in greeting, Auden said, to show the two kindly medical fellows that at last they could turn their minds back fully to their lifes' work of identifying the true essence of the human psyche with unerring scientific accuracy, "Hiya, Docs, glad to met you both. Phillip J. Auden, at your service. Just tell me what you want me to do for you, and I'm the man to do it!"

He didn't care.

He didn't.

He was an educated man, a Eurasian, the product of a Chinese father and an American mother, the best of both worlds.

ETERNITY . . .

On Tiger Snake Road, there was a nice patch of clean cement between the upturned basket and a pile of rotting fish heads on the sidewalk, and taking the big stick of yellow chalk from behind his head and squatting down, he wrote it carefully, beautifully, in a fine *cancellaresca* fifteenth-century Chancery hand.

It looked nice.

His coat hanger, when he asked it, thought so too.

5.

On the ground floor of the mall there was a fountain in the center of the atrium, but at 10:00 A.M.—the time the rich and conspicuous began their shopping day in the expensive boutiques of the place—it was still turned off. It had been turned off the day before after its delicate mechanism had been jammed by someone throwing a small coin into it for luck. A sign resting against its white marble base warned that, in future, the practice would not be tolerated by the management and would result in prosecution.

He was the man who prosecuted. Standing back a little from the fountain to keep his eye on it, holding his coat back a little against his hip with his fist to show potential shoplifters, muggers, and presumably coin tossers the butt of the holstered pistol he wore on his belt, George Shoemaker, glancing only for a moment in the direction of the fountain, asked, "What happened up there, Harry?" He had been a homicide cop for almost twenty years before becoming for the last three the chief security officer for the entire Lotus Flower Shopping Mall chain. The cost of his expensively tailored suit alone reflected the change. Shoemaker, holding a gold Mont Blanc pen ready above a tooled-leather Dunhill notebook to take the details down for his report, said to make it clear from the start, "The mall has nil liability on the inside contents of high-risk, self-secure businesses like banks, but we're probably going to be up for all the damage the entry team did to the door and floor and carpeting of the exterior."

Even his haircut looked like it cost more than he had ever earned in Homicide in a month. Shoemaker said, glancing down at his book, "I notice from the out-of-hours sign-in book in the security office here that you've had the bank auditor in all morning—so what did they get?"

"Nothing." He felt tired, gritty, and, compared to Shoemaker, badly dressed and seedy. He glanced over at the marble pool of the fountain. With the water on, the whole area would have been cool and fresh. Feiffer said as the man readied his pen to write, "All I know at this point is that from what the M.E. can judge from the condition of the bodies, that sometime between the approximate hours of 5:00 P.M. and 7:00 P.M. yesterday evening a person or persons unknown entered the premises of the Asia–America– Hong Kong Bank on the third floor after closing time, administered quick-acting poison to the nine members of the staff working in there, and then, after assiduously and carefully and methodically removing any traces of his existence, left again."

He watched Shoemaker write it down.

His fingernails were manicured. Feiffer said, "The door of the main vault was apparently still open at the time, the tills in the tellers' cages were still unlocked and full of cash, there were various personal items of value on the bodies, as well as cash and other small items of value in their wallets and purses, but none of it was touched." He glanced over at the empty pool and wondered what the mall management did with the coins the uncouth and common threw in there after Shoemaker and his staff hauled them off and ejected them unceremoniously out into the street. "As for the body count, it's nine, including the manager. Five male, four female, ages from approximately twenty to fifty-one. No signs of physical violence on the bodies. No interior damage to the bank. From your liability point of view only minor exterior damage around the main door area."

"Okay." He had no expression on his face at all. He

merely wrote it all down for his report. Shoemaker said without looking up, "Good. Thanks."

Feiffer said to encapsulate it for him, "Murder times nine." He watched the man's face, "You can say that at this point in the proceedings the police have absolutely no leads or suspects at all."

Shoemaker said without looking up, "I don't have to say anything. I'm out of all that."

"So what I'm doing next is—"

"I know what you're doing next." Looking up, he still had no expression on his face. Shoemaker said, by rote, "Next you're going to go over to the Morgue to watch everyone from the bank get cut up, then you're going to get Uniformed to go to all the relatives to get all the life histories of the victims to see if the manager or anyone else had personal problems, then you're going to follow up on the poison to find out what sort of poison it was—"

Feiffer said, "It was cyanide."

"—then, when all that gets you nowhere, you're going to put up posters in here asking if anyone saw anyone acting suspiciously between the hours of—what was it again? 5:00 to 7:00 P.M. on the due date—and then, when all that also comes to nothing, you're going to go back through Criminal Records looking for a lunatic, no-motive poisoner, and then, when all that fails too, you're going to announce the crime is still under investigation, and then— maybe ten years later— some traffic cop is going to stop someone for speeding and as he tells him the fine is a hundred dollars for going eight miles over the thirty-five-mile-an-hour limit, said speeder is going to ask out of curiosity what it is for killing nine people and tell everyone he did it because of the sun spots." He brushed at his expensive suit. Shoemaker said tightly, "I know what you're doing next, Harry. I had twenty years of what you're doing. It's all crap, and I don't miss any of it for a moment."

"Did you know any of the people in the bank? The manager, Mr. Lee? Any of the staff at all?"

"No, I didn't." He shook his head. "Why should I? Banks don't give staff discounts. I know the tailors and travel agents and the exclusive departments stores and the jewellers." He glanced for just a moment up to the third-floor gallery to the still-cordoned-off area of the bank, "And, anyway, places like banks and foreign-exchange agencies have their own internal-security arrangements. My responsibility stops at the entrance to the businesses. All I have to do is make sure low lifes and shoplifters don't get in to bother the customers." Shoemaker asked with heavy irony, "Did a low life or shoplifter do it? Did I miss something and fall down on my appointed task?"

"Whoever did it stood back and watched as nine human beings died one by one! Whoever did it watched as the last two of them—two women—crawled along the floor in agony to get water from the rest-room cooler because their throats were on fire!"

"I don't give a damn!" He was a tall, lean, well-tailored, manicured man in his late forties with what had once been piercing blue eyes. Now, the eyes had no emotion in them at all. Shoemaker said, "I don't even think about it anymore, Harry. I gave up on the idea of justice and fairness after the fourteenth raped and murdered ten-year-old kid—or maybe it was the twentieth or the twenty-ninth—but I gave up on it." Shoemaker said with his mouth hard and twisted, "I gave up on it because it didn't matter anymore which number raped and murdered kid it was because I didn't get whoever it was who raped and killed any of them anyway!" Shoemaker said, *"And I gave up looking at dead faces in the streets or in the Morgue pleading with me to find out what the hell happened to them!"*

Feiffer said softly, "They all drank the poison out of cups simultaneously, and then whoever gave it to them collected all the cups up, took them to one of the rest rooms and washed them clean in the sink, and then stacked them all neatly in a line—"

Shoemaker said, shaking his head, "Harry, I don't care! I just don't care anymore!"

He glanced over to the turned-off fountain. Feiffer said quietly, "They looked like dolls." Feiffer said, not to Shoemaker, but to the fountain, "Later this morning I have to go to the Morgue and see them all cut open and the top of their heads taken off so the M.E. can verify that they all—"

Shoemaker said suddenly violently, "You won't find out who did it, Harry! You're not ever going to find out who did it, because some maniac did it! And even if you do find out who did it, you'll never find out why he did it, because he did it because he was a maniac! And if he isn't you'll never put him away because some smart lawyer will make sure you never put him away! What'll happen is that they'll end up putting you away! Because you did something wrong when you arrested the poor little fucking maniac or you asked the poor little fucking maniac the wrong questions!" He was breathing hard. Shoemaker said, louder than he intended, "Cops don't win anymore, Harry—maniacs win. Because the whole fucking world is filling up more and more every day with more and more fucking maniacs!" He looked suddenly at the stilled fountain and then back again to Feiffer, "And anyone who gives a damn anymore or cares about anyone else—especially if he's a cop—is a fool!"

"Okay." He nodded at the man. Feiffer said softly, "Maybe you're right." He did not want to go to the Morgue. He wanted to stay until the fountain was turned on. Feiffer said with a smile, "You certainly made a bright move coming here." He thought of something Mansor had told him, "George, the bank auditor Mansor said he tried to phone the bank four times between about five and seven yesterday evening, but on the first three occasions he tried, all the phones were out of order. Does that happen much around here?"

"No." He looked back to the fountain, and for a moment his eyes were full of tears, "No. Not allowed to. Not here in the high-fashion, high-profile world of the Lotus Flower Shopping Mall—absolutely *verboten*." He glanced back and his eyes were clear again, "But I'll check for you if you like."

"It could be nothing, but—"

Shoemaker said, "Oh, no, everything is important in this place—everything." His fingernails were done each week by the Manicure Boutique on the second-floor gallery at no charge, and for an instant he looked down at them.

If there was something important he wanted to say, he did

not say it then. Shoemaker said, doing the job he was paid for, "I'll find out and get back to you. Okay?"

"Okay."

There was something he didn't want to let go. Shoemaker said as a statement of fact, "I was a good cop, Harry. I didn't take bribes and I worked my butt off on every case I ever got. I was a cop for twenty years. I've done my time caring about people."

"You're right." None of it was his fault. It was his fault only that he was the one who could order the fountain turned back on and he had not. Feiffer asked, to finish business with the man, "Do you need any copies of any photos of the interior for the mall insurance carrier—or anything?"

"No, all they'll want is a few pictures of the door. And they'll do that themselves." He was stiff, rigid, his face set. Shoemaker said quietly, "Twenty years. I did the job for twenty years and what did I get from it? Nothing. The first day I was on the job here I got a dozen suits, a new apartment, a car, and the fashion designer from one of the men's stores asked me, seriously, if there was any way I could get a dozen different color-coordinated grips for my goddamned pistol to go with each of the dozen suits!" Shoemaker said angrily, "Justice? The dead looking up at people like you and me as their last hope on earth for justice? That's what justice comes down to in the end: whether or not you've put in enough years of pure fucking hell to be entitled to carry a color-coordinated fucking gun so you don't offend the tasteful, clothes-conscious eyes of the rich!"

He looked away. He looked into the pool with the fountain where wishes were not allowed.

Shoemaker asked suddenly, "What were their names? The ones who were killed up there?"

"All of them?" He looked at Shoemaker's face and, suddenly, could not read what was in it at all. Feiffer said quickly, holding the moment, "Chiang. Sun. Wing. Chan. Lin. Mok. Fan. Wong and the manager, Lee." He watched the man's face but there was nothing and he merely stared blankly in the direction of the fountain.

He could not fathom what the man was thinking at all, or why he kept looking at the broken fountain. Feiffer asked, "Why? Why do you want to know? Does one of the names mean something to you?"

Ah, the remembrance of times past . . .

A—Zut!—la recherche du temps perdu . . .

Once, before RTG–68 had transformed him into Mr. Mulch, the meandering, moth-eaten, mad Maggot Monster of the Metropolis, in his other life as a person he had briefly fancied himself as Brother Christopher, a mild-mannered, manuscript-making medieval monk.

ETERNITY . . . Halfway down Tiger Snake Road, getting down on all fours under the filthy, rat-infested overhang of the loading docks for the closed, disgusting place, he pushed aside a pile of rotting fish heads and wrote it carefully and neatly on the sidewalk.

He wrote it in the fine, flowing Gianfrancesco Cresci Italian *bastarda* style from the mid–sixteenth century.

O'Yee shouted at the top of his voice to RTG–68, wherever and whoever he was, "Take that!"

He felt a little better.

He nodded to himself.

Directly behind him in the street, he heard the sound of footsteps and looked up quickly to see who it was.

Shoemaker said softly, "No." He turned back from staring at the fountain and suddenly his eyes were full of tears, "No. Nothing."

He put the notebook and pen carefully back inside the pocket of his expensive suit and if there was any more to be said nothing on earth was going to persuade him to say it.

He glanced back only once as it he made a final decision and all the tears were gone and his face was tight and hard like a mask.

He had made up his mind.

He turned to go. Shoemaker said evenly, "No. None of it, Harry. None of it means anything to me anymore."

It was nobody.

With the fish-market area closed for the day, there was no

one around and, except for a few hand wagons and empty fish trucks parked outside the loading bays, the entire street was deserted.

Squatting down on his haunches on the street, waiting for something or someone—God only knew what—to happen, in his best fin-de-siècle Vere Foster hand, O'Yee wrote an *E*.

He thought he heard a sound and looked up to see what it was, but it was nothing.

He wrote a *T*.

He wrote an *E*.

He wrote—

Suddenly, from out of nowhere, he heard someone come up behind him and he stopped writing and froze . . .

6.

The Institute of Yu wasn't a spaceship; it was a huge closed-in series of tiny, cabinlike rooms covering the entire ninety-thousand square feet of the eighteenth floor with a single corridor terminating at the far end in a single semicircular room with the walls lined with banks and banks of forty-two-inch TV screens and, dead center in the room facing all the screens, two custom-built console Star Trek captains' chairs set into swivel tracks on the floor.

The room was all fluorescent lights and glowing screens and plastic, like something out of the twenty-third century.

It was the nerve center of the Institute of Yu, the bridge, the TV screens their radar and sonar as they went where no man had gone before.

Standing identically by their identical chairs, in front of all their screens, the identical Yus were navigators of the mind—explorers. They were both so proud of it that as they glanced at all the screens they could not stop hopping up and down in unison.

They hopped. They glanced at each other.

They seemed so happy to have someone to show it all to.

They giggled in unison.

Leaning over one of the chairs and flicking on the power to one of the screens in the top left-hand corner of the huge electronic wall, the nearest Dr. Yu (it was Aaron, Spencer read it on his nameplate) screamed over the sudden full-living-color, full-deafening-volume picture of all the Mongol hordes from the north storming the Great Wall of China to wreak death, destruction, and a lot of yelling onto the entire peaceful population of China, "The Warrior Room! Room Number One! Our first and most basic! But still our most popular! Where a man lost in the turmoil and confusion of modern life—a square peg in a round hole—may indulge his secret passion of being the last lone heroic swordsman on the wall defending his nation against an army of invaders!" The screen was full of hordes of Mongols—ragged men with bad teeth and axes—swarming up one side of the Great Wall onto the ramparts. The camera had the point of view of someone looking down from the ramparts at them as they swarmed. Dr. Yu (Aaron? Douglas? They had change-hopped places and it could have been the other Dr. Yu) yelled in Chinese to the invisible lone swordsman whose eyes saw what the screens saw, "Fight! The fate of civilization rests on you! You are no longer the poor, unhappy stockbroker's runner you were yesterday! Today, you are the sole hope and guardian of two thousand years of history and the continuing survival of the greatest and most populous nation the world has ever known!"

They were in the psychodrama business. The room was an interactive TV fantasy setup, the Hordes on the screens that must have filled it on all four sides actors from the local movie studios. The film of the Hordes was outtakes from the latest epic—you could tell if you looked hard that the Hordes were second-string actors by the cheap battery watches on their wrists that, like John Wayne in *The Conqueror*, they had forgotten to take off.

You could also tell by the unearthly screams the Hordes made as the invisible swordsman slashed at them and the length of time it took them to die that they were on hourly rates.

The other Dr. Yu flicked a switch. He shrieked, "Room Number Two! The Alone on a Sinking Raft in a Storm Room!" (The storm was so terrible and the sea so high it made Auden reel and almost throw up.) "Only you alone with three other survivors—the capitalist gunrunner, the income-tax inspector, and the beautiful virgin! You are out of food! Which one will you eat?"

Then there was another flick and another screen was full of the pictures and sounds of what looked like the main street of a small Western town in the nineteenth century full of vicious-looking Chinese cowboys getting off a train a few minutes before High Noon. Auden said, "Let's stay on this one for a minute." Auden, glued to the set, seeing the scene as the man in Cabin Number Three saw it, asked in a whisper, "Who is it? Who's getting to be Gary Cooper in there? Who is it?"

One of the Yus (Who cared? Just answer the question!) said proudly, "Yesterday an unhappy lawn-mower salesman and father of two horrible children. Today, the surest gun in the West!"

Auden said, ". . . *wow!*"

Aaron said, "Here in the Institute of Yu we use psychodrama and cinema to delve to the deepest depths and discover what your true Yu really is." He turned off the screen. (Auden said, "Oh . . .") He nodded to his brother, "An invention of our mutual father. Many years ago, after he had made his fortune in real estate—a profession he loathed—it came to him that the real Yu—the real him (he glanced to Auden to see if he understood the pronoun shift, and then, seeing his gleaming eyes, realized he wasn't listening)—was but a chimera he had never truly known or allowed to roam free. He realized that, deep down, he had never released the secret Yu of his deepest fantasies and searched for his true potential and possibilities in those fantasies to verify once and for all whether he could have been in the world the person he had always dreamed of being. And that real Him—the true, secret, private Yu of his soul—withered daily, unused and unexplored. So, taking his fortune, he created the Institute of Yu—first for himself to delve into the depths of his most secret dream, and then, once his efforts were crowned with success, to the world at large."

Douglas said, "He created a haven, where, alone and unobserved except for the tender monitoring care of trained personnel such as ourselves, each person might live out his deepest fantasy and lock it into his memory as if it had really happened to him."

Aaron said, "The stockbroker's clerk, after he has saved China, will go back to his old life with the knowledge that he once saved China!"

Douglas said, "The lawn-mower salesman was, in another life, Gary Cooper in love with Grace Kelly!"

Aaron said, "Your own commander, worn down with his endless task of administering a police force, was once—"

Auden said curiously, "Yes?"

Aaron said, "Well, your commander has told you how we once helped him here—"

Spenser said, "No."

Douglas said, "Ah, so discreet." He turned to Douglas, "Clearly, it worked!"

Aaron said, "Yes!"

Auden was still thinking about shooting a lot of people in Main Street and then going off in a buggy with the young Grace Kelly already beginning to take her clothes off for their honeymoon. Auden said in a gasp, "My God, boys, you could make a fortune with this in California!" He thought about it for a moment. Auden said, "You could be *rich!*"

Aaron said, "Yes."

Douglas said, "Funny you should say that."

Aaron said, "As a matter of fact, we have already been granted green cards to take our project to the United States and be rich and successful and highly esteemed and surrounded by willing, scantily clad women of loose morality." He reached into his inside coat pocket and took out a single sheet of carefully folded paper from his billfold and handed it to Auden for them both to read, "Here is the notification."

It was a single sheet of paper from the American Embassy in Hong Kong confirming that the US State Department was prepared to offer permanent residence to both the Yu brothers in the United States of America. It was just a form letter with the names typed in, but it was what millions of people all over Asia would have killed for.

Aaron said after Auden had read the letter and handed it to Spencer, "But however—"

Spencer said, "But however you will not take up the

offer." He was the Scholar Type all right. Spencer said, to say what Aaron was about to say before he even said it, "Because you applied for it, not recently with your own new Yus, but long ago in your old pre-Yu lives when you both mistakenly believed that real and true success and happiness in life lay merely and solely in the attainment of money, sex, fawning respect, and physical happiness—am I right?"

By George, he thought he had it. Aaron said, "Yes!"

Douglas, nodding hard, said, "Right!"

Spencer said, "Ah, but wrong, *n'est-ce pas?*"

Aaron said, "Right. Our old pre-Yu dreams of money and success and meaningless mass sexual satisfaction in the United States, we discovered, were not our deepest dreams, but merely poor carnal substitutes for our deepest dreams. After spending less than one full day in Room Number Six—the room of Saintly Acts—we discovered that our true mutual Yu was merely to serve others *without monetary or physical remuneration and remain here forever as humble unheralded helpers of humanity!*"

Auden said, "Oh." It sounded noble. Auden said, "Oh. Right. Um— Good choice."

Aaron said proudly, "It was our dear Daddy who convinced us to search for our inner Yus beyond our outer ones."

Douglas said, "The saintly man he is!"

Spencer asked, "Where is your father now?" He smiled the sort of smile people smiled when the conversation suddenly turned from mortgages and matrimony to Mother Teresa. Spencer said, "I'd certainly like to meet a man like him."

Douglas said, "And he, you—the man who has his inner Yu already shining like a beacon from him: the Scholar and seeker after truth."

Spencer said, "Thank you."

Aaron said, not forgetting Auden, "And you: the Hero, the man of steel. As he sits alone in his little cell somewhere in hiding, how the knowledge that two such men are here to help must comfort him in his hour of desperation—"

Spencer said, "He's not here, then?"

"No." It was Douglas. He sounded surprised that Spencer had asked, "He is, of course, too distraught." He glanced at his brother, "The commander did tell you the situation and how you—what you were—" Douglas asked, "The commander told you why you were here, didn't he?"

Spencer said, "No, not a word."

"Oh." He drew himself up and stood tall. In the great room he looked small and lost.

Douglas said softly, so softly that Auden had to crane down a little to hear him, "You are called here because, like the Great Wall overrun by Mongols, like the villains succeeding at the end of the movie and taking Grace Kelly off to an arroyo to a fate of rapine and death, like a saint discovering in self-knowledge there is only disappointment and self-delusion, the Institute of Yu is failing. In the past two weeks, seven—not four, not five, not six, but seven—of our clients—"

Aaron said, overcome with grief, "—have tried, midway through their sessions, to throw themselves out of windows and kill themselves!"

Douglas said, "We caught them just in time, but we are only two men!" He was saintly, "We cannot all at once, help some of our many clients navigate the rocky shores of their unhappy lives to safe haven, find out why others strike the rocks and decide to end it all, and save them all at the same time!" His eyes were full of tears, "It is just all too much for us!"

Aaron said, almost in tears, "*And of course we cannot seal the windows to stop them because to do so would mean we have created not a free-choice world for them in which to find themselves, but a prison controlled by guards who do not trust them!*"

Douglas said, pleading, "Mr. Spencer, Scholar and Questor that you are, you have been sent here by your commander to save us, to sample every room, talk to anyone you wish, bring your great mind to bear on the problem—and find out why these poor souls are attempting one after another to throw themselves to certain death from the top of an eighteen-story building!"

Aaron said, "You have been sent here to save the entire future of the Institute of Yu! You have been sent here to save the future of catharsis and caring! You have been sent here to save all that is good in Man! You have been sent here

to save the very future of Man himself!" Aaron said to encapsulate it, "Mr. Spencer, you have been sent here to find
out, with your great brain, why, in the last two weeks or so,
our clients have been attempting to throw themselves en
masse out of our windows!"

Spencer said, "I'll do it!" You could tell by the set of his
face that the commander, God bless him, had chosen exactly the right man for the job.

Aaron said to Auden, still thinking about naked California
girls, "And you, Mr. Auden, our Hero, our Man of Sincerity
and Iron and true Fearlessness—"

Auden said, "Yes?"

Douglas said, "You, sir, have been sent here to stand alone
on the barely two-foot-wide catwalk on the outside of the
building and, if we miss any sad, lost souls bent on hurling
themselves down to eternity on the pavement and they get
out and begin to topple and fall—"

Auden said, "Yes?"

Aaron asked in a soft polite voice like the saint he was,
"Would you mind awfully at the risk of your own life *catch-
ing them* before they go?"

The elderly man with the smiling face standing looking
down at O'Yee's work on the sidewalk was clearly some sort
of eccentric millionaire keeping a watchful eye on his vault
of money in the Hop Sing Wa Investment and Insurance
Building, his half-drunk bottle of San Miguel beer, T-shirt,
and bargain-basement pants and plastic Taiwanese sandals
all direct from the Howard Hughes Blend-in Clothes for the
Billionaire Emporium on Rodeo Drive.

Either that, or he was a bum.

O'Yee, swivelling around on the ground, looked up into
his face. It was a nice, elderly southern Chinese face without
any trace of hardness or malice in at all.

The smiling face looked down at the letters on the pavement. The face, still smiling, said in Cantonese, "Did you
know that the letter *A* in modern Western script was originally pronounced as an aspirant *H* sound in ancient Phoeni-
can and was a phonogram representing a pair of ox's horns
on their side with a stave lying across them to represent the

ox's yoke? And that the Greeks turned the horns up on their points and called it *Aleph,* which is where the word *Alpha* came from, and why, now, all the letters laid out are called an *Alpha*-bet?"

He was a bum.

The bum said, "And that the earliest evidence of writing ever found is a limestone tablet from the city of Kish, dating back to about 3500 B.C.?" He was going to have a little chat. The bum said happily, "I'll bet you don't even know where Kish was."

Brother Christopher knew everything. O'Yee, looking back down to his sidewalk scriptorium, said, "It was in Sumeria."

"And did you know that, originally, people like the Sumerians wrote their thoughts down by drawing pictures on little lumps of baked clay called *pictograms*—but then they found out that a picture of, say, the moon could also be used just as easily to represent an abstract idea like *night* or *darkness*— the pictogram for *moon* being a drawing of one moon, and the pictogram for *night* and *darkness* being shown by two or three moons?" The bum said, "That was a very big leap for the human mind." He leaned down and lowered his voice. (There was no one else around in the entire street, but that was the way bums were.) "—Because then words began to take on a *magical significance* and could be used to communicate secret *ideas.*" He nodded. The bum said, "I'll bet you don't know which ancient alphabet which developed from all the disparate writings in all of human history is the basis of the Western alphabet used these days by over a quarter of all civilized mankind—"

O'Yee said, "The Roman alphabet of the first century A.D." Okay? Here endeth the lesson. Good-bye. O'Yee said, "Drop by again sometime." He went back to his letters.

The bum said cheerfully, "Isn't life amazing?"

O'Yee said, "No."

"Oh, but it is." The bum said happily, "—you stroll along a street in the worst part of town and see there some wreck of a man you think is in the last stages of dementia praecox and a drunk and a hopeless mental cripple—and what do you find? A person with a knowledge of the ancients!" The bum said, "You see from a distance merely some horrible, smelly little creature dressed in rags and the accumulated gleanings from trash cans, and yet close up what do you find beneath those rags communicated to you so clearly and easily through the illuminating beacon of human speech? You find a learned man, a historian, a sage, a monk!" The bum said, "Life is amazing!"

E-T-E-R-N-I—

The bum said, talking to the heavens, "Look at you! You're horrible! Who would have thought—"

-T-Y. *K-I-L-L!* . . .

The bum said quickly, "Oh, no offense!"

None taken. O'Yee said in a snarl, "Grrr! . . ."

"—who would have thought that in the last stages of your obvious physical and social decay your mind would still retain enough working brain cells even to be able to put two words together, let alone understand the historic derivation and magical significance of words? Who would have thought that someone so obviously weak and degenerate and disgusting and vile-looking would know even a smattering of the great concepts that made modern man who he is?" The bum, drawing a breath (he'd better enjoy it: it was going to be his last) said in wonderment, "Amazing! Truly amazing."

Brother Christopher knew a little more than a smattering. O'Yee said, to put the man in his place, "The letter *A* came from a Phoenician symbol that looked like a pair of ox's horns with a staff across them! Everybody knows that!"

The bum said, "Stave, but nice try."

"It was a staff!"

The bum said, "Stave. A stave is a stick or pole used for walking or climbing, and in regalia as a symbol of divine authority."

"That's a staff. A stave is a curved piece of wood forming the side of a cask or a barrel!" He was prepared to fight. He got up. O'Yee, scratching at where his tonsure would be if he had a tonsure, said with the full weight of his many years making magnificent manuscripts, "If letters have magical significance, then surely a staff would represent the yoke and strength of an ox better than a stave in representing the letter *A*—*because it would also represent the power and authority of the man who wrote it!"* QED. *Quod erat demonstrandum:* thus it is proven.

The bum said, "Phonogram."

"What?"

"Phonogram. You said *letter.* When the Phoenicians put a line across the ox's horns, they made the Sumerian pictogram into a phonogram. It was the Romans who made it a letter."

He was right. O'Yee, shrugging, said, "Whatever."

"You give in then?"

"I give in on the *letter,* but not on the *staff!"*

"Then I accept *staff* and will never again incorrectly use the word *stave* again."

"All right then." He was happy. He squatted back down with his chalk.

The bum, squatting down too, said, "You must have read a lot once."

"You too."

The bum said, "I'm a widower, and I'm old. I have plenty of time."

O'Yee said, "Oh. I'm sorry."

There was a silence. For a wizened, smelly, horrible-looking creature dressed in rags and carrying a coat hanger, the Eternity writer had soft, kind, brown eyes. And his writing—a form of the British Vere Foster script of the late nineteenth century, framed by the pile of fish heads at the Y—looked very nice. The bum, reading it in English, said, "Eternity, eh? How long have you been doing that?" The bum said quickly, still in English, "Forever. Right?" He grinned.

O'Yee said softly, "Yeah. Sometimes it seems longer."

It was a joke. The bum said, "Ha, ha!" When he laughed, he moved his shoulders up and down. His shoulders looked stiff and painful. Maybe he hadn't laughed much recently. The bum asked, "Did you really know all that about the alphabet?" The bum said quickly, holding his open hands up quickly to show he gave no offense, "If you say yes, I'll take your word for it as an honest man."

"I really knew that."

The bum asked, "And Chinese writing—calligraphy—do you know the history of that too?"

"Yes."

Life was amazing. "Did you know that the Chinese habit of writing in lines up and down a page in columns was originally inspired from the way an ox plowed furrows in a field?"

"No, I didn't know that."

"Oh, yes." The bum said, "I read it somewhere in a book on the history of world calligraphy from the public library." The bum said, "When I handed it back in at the desk the librarian said in all the years the book had been there only one other person had borrowed it." The bum said sadly, "People don't read anymore. What they do is watch. Watching is okay, but unless you read, sometimes you don't even know what it was you've been watching." The bum said, "I like the bits in books where the author tells you what the character you're reading about is thinking, and it isn't what you'd think he was thinking at all, it's something different and private and amazing. Do you like those bits, too?"

"Yes." He shrugged. As he shrugged, he clanked. O'Yee said, "Yes, I like those bits a lot." He looked at the bum's face. It was a nice face. O'Yee said, "My problem is I seem to read books no one else has ever heard of and no one but me thinks are any good!"

The bum said, seeing it at last, "Ah! Now I see what you are! You're a *poetry reader!*"

"No! No, I'm not!"

"You are!"

"I'm not!"

"You are! You're a poetry reader because you have a soul that cries out for a cooling draught!"

"I don't have a soul that cries out for a cooling draught!" Or did he? Sometimes, when all the world was against him . . . He kneaded his hands hard together at his chest and clanked. O'Yee said sadly, "Well, maybe sometimes, maybe just a little . . ."

The bum said with firm, manful contrition, "I apologize for what I said about you looking horrible and wizened and smelly. I only watched and did not read. Now that I know your thoughts—" The bum said, "Now, I believe now, totally, that you really did know all that about the alphabet." The bum, holding out his hand, said, "Franklin Feng. Call me Frank."

"Christopher O'Yee."

They held their hands together for a moment. It was a very hot day and Frank's hand was wet and sweaty. O'Yee's was gooey with chalk.

"Christopher . . ."

"Yes?"

Franklin Feng said in perfect English with his eyes suddenly glistening with tears, *"Great Heaven, Christopher, with no time left for poetry or good fellowship or talk, I hate the way the world is going these days! Don't you?"*

Auden said, *"What barely two-foot-wide catwalk on the outside of the building?"*

Spencer said, "He's joking. It doesn't matter to him." He looked at Auden. Spencer said, "He's a true hero. He'll be glad to do it."

Auden said, "I didn't see any barely two-foot-wide catwalk on the outside of the building."

It threw him for a moment, but then he saw it: it was a little *joke*—Hero Humor. Aaron said, "Ha. Ha. That's because it *is* only barely two-foot wide and not meant to intrude on the sheer, monolithlike appearance of the building this high up." He reached down and, at a touch of a button, a long drawer under his chair slid out. He was still grinning at the Heroic Jest, "Naturally, you will probably scorn even the least assistance, but just in case, and to please us, perhaps you might allow us to supply you a few little items that may assist you—" He looked up at Auden. The man was built like an oak door. Aaron said, "You probably only need nothing more in your venture than your courage which you have in overflowing measure and your True Grit, which you already have in great sackfuls, but perhaps you will allow us to—"

Auden said to Douglas, "What barely two-foot-wide catwalk? I didn't see any barely two-foot-wide catwalk." He looked at Spencer, "Did you, Bill? Did you see a—"

Aaron said humbly, hoping the man would take the gifts, "A few minor aids that may assist you—if you don't object." Maybe with people like Auden it was like asking Sir Lancelot on his way to the Crusades if he'd like to take along a few pointed paper airplanes to toss in the general direction of the retreating rear guard of the Saracen army after he'd torn the best shock troops of their cavalry to pieces in hand-to-hand combat solely with his bare fists and battle-ax, but he tried anyway. "A walkie-talkie to stay in contact with Mr. Spencer should you wish, improbably, to consult on some point of physical prowess with him; spare handcuffs to restrain, if necessary, the poor soul or souls hovering on the edge of the window or windows until you can shove him or them back from the brink; a solar topee hat for the sun and also so that anyone seeing you from the street from far below will merely assume you are a window cleaner and not interfere with you in your task; a mixed wad of multicolored artisan's rags to further fix the point; a large, heavy-duty rubber band to hold the hat down in the event of high winds—and a brand new Little League aluminum baseball bat for the birds."

He offered these things humbly. He waited for the great man to merely scoff at them.

Auden said to anyone who might listen, "What—?"

No one listened.

Aaron said in admiration, "The Hero! See how his face is frozen in determination! See how he continues unceasingly to make light of what to mere ordinary men like ourselves would be the prospect of unspeakable fear and almost certain death! See how he looks at us all dully as if he does not quite comprehend how awful a death by falling from eighteen stories to the street below could be for any of we merely mortal men!"

No one listened.

Douglas said, "Yes!" He was beside himself with admiration. He looked at Spencer. Douglas said, "What a man!" He almost yelled, leading the crowd of admirers to a frenzy, "Will he do it?"

Auden said, "Bill—?"

No one listened.

It was a wow of a job, a chance to delve deeply into the dark recesses of the human mind, to go boldly where no man had ever gone before, to— He looked at the blank screens on the wall, each of them connected to a room of wonderment. Spencer roared, "Yes! He'll do it! Nothing frightens him!"

He never ceased from gaiety. He even did it with his nearest and dearest friend. Auden, putting his hand suddenly to the side of his face as if he equated the whole terrifying, awful prospect *with nothing more than a simple trip to the dentist to have a tooth filled* said, playing the part wonderfully, making them all laugh—oh, what a card he was!— "What—? What—?" He looked hard at the gifts from the Magi to try to work out what they all were.

He couldn't work them out.

Auden said, in sudden terror, still making everyone chortle, "What *catwalk?* What *high winds?* What— What— *birds?*"

With Frank gone, sitting alone on the street in front of the smelliest, dirtiest loading dock of the smelliest dirtiest fish market anywhere in the world, O'Yee looked up, but there was no help in heaven, only a window cleaner getting out gingerly from a window on the top floor of the Hop Sing Wa Building onto what looked like a frail window-cleaner's catwalk about two-foot wide.

From that distance, it was hard to tell, but the man seemed to be carrying something silver in his hand, and, for a moment, wallowing in the lost dreams of his childhood, O'Yee thought it looked exactly like a brand-new, aluminum, American Little League–size baseball bat . . .

Ah, the snows of yesteryear, dreams of things that might have been . . .

Either that, or it was a huge, silver, succulent, freshly caught fish.

He looked up again and squinted his eyes to see it.

Yep, that was what it was all right. It was a fish.

Forty thousand seagulls couldn't be wrong.

Coming suddenly out of every eave and nook and cranny and rafter in the fish markets behind him, cawing and screeching, and, mad with hunger and blood lust, they rose up in a single formation towards the catwalk on the eighteenth floor of the Hop Sing Wa Building to get it.

7.

In the Morgue, Dr. Macarthur took up something from the instrument table next to him, and then, as Feiffer looked away,
there was the sound of metal cutting into flesh and bone and
sinew, and then, as if the dead figure on the stainless-steel
postmortem table still lived, there was, in that awful windowless
room, the sound of a sigh.

It was a sigh of triumph. Macarthur, bending down to peer
hard into whatever it was he had exposed inside the corpse
with his saw, said, justified, "Ah. Right as usual."

What he had cut through with his surgical steel saw on the
first corpse—Mr. Lee—was the throat and windpipe. Bending down into the cavity, pulling back the subdural tissue
with his gloved fingers, he shone the light from a silver ENT
flashlight deep into the cavity and lit it up.

Dressed in his postmortem leather apron, peering down
into the opening in the naked flesh under a huge ceiling-
mounted overhead light, he looked like a meat inspector in
an abattoir checking a carcass before giving it his stamp of
approval.

Under him, Mr. Lee looked cold and waxy. Mounted in
the light there was the microphone for a tape recorder, and
Macarthur, speaking up to it, said for the record, justified in
his original on-the-spot diagnosis at the bank, "As expected,

the interior of the throat demonstrates the characteristic burned appearance of the ingestion of a toxic substance—in this case—" He bent closer into the laid-open throat and seemed to thrust his hawklike nose in to actually smell it, "potassium cyanide." He looked up again to where the microphone was, "Note the typical dusky color of the skin of the face associated with toxic asphyxiation and the constriction of the blood vessels leading up into it."

On the table, he had the neck and throat open like some ghastly full-colored illustration in a medical textbook. Straightening up a little and turning to glance back at Feiffer standing back by the line of gurneys where the other eight bodies lay under morgue sheets awaiting the same treatment, Macarthur asked, "Which one is this? Male, Chinese, well nourished. About fifty."

It was Lee. Even with the air conditioning going full blast, without windows to ventilate it, the autopsy room smelled like some sort of awful secret place in a pyramid full of the heavy thick odors of decay and evisceration and death, and, wincing with the smell of it, and with the smell of Macarthur's cigarette burning away in a glass ashtray set across the blood drain hole at the foot of the table, Feiffer had to fight hard to get his breath to answer.

Feiffer said, almost gagging with the effort, "It's the manager, Mr. Lee." He still had Lee's folder from the bank, but with the dead parked on their gurneys everywhere in the room, with all the steel tables and shelves full of the things of the dead or the devices to be used on the dead, there was nowhere to put it down and open it. "He was one of the five bodies found in the main customer area of the place."

There must have been some sort of automatic scales mechanism wired up to the stainless-steel table because Macarthur said without touching anything or adjusting anything or even turning back to the table, "Body weight one hundred twenty-nine pounds three ounces." He turned and looked up to the microphone again, "In my opinion, considering the body weight of the subject and the widespread area and depth of toxic burning present in the throat, death was almost instantaneous—notwithstanding, judging by the presence of traces of another, so far unidentified, substance still lodged in the burned area of the soft tissues in the throat, that the poison was not administered straight but masked or mixed in with something else." He glanced up at the light. With all the best graduate students from the university choosing careers, not in the low-paid area of government pathology, but in the glamor fields of pediatrics or neurosurgery—or anything that might get them an overseas appointment before the Communists took over—he had to keep it simple for the unqualified nurses' aides who transcribed his notes these days: "Obviously, nobody could have drunk a lethal amount of potassium cyanide without it being masked by another substance to disguise its taste and instantaneous burning sensation."

He did not want to come forward and have to look down at the thing on the table under Macarthur's overhead light. Standing by the next gurney in line, raising his voice a little to make it carry into the recorder, Feiffer asked, "What do you think it was masked with, Tony? Any ideas?"

He turned to look at him. He would have liked Feiffer to come and stand at the table with him and keep him company, but obviously he was not going to. "It was masked with the substance apparently still residually lodged in the soft tissues of the throat." He turned back to the table, and just for a second, Feiffer saw Lee's entire neck section laid open like a gutted fish. Macarthur, cutting even deeper into it with a scalpel, said for the tape, "After all the preliminary examinations are completed here, a thorough chemical sample analysis by the laboratory should reveal the exact nature of the masking agent." He dug down and freed a lump of the substance from the throat and held it up on the blade of his knife, "Small sample of substance removed. Substance is of white granular appearance still retaining traces of a clear liquid and of another substance that—" Macarthur said suddenly, turning around to show Feiffer the smear on the curve of the glittering knife, "It's sugar!"

Feiffer asked, "And the liquid around it?"

Macarthur said, "Water. And the other substance—the one that seems to have lodged higher up in the throat—the other white substance in the throat that *isn't* sugar—"

Feiffer said, "Is what?" There was no alternative. He went forward and, standing beside Macarthur, looked down at the dissected, opened nightmare creature on the table that had once been Mr. Lee.

He thought about it for an instant. Macarthur said slowly, "Is—I don't know." He reached down into the throat with the knife, and, with a twist, cut out a core of tissue and held it high up to the light to look at it. "I'm not sure. Judging by the signs of rapid chemical decomposition of some of its grains brought on by contact with the sugar and water—and probably saliva—it's some sort of calcium derivative: a carbonated form of calcium."

"Which means what?"

He didn't hesitate. He didn't care about what happened after the Communists took over the Colony. He had been the government medical officer long enough to qualify for a more-than-adequate pension, and, at home in England, he had a house in the country with enough room to set up a small part-time medical practice that he had almost paid off, "Which means, death was caused by toxic asphyxiation due to the oral ingestion of a respiratory-inhibiting agent—in this case, cyanide—mixed in with a solution of water and sugar and calcium carbonate—or, in any event, a calcium derivative that gave off carbon-dioxide gas when it was brought into contact with the water." He turned for a moment to Feiffer, "In my opinion, using the present subject as a control, as someone who clearly died instantaneously, the people who crawled away to the rest room to die either didn't get the same dose as he did, or they had a larger body weight and it took longer to work through their systems, or—" He thought about it for a moment. Macarthur said slowly and carefully, "Or they didn't drink as much of the solution, or—or they only sipped at it, or— Or some of them weren't given as much of the poison to drink as others, or—" Suddenly, he knew what the solution was. Macarthur said in triumph, "I know what it is!"

"What is it?"

God, he was going to miss it. He was going to miss the joy over the years of passing on what he had learned. He was going to miss the thrill of the inferential leaps that turned a good pathologist into a great one. Macarthur said, to make the moment, "What is it?" He was going to miss giving evidence in courtrooms and stilling them with the power of his irrefutable, calmly delivered scientific logic. Macarthur asked, "What is it? What did nine people in a bank drink simultaneously that completely and totally masked the taste and smell of the potassium cyanide in it that killed them? *What does a combination of water and sugar and carbonate make?*"

"Some sort of soda solution, or—"

"Or what else?"

He looked down into Lee's face. In the bank, all of them had drunk the poison all at once, as if it were—

Feiffer said in a whisper, "Oh, my God!"

"Yes! Yes!" Macarthur said in triumph, knowing he knew, "So what is it, Harry? What is it that nine people all drink together—in unison—in a bank that kills them? What the hell is it that makes the doses vary? What is it masked by? What is it that they think they are drinking? What is it that someone drinks *at exactly the same time as someone else that cannot be refused?*" Macarthur, listing off the points with his fingers one by one, said, to savor the glory and simplicity and elegance of it, "Sugar. Carbon-dioxide gas. All drunk simultaneously in solution form as if at a single command— What is it?" Macarthur said in his glory, in his finest moment, "It's *champagne!*"

He had been, he always thought, the best teacher, the finest cutter there had ever been.

Macarthur said, grinning with victory, "Harry, when I leaned in to look into the throat with the flashlight, I actually *smelled* it!"

Feiffer said softly, "So when they drank the poison—God in heaven, they—"

"Yes! Yes!" In the Morgue, surrounded by all the cold, naked dead, Macarthur said in triumph, conscious only of his own brilliance, "Yes. A moment before they died they thought—they all must have thought because they all drank it together—that they were there, not to die, but to celebrate or commemorate something—something *wonderful!*"

Maybe he should have helped in some way: before he had been cast down by an uncaring world into the slough of slovenliness via the pit of no pity, he had been a policeman who helped people.

He had. Once, as his Irish-American mother had confided in him on her third glass of gin, he was the greatest of the great Chinese-Irish cop O'Yees. (Maybe it was her fourth glass—he was the only Chinese-Irish cop O'Yee.)

Once, if he had seen some poor window cleaner fighting for his life against a sea of seagulls on what looked like a barely two-foot-wide catwalk on the eighteenth story of a building, he would have thrown personal safety to the winds and rushed up there to do something to help.

Ah, the dreams of yesterday . . . The things that might have been.

Now, thanks to RTG–68, all that was gone, and he had to be content to sit alone and unimportant among the fish heads and only watch as the poor soul up there fought for his life with bat and fish and fists and shrieks that made his ears ring and let the seagull feathers fall where they may . . .

They were extremely big seagulls.

The feathers, as they wafted to the ground, looked heavy.

In the Morgue, Feiffer put Lee's folder of the last day's business open on top of a stainless-steel tray of clamps and resectors laid out ready for an autopsy to come after the ones from the bank were completed. They were all clamps and re-sectors of tiny size: they were the opening and gutting mech-anisms for a baby. Under the open folder, with the vibration of the electric sternum saw Macarthur was using to open up the chest of the second body from the bank, they tinkled and moved from one end of the tray to the other like tiny silver soldiers.

Inside the folder, there was nothing of importance or sub-stance, only the thing that Mansor with his accountant's mind had collected that he thought were important. There were only stapled-together sheets of filled-in bank forms: loans granted or denied, cash and check amounts paid out or paid in and reconciled, overseas drafts sent or received, agio payments received on transactions in foreign currency or for-eign currency requiring agio payments to others, and, here and there, interspersed throughout it all, pages and pages of

memos, notes, and aides-mémoires written on blank sheets
of paper in both English and Chinese in Lee's spidery hand
that listed all the dealings of the bank in full and exhaustive,
careful detail.

They were the pages, all the details, of the last day of Mr.
Lee's life.

In all the side and top and bottom margins of all the memo
and note pages there were little blocks of sums and calculations everywhere written in pencil, estimates, projections,
additions and subtractions, and, where he must have sat
through some interminable interview or for some other reason been stuck at his desk bored beyond description, a single
page covered in doodles of triangles and squares and what
looked like little curved pagoda roofs free-floating in the sky.

There was nothing in the folder with the number I–797–6–
29–88 on it, or anything with a logo or trademark or a
colophon resembling the wings of a hawk or a bird of prey
printed on it.

Attached to the inside cover by a blue-plastic paper clip
there was a single sheet of paper breaking down the events of
the day's business—the highs and lows of commerce—with
Lee's signature at the bottom of it, and Feiffer, moving the
folder on the tray and making the instruments under it tinkle,
bent down to read it.

*Cash Reserves at Start of Business Day (including nego-
tiable instrs, T/Cs, etc.):*
Lee had written in: *$HK 5.21 million.*

Cash Reserves at End of Business Day: *$HK 21.1 Million.*
(do. above)

Remarks: *None.*

It was nothing special, just another day.

Staff Performance:
   (a) Counter. He had written in the space   *Satisfactory.*
   (b) Clerical and Other.   *Satisfactory.*

Absentees: *None.*

Manager's Comments or Recommendations: *None.*

Time of Opening for Public Business: 8:59 A.M.
Time of Closing for Public Business: 5:01 P.M.

Remarks:

At the postmortem table, Macarthur said in triumph, "Look at this! More of the calcium substance in this one's throat, a lot more!" He reached over and threw his bloody scalpel onto the steel tray at the top of the table and took up from it an electric cranium saw and flipped it on and made it whirr, "Now, let's take the top of the skull off so we can examine the brain and see just how long this one lasted!"

He never looked at the faces of the dead, merely identified their sex, race, general appearance, and age for the tape.

He identified this one.

Macarthur said, glancing quickly over the naked dead creature on the tray, raising his voice slightly over the whirring of the saw, "Female, Chinese, about twenty to twenty-five, demonstrating slightly uncharacteristically pudgy face and hands development for general body shape. Probably caused by late retention of residual so-called baby fat . . ."

Maybe it was all some sort of plot to make him resign so RTG–68 could have his job, and his wife, and his children, and his socks—and anything else he wanted . . .

O'Yee, deep in paranoia, said, "Yeah! That's it! That's it all right!" The screaming and bashing and bird battery from the eighteenth floor above him was so loud he could hardly hear himself think, and O'Yee shrieked at the top of his voice to the desperate man up there hacking away at the flotilla of birds with his fish, "At least you've got a job where you get treated like a man!"

The window cleaner, covered in pigeons, shrieked back down, "Ooohhh!"

Once he had been a cop: a man dedicated to the aid and

assistance of others, a defender of justice and truth. Now all he was was a bum.

The bum shrieked back up to the window cleaner, "*Ooohhh* yourself!"

The window cleaner screamed down eighteen floors, "Aaaahhh!"

How the hell could you be expected to think when the air was full of falling feathers?

The bum screamed back, "*Aaaahhh* yourself!" The bum screamed up eighteen floors, "And mind where you throw your goddamned feathers, will you!"

The window cleaner, only a tiny dot in a skyscape full of birds, shrieked down, "Aaar! Oh! Aaarrgghhh!"

O'Yee shrieked back, "*Aaar! Oh! Aaarrgghhh* yourself!"

It felt good.

He did it again.

So, over and over again, flailing and whacking at the birds with his silver fish, way up on the eighteenth floor on a catwalk barely two-foot wide, did the window cleaner.

The window cleaner shrieked in a cry of ultimate, torn-to-pieces horror that not even O'Yee was able to emulate in its total, wild, terrified desperation, "Oh! Oh! Oh! Aaar! Oh! *Aaaaarrrrggghhh!*"

Inside the bulk of the folder there was a single sheet of paper listing all of Mr. Lee's appointments for the day.

9:00 A.M.:	Mr. and Mrs. Kwai.
Re:	Advice on rollover of fixed deposits.
Result:	Advice to rollover accepted.
Further Action:	Counter staff advised to execute rollover.
10:00 A.M.:	Telephone Temple Lamp Company (Mr. Lam).
Re:	Additional collateral required for refinancing of loan.
Result:	Additional satisfactory collateral offered.
Further Action:	Refinancing approved subject to verification and lodgement of deeds to additional collateral.

It was a list of appointments and events on a day when nothing had happened, when there had been no drain on cash reserves, no absenteeism, no recommendations, and nothing out of the ordinary at all.

It had been a day like any other, just another day in the week.

11:00 A.M.:   No appointment.

Maybe he had strolled out to the main counter and talked to one of the customers for a while, or checked that there were no absentees, or—

12:00 noon: Lunch.

And then maybe gone out somewhere into the mall, or out into the street and had his lunch, or—

In the Morgue, the smell of burning hair and bone as the cranium saw cut into the girl's skull was overpowering.

1:00 P.M.:   Transfer of funds to Bank of Manila requested.

He had not even bothered to fill in the spaces on that one, but merely scribbled the details on the page as, one by one, he must have gotten them: *To branch: Roxas Avenue. Sender: R. K. Olivera (Phil. citizen, HK Central Bank permission N/A). Recipient's Name: M. J. Olivera. Amount: Phil. Pesos P2,280.*

It was nothing, just a remittance home from some overseas worker's wages to his family. It was no appointment at all, just something Lee must have stopped at the counter to do on his way back in from lunch to help out one of the tellers.

1:30 P.M.:   Mr. and Mrs. Tak.
Re: Apartment purchase loan.

It had been approved.

2:00 P.M.:   Henry James Wu, age 19.
Re: Extension of credit (college fees).
Approved.

It was nothing. It was the daily, ordinary stuff of the ordinary, mundane business of the bank. It was about people buying homes, students, small companies expanding, Philippino expatriates sending part of their weekly wages home to their families. It was nothing, insignificant.

3:30 P.M.:   Check cash reserves, confirm totals of foreign currency exchange. Check appointments for tomorrow.

It was nothing.

4:00 P.M.:   Begin reconciliation all transactions.

It was all nothing.

4:30 P.M.:   Complete all transaction reconciliations and verify figures with counter staff.

There was nothing at all!

5:01 P.M.:   Bank closed for public business.
Date: And he had dated it.
Initialed: And initialed it: *T. M. Lee. (Mgr.)*

And then, probably less than fifty minutes later, everyone in the bank, including him, was dead.

At the table, Macarthur had the pudgy girl's brain exposed.

Behind him, still staring at the appointment list for something, anything that might tell him what they all had to celebrate that day, Feiffer heard him, in precise, full, awful detail, begin recording his observations.

8.

The normal, ordinary, respectable seagull is the *Larus argentatus*—a nice-looking bird of about three pounds weight with a white head and clean wings and a general appearance of having been raised on a nice clean white navy ship with three squares a day and a little saluting of the flag on the stern before bedtime.

What continued to come up towards the catwalk at the speed of light in hordes, in armies, in armadas, screaming and cawing, didn't have a *Larus argentatus* among them. (Or if they had once, they had eaten it.) What continued to come up were *Larus cutthroatatus:* fish-market seagulls, seagulls who shot it out with gangsters, seagulls with tattoos.

These seagulls weren't human. These seagulls, all forty thousand of them, were the Hell's Angels of seagulls, seagulls so tough they had hairy armpits, seagulls so bad that after they had sunk twenty-thousand-ton Japanese trawlers pulling into the fish markets and eaten the crews raw they sat around on pylons smoking cigars and drinking straight-up diesel fuel.

And they were big—a lot bigger than three pounds.

And they weren't white.

They were a kind of gunpowder color.

And there were a lot of them.

On the catwalk, Auden yelled to the closed window behind him as the entire world went dark with them around him, "Bill! Bill!" but Spencer had gone off into one of the rooms of Yu with the two Yu brothers and there was no one there.

Auden, raising his baseball bat above his head to fend off the first wave, yelled at the top of his lungs in a voice that carried across the ocean to Australia, but not across the corridor to Spencer, "Bill! Bill! *Bill!*"

Ducking, he took a single swipe at the first seagull in line—a huge, horrible-looking dirty object with one blind eye and what looked like a wooden leg where his claw should be—and got it square in the head.

It was a hell of a swat with the business end of the bat that would have killed three men.

It didn't kill the seagull.

With a ringing, solid sound of aluminum hitting steel, as the seagull wheeled over him to tear him to pieces a second before the rest of them got there to pick over his bones and clothing, the bat simply—making every fiber in Auden's arms shake with the vibration—bounced off.

He was the Eternity Man.

He didn't care.

Shuffling his way down Tiger Snake Road, swinging his coat hanger as the sky filled yet again with the armada of seagulls flying back the other way cawing and wheeling in triumph over whatever prize they had wrested from the window cleaner up on the eighteenth-floor catwalk, O'Yee, heading for whatever it was that cruel fate had in store for him, clanked ever on to nowhere and nothing.

He clanked on all the way to the eastern end of Tiger Snake Road then turned right onto Wyang Street and—almost as if it was exactly what cruel fate had in store for him and the man had been waiting for him to come—instantly tripped over Franklin Feng taking a nap on the sidewalk and fell over headfirst dead center into the hard, horrible embrace of his open, ancient, welcoming arms.

In the Morgue, looking away from where the pudgy girl's cut-away hair hung down over the back of the stainless-steel table in matted, bloody clumps, Feiffer turned the appointment record sheet over.

Written in pencil on the back, there was a list of telephone calls scribbled all over the page that, beginning at a little after 10:00 A.M. and continuing right through until almost the last moment of his life, had made Mr. Lee angry.

It was a list of calls to someone called . . . "Tolliver."

On the sidewalk at the corner of Wyang Street, wrestling to keep him in his grip, Frank Feng screamed to O'Yee, "I have to know! I have to know! *What in the name of heaven is the coat hanger for?*"

He got loose. Loose? He was never going to be loose.

O'Yee screamed back, "I don't know! I don't know! *I don't know!*"

He could have sat down and wept.

He did. He sat down beside Frank and wept.

He was only a cockroach: how did he know the machinations of men?

O'Yee said sadly to his friend, the only person on the face of the earth who cared about him enough to ask, "Frank, I'm forty-six years old. And suddenly"—he balled his fist and knocked it against the twenty-five feet of half-inch chain that bound him around his chest, "And, suddenly—I don't know anything anymore!"

Heroes fought like lions.

Lions fought like tigers.

Audens about to become Seagull Leavings fought like they were about to be eaten alive.

On the catwalk, bashing and swiping at the seagulls as they swarmed around him like Stukas, Auden screamed, "Take that! And that! And that!" They took it. In their sea chests back on the pylons, these seagulls had Iron Crosses: they had been in battle before.

And they knew tactics. They didn't come in one at a time, or even two at a time, or even three at a time. They came in in waves, in droves, in hordes. They came in like regiments of obedient Huns given a single order to do or die. They came in in a typhoon of flapping wings and screeching war

cries, in a hurricane of flying feathers and balled-up claws
and razor-sharp beaks.

They came in for the long, juicy, baseball bat–sized silver
fish.

Well, they weren't going to damn well get it! On the catwalk, Auden, swiping at a bird so beaten up and ragged he
should have been called Spike, roared, "Take that!" and hit
Spike so hard the next time Spike walked the poop deck he
was going to do it on crutches. Behind Spike there were a
dozen more Spikes just like him to take his place. He hit the
next one on the head and made it reel, then the second on the
tail feathers and shot its rudder away, then the third and
fourth he missed, and then the fifth caught hold of his bat
and shook it, and as he swung at the sixth and seventh in
line, the fifth came off the end of the bat like a cannonball
and hit the sixth and seventh amidships and sent them
foundering back to the rear of the armada in flames.

Fifteen others he didn't get hit him on the hat and began
pecking. They pecked through the linen covering to the cork.
They pecked through the cork. One of the pecks in the cork
was just in the right place over where the little storage bin in
his brain was that held his last major thought.

The last major thought he'd had was "Hero."

His heroes had always been old salts and sea captains.

He had read a lot of books about them when he'd been a
lad.

And pirates.

He knew how they talked.

Auden screamed, "Ah, too much for 'ee, aye, ye scum of
the seven seas?" The eighth and ninth hit him square in the
crow's nest and hoed his hat in a dozen places. "More used
to fat, unmarked merchantmen sailing around in the old Ja-
makey Sea and givin' up at the first shot across the bows, are
'ee? *Ye black-earted from 'ell bilgewater bollard sea-brig-
ands with ye black flag an' ye even blacker 'earts!*" (By this
time, the birds on his hat had gotten through the cork and
were pecking at his head. After a while, all those little pecks
echoing in the brainpan added up.) Auden screamed, "Mid-
shipman Auden of His Brittanic Majesty's eighty-gun ship
Oak Door don't give up so easy as 'em as what ye been used

to does, does 'ee?" The pecking reached something vital inside his brain and fused it. Mowing down four of them in a single forward sweep and them mowing down another four on the return, Auden roared, "I'll sweep the old Caribee free of all of 'ee and see 'ee all hangin' from a yardarm at Port Royal afore I'm done with 'ee!"

The thing inside his head the pecking had fused was the remote-control channel changer for his brain. Stuck on *Search*, it kept changing channels and Heroes.

It changed to Heroes at the Charge of the Light Brigade. "Seagulls to the right of them, seagulls to the left of them . . ." Colonel Auden of Her Majesty's Death's-head Hussars, roared to his regiment of trembling troopers, "Follow me, lads! Into the Valley of Death—*ride for the sea-gulls!*"

He got one: a huge, hairy Slavic-looking Cossack one named—he'd bet—Dmitri—and with a mighty wallop sent him cartwheeling back towards Moscow.

His channel changed. He was Major-General Auden at the Battle of the Bulge. Major-General Auden roared, "Send more seagulls!" He hit an entire panzer thrust of the filthy invaders with a mighty swipe from his bat and sent them scuttling—Nazi swine!—and then his brain changed channels again, and deep in blood lust, full five-star General and famed Commander in Chief of the Pacific Theatre Douglas MacAuden thundered, "I have returned!" and clobbered an entire formation of kamikaze Zeros in one go and sent them fleeing back out to sea.

Auden said in his deepest voice, "Never in the field of human conflict has so much been owed by so many to so few . . ."

He was in heaven. He was on the catwalk of the Institute of Yu moving through one Yu after another faster and more deeply than any man had ever moved through all his Yus before. He was at *satori*: his Essence—Zen in the Art of Seagull Slogging.

He hit one.

He hit another.

Auden shrieked, *"Aaaaiiiya!"*

Someone else just by him at an open window shrieked the same.

Auden said, "What?" and covered from head to foot in raging, beating, flapping, pecking seagulls, turned quickly, bat in hand, to see who it was.

"Tolliver"—he or she—was a doctor of some sort.

Put together from its chaos of circles and squares and underlinings all over the page, Lee's angry, scribbled list read in order:

10:10 A.M.—Call Dr. Tolliver.
Result—Unavailable.
11:00 A.M.—Call Dr. Tolliver.
Result—Unavailable.
11:55 A.M.—Call Dr. Tolliver.
Result—Unavailable.

And then, at twelve noon, according to his appointments list for the day, Mr. Lee had gone to lunch.

And then begun calling again.

At one, he had helped a Philippino named Olivera transfer some money home to his family in Manila, but it was a transaction that must have only taken a few moments because, less than fifteen minutes later, he was back on the phone again:

1:12 P.M.—Call Dr. Tolliver
Result—Unavailable.

Then the style changed as Lee's patience must have run out:

Tolliver—2:10 P.M./Unavailable.
Tolliver—2:30 P.M./Unavailable. Message left on answering machine to return my call as soon as possible.
Tolliver—3:01 P.M./Message left on machine to return my call urgently!
3:45 P.M. *No callback.* Message left that withdrawal of all credit imminent. Personal attendance at bank required this date!

4:55 P.M. Message left as above. Require Dr. Tolliver make
       urgent appointment with me *this date!*

And then there was nothing. And if Tolliver had made an
appointment and come to see Mr. Lee about his loan, he had
made the appointment and come to the bank after it was
closed, when suddenly, according to Mansor, all the phones
had been out of order and, maybe less than forty minutes
later, everyone in the bank was dead.

Tolliver. It was just a name, with no address and no first
name or initials, nothing to show whether it was even a man
or a woman.

At the table, Macarthur had the pudgy girl's brain out on
the table, dissecting one of the lobes with a scalpel, and Feiffer asked him because at the moment he had no one else to
ask, "Tony, I don't know if he or she is even medical, but
have you ever heard of anyone in the Colony named Dr. *Tolliver?*"

He was a nice old guy, old Frank, and he looked, in the
comforting setting of the mounds of trash and fish parts piled
up against the corner of the street he rested his back against,
just like O'Yee's—

He did. With his kind face and soft eyes, he looked just
like . . .

He sighed. Under his breath so no one heard, O'Yee said
softly, "Oh . . . Ba-aa, *Ba-aa* . . ."

It was soft, like a sigh—in Chinese, a small child's word
for "Daddy."

Sometimes, especially now as he grew older, he missed
him more than he could bear.

The scream of *"Aaaaiiiya!"* was from the stockbroker's
clerk Warrior from the Great Wall Room, getting out an
open window with the clear intent of committing suicide,
and, by Jimmy, by Corn Cob Pipe, the Old Soldierman the
Yus had placed their faith in to save the Pacific—the Hero of
Heroes—did his job as God had given him the light to see it.

He saw the light.

Dressed in full leather armor and carrying a long Chinese sword, he saw—

He saw a seagull poacher.

Auden shrieked, "You bastard! *Get away from my seagulls!*" and in a single heroic movement—the stuff epics were made of—drew back his bat and smashed the man square on the horned helmet to blast him back inside and, in a flurry of feathers as the entire formation of seagulls fled in fear, clambered in after him to beat him to death on the floor of the corridor with his fists.

In the Morgue, Macarthur, holding part of the pudgy girl's dissected brain in his gloved hand, said with a smile, "Sure, I've heard of him. I knew him slightly. He used to teach at the university when I did. He used to be a full-time academic. Like everyone else when it looked like the Communists might take over earlier than expected he tried to get a placement overseas, but he just wasn't in one of the zippy-doo Academic Doctor for God fields that everybody seems to want these days so he left teaching and went into private consultancy work." He glanced down at the brain and tested its weight, "Why do you ask?"

"What field is he in?"

"Toxicology." He looked down at the brain and then back up again to Feiffer, "He's in the field of toxicology—poisons."

Inside the awful place full of all the dead and all the smells of the dead, for a moment there was no sound at all.

"Why?" In that dreadful, ghastly place, Macarthur asked with sudden alarm, as if he did not want to hear the answer, "Why? What is it?" He saw Feiffer look down again at the single sheet of paper, "What is it? *What is it you've got there in your hand?*"

9.

It was as if he had been waiting to hear it all his life.

Frank said, "You called me *Baa-aa!* 'Father!'"

"No, I didn't!" O'Yee said, "No!" He hadn't. He had not. He hadn't. It was merely the sound of one of the gods in heaven sighing at Man's condition on earth, or the sound of a tree falling in the forest with no one to hear it—or a snarl or a growl or a belch or a mistimed kick from one of the thousands of people trying to make their way down Wyang Street to their places of business and wishing the two stinking smelly bums sitting on the sidewalk would get the fuck out of their way. O'Yee said, shaking his head, "No."

Frank said, "I heard you! I heard it said! I head the word *Baa-aa!*"

"No! No!" He tried to look away, but could not. O'Yee said, "No, it was not I!"

He had such a nice face. A woman carrying shopping bags took a kick at the nice face as it bent down close to O'Yee's, but the nice face—above such worldly things—ignored it. In its eyes, the face yearned for something. The face looked like it had found it. Frank, reaching out to O'Yee's shoulder and holding onto it with a grip of iron, said in his joy, "Yes! I heard! I heard it said. It was you! It was *you!*"

"It was not I. The word was not mine, but another's."

"No, it was you."

"No, it was not!" He couldn't look into Frank's face. O'Yee, looking away, not even seeing or lip-reading the seven-generation curses being heaped upon him and his friend by the witches and harpies in the street who masqueraded as simple shoppers trying to make their way down a public throughfare without having their eyes or noses assaulted by the sight of the Obnoxious of the World lying about in their paths, said with his hand raised in an oath, "It was not I, I swear—it was not I!"

"It was you!"

"Upon my life, it was not!"

It was beginning to sound to O'Yee like the final scene in *Cyrano de Bergerac* as the dying Cyrano protested to Roxanne that he had never written the love letters to her that had won her heart for another.

It was beginning to sound to Frank like a lovely passage in a commentary on the perfection of the soul of the true Buddha-follower, where the gentle older and more mature soul, taking it in the cupped palms of his hands, conveyed the striving, imperfect soul of the lesser, younger man safely through the stages of change and birth and rebirth to—

It sounded to a coolie pushing a cartful of rice sacks *who had to work for a goddamned living!*—like two freeloading bums about to demand money from him to let him get past them on a public thoroughfare that his taxes paid for.

The coolie, aiming a kick from his sandaled foot at Frank's head and only missing by a fraction, yelled, *"Sut ne go tao!*—I'll cut your heads off!" He would have stopped for a moment or two to kill the pair of them, but he didn't have time—and, anyway, as the old bum bent in closer to the younger bum, there was room to get his cart by, and as he got it by in a rush that got him a string of seven-year curses from a second roving coven of witches in front of him masquerading as a second gaggle of weighted-down middle-aged shoppers struggling with their plastic bags of packaged food, fresh fish, bagged rice, bottles of bat's blood, and eyes of newt.

Frank said with his face only an inch from O'Yee's, "You-called-me-Daddy—*Father!*"

"No!" His father was dead.

"Your soul hungers!"

"No, it does not!"

"You read baleful poetic ballads—sad songs sung in verse about the lost joy of innocence and the warm, loving comfort and ease of—"

"I deny it completely!" (Once you got old C. K. O'Yee into character, he was lost in it forever. And every time he saw Jose Ferrer do *Cyrano* on the late-night movie, he was useless for days.) "By my plumed hat, I tell you it is not true!"

Frank said quietly, "I can tell by the mere posture of your body that you have been worn down and beaten by the world of the city and that you yearn to return to the primeval world of Nature where you were once a man and there were probably women who would find you attractive."

He shrugged. O'Yee demanded, "How can you tell that?"

"I can tell that because you shrug a lot."

He shrugged. O'Yee said with a shrug, "You just got me upset, that's all. You asked me about the coat hanger and I—" The late-night movie had finished, and suddenly he didn't want to be there anymore. O'Yee said in protest, "You just got me upset asking me about the coat hanger and I didn't know what I was saying!"

"Consider this coat hanger of which we speak!"

He considered it. It was a coat hanger. He didn't shrug. He made sure he didn't shrug. O'Yee said, "What's wrong with it?"

"Quick, without thinking, what's it made of?"

"I don't know." O'Yee said, "Metal wire."

"Is it?"

"Sure. Cheap, second-grade metal wire . . ." He was heading for something significant here. O'Yee said, "It's a *coat hanger!* What do you expect?"

"What do I expect from a man such as you—the man whose soul calls out to me in its darkness, *'Baa-aa, help me find myself for I am lost'?* I expect, at the very least, that the coat hanger he carries should mirror the man he ought to be with my help—and the true mirror of that man is not cheap, second-grade metal wire, but—" On his knees, he raised his arms to heaven, "But *Rattan!*" He fixed O'Yee with a glittering eye. He reached his finale, his spellbinder—why the Academy had handed out the Oscar to Ferrer when they could have given it to Frank was a mystery only the judges knew—"For you are not in your truest of true souls wire, but *rattan!* the Latin for which is—"

O'Yee said, *"Daemonorops oblonga."*

He reached his pitch, "Otherwise known as—"

O'Yee said, "Bamboo! *Bamboo! The strength of Asia! The deep heart of the jungle and all things natural and primeval! The plant that begins in the darkness and entwines itself around boles and branches searching for the light and which cannot be cultivated and which will not regenerate itself other than in the deepest, most secret forest!"*

"Yes!" He was Baa-aa. "Rattan does not *shrug* at life! Rattan fights for the light! Does *wire?"*

"No! It does not!"

"Do *you?"*

"I—" He should. O'Yee said, "I should, but I don't!"

It was the apogee. He was covered in sweat. Bending down from his knees, Frank, his face full of care, building up credits in heaven for good works so fast the celestial accountants had to call for computers to keep pace, roared to the street full of people in a voice so piercing the street full of people became a street no longer full of people, "Christopher O'Yee, fellow seeker of life's secrets on the sidewalk, tell me . . . tell me plainly"—he clasped his hands together in prayer to muster all his strength to see his friend through to the end— "Tell me—deep down—who are you? What is your secret? Who are you? You are not what you seem to be at all. *Who are you?* Who are you *really?"*

In the tiny clerical and administrative office of the Morgue, Feiffer found the entry for Tolliver in the two-year-old copy of the *Scientific Who's Who* the administrative and clerical staff kept on their reference bookshelf, and taking it over to the single desk in the unattended glassed-in room, laid it open under the twenty-watt halogen table lamp on the desk to read it.

The entry took up almost a full page in the book:

* * *

TOLLIVER, Dr. E. G. A. (Edward George Arthur),
b. Cirencester, England 1941. Educated: Clifton School,
Bristol (Lassiter Science Prize, 1958). Degrees: MBBS,
London, 1963 (University Medal, Toxicological Analy-
sis); PhD, Harvard Medical School, USA, 1967 (Thesis:
"The Clinical Toxicology of Phosphorous Additive to
Arsenious Oxide Derivatives").

Publications (USA): "The Basics of a Toxicological
Approach to the Detection of Oleander Plant Poisons in
Human and Animal Tissue with a Specific Reference to
the Yellow Oleander," *New England Journal of Medi-
cine*, 1969. Reprinted in revised and updated form in the
Encylopaedia of Tropical Medicine in Section III:
Forensic Toxicology, New York, 1971.

Publications (UK): "An Analytical Model for the Detec-
tion of Poison in *The Science of Forensic Medicine*,
O.U.P., 1977; "The Chemistry of the Cyanides" in
Pathology,. Volume III of the BMA series, *Notes for
Medical Students*, third ed., 1978.

Lecturer, School of Tropical Medicine, Sydney, Australia, 1970–1975; Guest lecturer in Toxicology, London University, 1976, 1977, 1978; Gordon Professor,
Medical Toxicology, Hong Kong University, Hong
Kong, 1980–1991.

In private practice since 1992. Presently (1993) Chair-
man and Owner, Hong Kong Analysis Laboratories,
Hong Kong.

M. Veronica Everson, London, 1977. Divorced 1979,
no children.

Clubs (1991): Hong Kong Club (HK), Hong Kong Golf
Club (HK), Harvard Club (USA), Garrick Club (UK).

Hobbies: Golf, Oenology.

Address: (Private) c. British Medical Association Overseas Box, London WI; (Business) HK Analysis Laboratories, Cathay Pearl Bldg, Aberdeen Road, HK.

With his hands resting across the open pages of the telephone book–sized tome, Feiffer looked down for a second
time at the entry. He had the wad of Lee's papers from the

bank in the folder beside the book and he reached over for it, and holding it above the book under the light, leafed through it to find the outstanding-loans list, the daily breakdown on the major loans the Asia–America–Hong Kong Bank had out and what was being done to repay them.

There were only four loans listed to be dealt with or reviewed that day, all with the sums owing converted into market-rate US dollars to keep them stable.

The list read:

Action on Outstanding Loans

1. *Debtor:* Industrial Electrical Supplies, Ltd
   (Singapore and HK).

   Amount of Loan in $US: $US 1,523,000.
   Amount Still Outstanding: $US 1,323,000.
   Current Status of Collateralization and Repayment:
   Satisfactory.

   Contact: T. W. Kwan   (CEO Singapore).
   Action Required: None.

2. *Debtor:*   Mercantile Credit, Inc. (Macao and HK).
   Amount of Loan in $US: $US 1,350,000.
   Amount Still Outstanding: $US 1,118,000.
   Current Status of Collateralization and Repayment:
   Satisfactory.

   Contact: A. S. Singh (Exec.-VP Macao).
   Action Required: None.

3. *Debtor:*   Cavite Import-Export Co. (Manila and HK).
   Amount of Loan in $US: $US 1,400,000.
   Amount Still Outstanding: $US 1,212,250.

(It was all written line after line in the appropriate spaces or boxes on the printed form in Lee's neat, unhurried, meticulous hand.)

   Current Status of Collateralization and Repayment:
   Satisfactory.

   Contact: A. J. Alvarez (Pres).
   Action Required: None.

And then—*4.*—there was the loan to Tolliver that had driven Lee to scribble the phone log all over the back of a page in mounting frustration.

4. *Debtor:*   Hong Kong Analysis Laboratories, Ltd.
                                          (Hong Kong).
    Amount of Loan in $US: $US 250,000.00.
    Amount Still Outstanding: $US 235,150.09.

(Not, like all the others, a rounded-off figure, but the figure to the exact penny.)

    Current Status of Collateralization and Repayment:
                                  Highly *Unsatisfactory!*
    Contact: Dr. Tolliver.
    Action Required: Cancellation of All Credit Facilities This Date! Full and Total Repayment Required This Date!

And then from the time—presumably first thing in the morning at the start of business—that Lee had made his decision about Tolliver's loan, he had tried to get the man to come in during business hours to tell him what arrangements he intended to make.

And failed at it.

And gotten in, after business hours when there was no record of it, not Tolliver the debtor, but Tolliver the mass murderer.

And, with all the members of his staff, died.

Under the twenty-watt light on the desk, Feiffer read first a single word on the loans page under Tolliver's name.

He read *Debt.*

He read for that word:

Motive.

He read on the list of telephone calls, *4:55 P.M.*

He read for that:

Opportunity.

He read in Tolliver's entry in *Who's Who: Toxicology.*

He read for that:

Means.

He heard a sudden high-pitched whirring sound start in the postmortem room where Macarthur was and he looked up from the papers through the glass windows to see Macarthur carefully lean down over the naked, dead girl on the table with a long, gleaming surgical power saw to begin splitting her open from end to end to get at the heart and stomach.

He read in *Who's Who,* right at the end where the man's hobbies were listed, *Oenology.*

He read for that:

The study and collecting of *wine.*

He read for that:

Means.

He read for that: *Champagne.*

In the street, Frank yelled to the trembling, fragile soul of O'Yee, "Be free! Divest yourself of all that you are not! Throw away your coat hanger! Throw away your chalk! Throw away your chains!"

O'Yee's trembling soul yelled back, "I can't!"

"You must!"

"I can't!"

"You *can!*"

"I *can't!*"

"You *must!*"

"I *mustn't!*"

"You have to!"

"I can't!"

"Why not?"

"I— Because . . . because—" He said it. O'Yee shrieked, "Because of— Because of orders!" He wished he had died before he said it. He knew how it sounded. O'Yee shrieked, "Because of *orders!* Because of *orders from above!*"

There was a silence, then Frank said in a gasp, "Oh!"

He had not realized how fragile and trembling the ragged little man's soul really was and how fast he had tried to take him on the express train to enlightenment.

Frank said softly, full of self-reproach, "Oh, I am so sorry."

He was a nice man, Frank, with a warm, loving voice just like his poor dead dad's.

And just like *Baa-aa,* he understood how sometimes things just had to go slowly, and in the darkness, sometimes one faltering step at a time.

Frank, his face softening as he stepped out of the driver's seat of the streamlined atomic-powered monorail *Perfection Pell Mell Limited* and carefully settled his mind into the cab of the slow, all stops *Delunaticking by Degrees* local on the other side of the platform, said, "Okay. Yes. Fine. One thing at a time." He reached out gently to O'Yee's shoulder and gave it a little pat.

Frank said softly, his heart full of love and pity for the poor, lost, ruined, hopeless soul, *"Eternity:* now that's a nice, good long word with plenty of letters in it . . ." He patted O'Yee again gently and softly on the shoulder to keep him calm, "Why don't you get out your chalk and show me again just how nicely you can write it on the sidewalk—?"

O'Yee said, "It's the truth!"

Frank said, still smiling, "Yes, of course it is." He patted again at the poor, mad little mutt.

Frank said softly with his great good heart bursting with love and good works, *"Eternity*—let's see how nicely you can do it if you really try hard. Okay? Ready now? E . . . T . . . E . . . R . . . N . . . I . . . T . . . Y: *Eternity* . . ."

It was the astronomer Carl Sagan who pointed out that the great principle of biology, first propounded by Darwin and Wallace in the nineteenth century, is evolution by natural selection, and that it is only by the preferential survival and replication of those organisms that are by accident appropriately fully adapted to their environment that contemporary life forms in all their wonder and beauty and elegance have emerged.

The ultimate wonder and beauty of these contemporary life forms is, of course, the brain, and, clearly, the development of an organ system as complex as the brain is inextricably tied to the earlier history of Evolving Life, its fits and starts and dead ends, and the long, tortuous adaptation of organisms to conditions that change over and over, leaping forms that once seemed supremely adapted to what once was, extinguished in an instant by what now is.

Evolution is adventitious in the extreme, and, indeed, it is only through the deaths of an immense number of slightly maladapted organisms that we are, brains and all, here today.

But in the Institute of Yu, pecked to pieces in the brainpan region, gone tomorrow.

In the corridor of the Institute of Yu, Spencer said in horror to the glazed dinosaur that once had been Phil Auden, "You brained him! He's out cold! How the hell are we going to find out why people are trying to commit suicide by jumping out of windows if the very first time one of them actually tries to jump you brain him with a baseball bat and practically kill him?" He looked down at the laid-out Warrior on the floor. In his suit of leather armor and horned hat he looked like a trilobite trampled by tyrannosaurus. Spencer said, "The idea is to grab these people and get them in alive so we can find out why they wanted to commit suicide in the first place, not bludgeon them into the next world with a baseball bat!"

The Primeval Beast looked at him.

The Primeval Beast didn't like that.

The Primeval Beast, looking around for pterodactyls, said, "Uh!"

Spencer said, "Are you all right?" He looked awful, sort of . . . pecked.

Auden said, "Uh!" He glanced out the window for the birds. Auden said, "Mmm, humghh!" Auden said, "Hah!" (Maybe it was meant to be a self-deprecating laugh of apology. Maybe not.) Auden said, "Hoomggh!"

He knew what they said about him in the caves all right, but they were wrong.

Auden said to all the other inhabitants of the Stone and Flint Age his brain shared space with, "*Uh!!!*"

He had a normal sex life.

He did.

He did! By the happily humming reptilian-ancestoral limbic system of his brain stem, he did!

Auden said, "Uh! Uh! Raaghhh!" Inside his head the last living cell in there made some sort of tenuous connection.

The tenuous connection was that what was now happening to his brain had something to do with the gallons of Novocain the dentist his mother had kept taking him to had pumped into his gums when he was a kid. Auden said to the tenuous connection, *"Gnaaarrrrr!!!"*

Leaving Spencer to drag the flattened armored Warrior of the Great Wall back into the Great Wall Room to try to bring him around, baseball bat in hand, he went back out the window onto the ledge on all fours to show the birds just how normal his sex life really was.

He wanted to tell him. He wanted Frank to know the truth.
He wouldn't have believed him.
All he had to prove who he was was a mad letter and a coat hanger and twenty-five feet of chain and a stick of chalk and a gun.
And a mission to write the word *Eternity* on the sidewalk.
He wrote it slowly.
O'Yee, writing, said in a snarl, "Ohh—!"
At last, his feeling towards RTG–68 was plain, clear, pure, uncomplicated, consummate.
He hated RTG–68!

10.

He thought it couldn't have been that easy.

If it had been that easy, what Feiffer would have got when Tolliver opened the single door to the lab on the third floor of the Cathay Pearl Building on Aberdeen Road would have been a monster.

What he got instead was a big, bent-over, shambling, silver-haired man in his early fifties with watery blue eyes and a sallow complexion dressed in a rumpled gray suit that looked as if it had become between the time he had bought it and now at least one size too big for him.

He got Dr. Edward George Arthur Tolliver.

At the door, he waited while Tolliver looked hard at his police ID. There was a small rectangular brass nameplate on the half-open door behind him that read, in English and Chinese, Hong Kong Analysis Laboratories, and below that, next to a plastic button push, larger than the name of the firm itself, again in English and Chinese, Please Ring.

Behind the man, as Feiffer looked past him, there was a single reception room with a desk and telephone and answering machine on it and an overflowing wastepaper basket beside it full of what looked like crushed and discarded cartons and boxes from take-out meals and food-stained screwed-up paper napkins. By the side of the basket there were two empty half bottles of—for a wine connoisseur—repulsively cheap wine.

The man already knew what had happened at the bank. On the desk above the wastepaper basket there was a portable radio playing softly on the local news channel. To one side and a little ahead of the desk in the little room, there was a closed door leading off somewhere to the right, and, on the other side of the desk, another door, also closed.

It was as if, standing a little out in the corridor, the man at the door had to stare at the photograph until it became familiar and safe before he invited the man holding it into the first room.

He stepped back inside the room.

He had a soft, cultured, almost trans-Atlantic accent.

Tolliver asked, "Do you smoke?"

Behind the desk, there was a sign on the wall in both Chinese and English that read FLAMMABLE CHEMICALS IN USE. ABSOLUTELY NO SMOKING! The sign was in plain view, tacked to the wall to one side of a metal bookshelf filled with papers and books and what looked like complete runs of scientific extracts.

Feiffer said, "I can see your sign." Apart from the telephone and an answering machine and the residue of food eaten there, the desk in the room where the receptionist should have sat was bare. He glanced around for them, and the two wire In and Out baskets that should have been on it were stacked unused in a corner on top of what looked like a sealed ream of computer paper and an unopened cardboard box of business-sized envelopes.

In the little room, following Feiffer's eyes as he looked at it, Tolliver touched for a moment at the side of his head in the exact corresponding place where the corner would be if his head had been the room itself.

It was as if he had a map of the room inside the skull and he navigated himself by it. As if he heard it for the first time, he touched to the back of his head as if that was where the sound of the radio on the desk behind him was coming from.

Tolliver asked, "Does the radio disturb you?"

It was very low, almost imperceptible, an English-language news station giving the day's weather and road conditions for the Colony. He looked hard at the man's face, but could not read what was on it or what sort of sound he heard from the radio in his head. Feiffer said, "Dr. Tolliver, yesterday morning at approximately 10:10 A.M., the manager of the Asia–America–Hong Kong Bank in the Lotus Flower Mall, Mr. Lee, put in a call to you. The call was to ask you to make an urgent appointment with him that day to discuss the state of an outstanding business loan of approximately a quarter of a million US dollars. The note he made on his phone sheet following that first attempt to contact you was 'Unavailable.' "

The man looked hard at him, but it was as if he looked through him, and there was nothing on his face.

Feiffer said, "He then tried to call you again at 11:00, with the same result."

As if he listened to something else.

Taking out his notebook and holding it open so the man could see the copied notations on it that covered the entire page, Feiffer said as a matter of record, "He then tried to contact you approximately ninety minutes later at 11:55 A.M., and then again at 1:12 P.M.—both times with the same result—and then again at 2:10, then, twenty minutes later, at 2:30, then again at 3:01, again at 3:45, and then, finally, five minutes before the bank closed for public business, at 4:55 P.M." He looked up to the man's face, "On at least four attempts—at 2:30 P.M., 3:00 P.M., 3:45 P.M., and finally at 4:55 P.M.—Mr. Lee left a message on your answering machine for you to contact him urgently. Did you get any of those messages?"

"Yes." It was as if he was not truly alive. He touched at the back of his head. He did have a map in there. He touched at the place where he had gotten the messages. He had gotten them sitting in the chair behind the desk as he stared at the mess and desolation in the room with his gone, watery eyes.

He fell silent. He was like a zombie: the shell of what once had been a living man. He was not even that—he was inanimate, not standing separate from the little room but part of it. He saw Feiffer put his notebook back into the inside pocket of his coat and saw, as he did, a pack of cigarettes and a plastic lighter in his shirt pocket, and, instantly, as he followed the geography of it along his nerve endings, touched at the right side of his head where on some sort of reflected imaginary wall on his brain the No Smoking sign was.

Standing there in the room, staring into the distance, he was still, unreal, like a chimera.

Feiffer asked carefully, "How many of the messages did you get?"

He answered the question. Tolliver said with no tone or expression in his voice at all, "All of them. I got all the messages, at 2:30, at 3:00, at 3:45, and at 4:55." Maybe he was a monster. Tolliver said, "There were other calls during the day, but whoever it was didn't leave any messages."

He blinked, remembering it, not from the playback of the answering machine, but from somewhere deep inside his head where it had really happened.

"Did you try to call back on the first message at 2:30?"

"No."

Thy rod and thy staff they comfort me. For some reason, it ran through Feiffer's head, and all he wanted to do was reach down under his coat and lay his hand around the butt of his revolver to make sure it was still there. Feiffer said, "Were you here when the message came in at 3:01?"

He had been. He saw the man barely perceptibly lean his head back towards the desk to recreate in his head where he had been.

But he did not answer.

Feiffer said, "When the second call came in at 3:01 where were you? Still sitting at the desk?"

He said it in a whisper, "Yes."

Who the hell was he? What in God's name did he have standing there in front of him? Feiffer said tightly, "But you didn't call back, did you? Or after you got the message at 3:45—did you? When did you call back? Did you call back after you heard the message at 4:55? Is that when you made an appointment?" He felt a growing tightness in his chest, and for some reason he could not seem to get his breath. The man just stood there, looking at him and through him. Feiffer said, with the fingers of his right hand aching to reach for the comfort of the gun, "Dr. Tolliver, did you make an appointment to see Mr. Lee sometime after the bank had closed that evening, sometime between the hours of 5:00 and 7:00 P.M.? And did you go to the bank and keep that appointment?"

"No." His eyes looked up, and it was as if he listened back over the top of his head to the radio, or recollected listening to it and recollected hearing on it for the first time that everybody inside that bank was dead, "No, I called, at last"—he had waited there, all day, through all the ringings of the phone—"at exactly five minutes after five, but I couldn't get through because all the lines to the bank were busy." Tolliver said with absolutely no tone at all in his voice at all, "So I didn't make an appointment then, or any other time."

He terrified him. He had never met a mass poisoner before, and he utterly terrified him.

The reception room was the man himself. Bare, disused, awful somehow, in some sort of mad, distant, unhuman way, it was an exact, mapped, stifling copy of some sort of reception room and entrance to the mind of the creased, pale-eyed man facing him.

Leading off from both sides of the room, there were the doors to two other rooms, with no signs or notices on them at all to show what they were for or what was kept in them.

He saw Feiffer glance at the door to the right near where the No Smoking warning was, Tolliver asked, "Do you smoke?"

He looked hard at the man. Feiffer said tightly, "Dr. Tolliver, according to your entry in *Who's Who*, your particular field of expertise is toxicology—" He thought he already knew the answer before Tolliver gave it, "Where do you keep your *poisons?*"

It was a difficult life sometimes, but occasionally it had its compensations. At the open doorway to the Great Wall Room, watching as the Doctors Yu carried the poor, flattened Warrior off to their control room for a little emergency bringing around, Spencer said sadly because it was the correct and moral and good thing to say, "Well, if I can't get anything out of him, I suppose I'll just have to work out the answer to the question myself."

The question was: why in the name of all that was therapeutic and mind cleansing would anyone happily at work in the Great Wall Room finding their true Yu want to throw everything away by throwing themselves out of an eigh-teenth-floor window?

Ah, that was the question.

At the open doorway to the room, Spencer heaved a sigh.

Spencer said happily, "Hee, hee, hee!" Spencer said in his joy, "What a question!"

God, he loved it! The only thing better than being a detective was being a detective in the Institute of Yu.

He detected not at all, three rooms along the corridor from the Great Wall Warrior Room, a door open just a fraction and a man wearing a flowered shirt and carrying a surfboard under his arm peek out, glance for a long, loving moment at the closed window facing him across the corridor, and then, just as quietly as he had opened it, pull the door closed again.

It was the second room inside Tolliver's head, but it had become unfamiliar to him: he had not been in there for some time. As he opened the right-hand door and went in ahead of Feiffer, he stood there in the open doorway for a moment looking in, blinking hard to bring it back to memory. It was almost as if it was no longer part of his present life and he had to recall what it once might have been in the past.

The second room was the laboratory, where all the chemicals and poisons were kept.

It was a windowless room four times the size of the reception room full of benches and shelves and work areas laden with computers and centrifuges, microscopes, burners, scales and microscales and Rube Goldberg–looking unidentifiable machines and devices in glass and stainless steel with tubes and pipettes and reaction chambers attached to them, and everywhere on the walls, charts and tables and diagrams and schematics of chemicals and their molecules and their solution forms and the compatibility or otherwise of yet other chemicals and molecules and solutions forms to them.

There were no notes or papers anywhere on any of the benches, and everything was covered in dust: there was nothing in progress in there.

The room had been left the way it had been on the last day anyone had used it. Everywhere, lined up on the benches or on shelves or in cabinets, there were rows and rows of dark half-gallon and pint glass bottles, covered with dust, full and half full and a quarter full.

All the bottles were labelled.

They were bottles of strychnine, arsenic, prussic and hydrocyanic acid, thallium—the labels chilled Feiffer to the bone.

Once there had been staff of at least a dozen in there. Tacked up on a wall above a row of chairs along the rear bench where at least half a dozen people had once worked over a line of what had been once brand-new state-of-the-art high-resolution electron microscopes the No Smoking sign, again, was written in both English and Chinese, with below it another sign presumably stating the same in what looked like Hindi and Arabic.

Once, the place had employed people from all over the world, once, probably the best and brightest people there were to be had.

Now, like the man himself who had once run it all, all it was was dust and disuse and decay.

He didn't wait for him to speak. Feiffer asked tightly, "Where's your potassium cyanide kept?"

From somewhere a long time ago, the words registered in his mind like an echo. Tolliver asked, "Is that what was used at the bank?"

It hadn't been on the radio. All that the press had been told by Headquarters was that a poison had been used, but not what kind.

"Yes." He looked up at the man's eyes. "Where do you keep it?"

It was in a single, dark, half-gallon bottle sitting with three other smaller bottles of indeterminate contents inside a steel-and-glass cabinet against the far wall. Tolliver said, indicating it with his eyes, "There. In the case against the back wall."

He was a policeman. Feiffer asked for a policeman's information, "By law, how much of it are you permitted to keep on these premises at any one time?"

He had to force himself to remember. He looked hard at Feiffer to also remember whether the man asking him was a scientist or a policeman. Tolliver said, "In layman's terms, in imperial measure, approximately . . ." He had to make his mind work on the calculation, "—two and a quarter pints."

Even given in a one-hundredth part in solution, it was enough to kill ten thousand people. Put into a water supply or a dam, it was enough to kill everyone in the Colony and still have some left over.

On one of the shelves near a line of dark bottles marked in a line of pure horror, Ergot (Systemic), Hydrocyanic (Sysmetic and Corrosive), Iodine (Systemic), Pilocarpine [JABORANDI] (Systemic), there was a pile of thick leather-covered books lying on their sides—ledgers and accounts books and the official pharmaceutical-trade poisons record book issued by the department of public health—and Feiffer with his eyes still on it to let the man know he had seen it, asked directly, "And how much of the approximately, in layman's terms, two and quarter pints of potassium cyanide that you're entitled to have on hand at any one time is missing or unaccounted for?"

He was like some sort of huge, shambling, disoriented bear just out of hibernation, blinking and shaking his head as if he kept trying hard to remember something he had forgotten or maybe never even known. *It was as if none of this was even happening to him.*

Feiffer shouted at the man, "Do you hear what I'm asking you? How much potassium cyanide is *missing?*"

The sound seemed to suddenly confuse him, and he rubbed at his shirt with the flat of his hand and looked back in the direction of the reception room as if the sound had come from in there. Tolliver said, "Um . . ."

It confused him. He glanced at the No Smoking sign.

He was on the edge of tears. Maybe the No Smoking sign was all he could understand anymore. Tolliver asked, "Um . . . Do you smoke?"

"How much of the potassium cyanide is *missing!*"

"None!" He came alive. Tolliver said, "None! *None!*"

All Feiffer wanted to do was get his hand to the butt of his gun. "Yesterday evening, between the hours of 5:00 P.M. and 7:00, did you go to the Asia–America–Hong Kong Bank on Wyang Street and there, administering it in a solution of some sort of wine or champagne or something very similar, use the same sort of cyanide as you have in that bottle there to kill nine human beings!"

Tolliver said, "No!"

"*How much of your potassium cyanide stock is missing?*"

"None!"

"*How much of the original amount granted into your possession by law can't be accounted for by normal scientific use?*"

"None!"

"In that case, I want the poisons record book!"

Tolliver said, "Some! Some is missing!" He was trying to think, trying to come back. And then his eyes became bright and he did come back for an instant, "It's missing from normal loss by evaporation!" Then suddenly his huge body changed and became slack and he was gone again for a moment. Then he came back—he came back to being the man he had once been in that room, the man who had once answered questions in there all the time for all the people who had worked for him and looked up to him as the final authority, "And spillage! Normal evaporation and spillage and oxidization, and—" He put his hands flat against the sides of his head as if to fix himself back in the room, to remember all the things that he had once known in there, "And staff loss!" He glanced down at Feiffer and, for an instant, almost seemed jocular, "The youngest members of the male staff in poisons labs always take a little away in bottles to impress their girlfriends, to—to—to show them how powerful and lethal and potent they are, and then they—and then afterwards they dilute it to harmlessness and flush it away in—in—"

Feiffer said tightly, "The No Smoking signs are in English and Chinese and two other languages for your staff. *Where is your staff now?*"

"Gone." He looked around, "Everything is gone, finished."

"Why? What happened?" He had gotten nothing. He had gotten nothing more from the real man standing in front of him than he had gotten from the open pages of a book, from the *Who's Who*.

He was a zombie, a shell—inside Tolliver's body there was no one there.

Lined up, in rows and cabinets in the room, all the dark, secret poison bottles and all the labels on them chilled him to the bone.

Standing in front of the man, facing him, Feiffer demanded, "What sort of man are you? What happened here to do this to you?" He thought he knew where the secret was. *"What the hell's in that other room off the reception room?"*

On the sidewalk, O'Yee wrote in a hand totally without character E-t-e-r-n-i-t-y: *ETERNITY*.

It was so totally without character that even the people struggling by with their shopping and parcels, even the coolies pushing their carts, did not bother to look down to see what it was.

Only Frank cared.

Only Frank stayed there with him as if his life meant anything at all.

Only Frank, feeling his pain, patted him gently on the shoulder to comfort him.

Only Frank, full of love and care, said softly in a whisper, "It's all right. It's all right. I'll stay with you . . ."

His face was a soft, kind face. Frank asked, "Okay?"

He did not look up from his writing. O'Yee said in a whisper, "Yes. Okay." He went on writing. He wrote for the second time in a hand with no character or hope in it at all, *ETERNITY*.

Concentrating hard on it, he failed completely to notice a sudden, fleeting change in the expression on his friend Frank's soft, kind face.

He failed completely to see it suddenly go hard.

He noticed not at all, Frank, still standing behind him, suddenly reach down into the pocket of his ragged pants, take out a little gold key, and then, after looking at it carefully and turning it over twice in his hand, put it back into his pocket again and purse his lips.

It was the third room in the three-room business. It was the room that had once been the toilet and changing room for

the staff. In the room, originally, there had been little more
than a row of metal lockers with a bench in front of them for
the staff to sit and change their street shoes, a sink, a sign on
the wall again ordering No Smoking, and in the far corner, a
single toilet cubicle.

Now, the room was full of wastepaper baskets full of
crushed cardboard cartons and paper cups from take-out
meals, boxes of unwashed clothes and socks and underwear,
and, in the center, a single army cot piled high with a mound
of gray, army-style blankets, a thin, poor-quality sleeping
bag, and a once-expensive frayed topcoat folded twice to
make a pillow at the head.

The room stank. It stank of food and sweat and dirty socks
and, from the open door of the toilet cubicle, human excreta.

It stank—and as he looked at him, he smelled all the
smells on him too—of a man one step away from the streets.

The third and last room in Dr. Tolliver's business was the
third and last room in his head. It was who he was, what Dr.
E. G. A. Tolliver MBBS PhD was—what he had become.

It was the room where the man lived. There was no
shower or bath in the room and he must have had to wash
one part of his body at a time with the cold water from the
sink and, in the absence of any sort of towels or soap or flan-
nels in the place, use what must have been the last of the toi-
let-paper supplies for the open toilet to dry himself.

Standing by the cot, Feiffer looked back to Tolliver, but
there was nothing there to be read on the man's face and he
had long ago reached the point of forgetting what his life had
been before the room, and, standing at the open doorway, the
man who had been Dr. Tolliver merely looked around at it,
not in disgust or shame or humiliation, but in case there was
something that he had missed finding—another blanket or a
toothbrush or perhaps some scrap of food stuck to one of the
cartons in the trash he had overlooked and could take out and
salvage.

There was nothing.

When he had read the man's entry in *Who's Who,* Feiffer
had expected that what *oenology*—wine collecting—would
mean was that in a huge rambling stone house somewhere up
among the houses of the rich on Victoria Peak there would

be a deep, cool, specially built stone cellar holding racks and racks of dusty dark bottles with rare and expensive labels.

When he had read all his triumphs and postings and honors, he had expected the man would have the faint, mellow smell of success and expensive cologne about him. He had expected that when the man moved to get up from his thick leather chair to meet him, his tailored clothes would make a rustling sound and, always, at any angle, have perfect creases and shape.

He had not expected he would shamble, and that his eyes would be pale and he would stink like an old incontinent bum who had pissed in his pants on the street.

In the room, everything stank. It stank like a cesspool. It stank of diarrhea and bad food and fear.

It stank of what Dr. Tolliver had become and how he had become that way. It stank of failure and ruin and desperation.

He knew what had happened to him: he had seen it before. It was in the room and in his eyes and the way he surveyed the loss of it all without recourse. Feiffer said evenly, "You were a gambler, weren't you? You lost everything. Didn't you?"

He didn't need to ask why the man had left the university. He knew. He had lost everything gambling, then began stealing, and been discovered at it, and then in order to get out without criminal charges being pressed against him, cashed in his pension and everything else he had left and turned it over to the university to make it right.

Feiffer asked, "Did you have to sell your house to make restitution at the university?"

In the room, Tolliver's eyes strayed to the No Smoking sign on the wall and stayed there. He registered no surprise at all at the question. Tolliver, still gazing at the sign on the wall, said, "Yes."

"Then what did you use for collateral for the loan from the bank?"

"Expectations and debts due."

"What expectations and debts due?" Because he knew what the bank had not—the terrible worm in the soul of the man that would not let him alone—he already knew the answer. Feiffer said, "You won, didn't you? You had a massive win somewhere where gambling is legal and gambling debts go through the banking system listed as investment returns, and you showed the bank that for your collateral, didn't you? Along with a letter of recommendation and trust from a university that felt it owed you at least one last chance in the private sector—or at least wanted to make certain you kept out of theirs—and the bank gave you the loan to start this place up, didn't it?" Feiffer asked, "Where did you do your gambling? Macao?"

"Yes." He looked only at the No Smoking sign.

"And because of who you were, the bank expected you'd succeed, didn't they? So they didn't ask for the collateral to be physically lodged with them, but only took a copy of the Macao deposit bank advice and left it at that?" Feiffer asked out of curiosity, "What did you tell the bank the win was?"

There was so much to confess that it didn't matter anymore. Still gazing at the sign, he only shrugged. Tolliver said with no tone in his voice, "I told them that it was part payment on a continuing long-term contract with the Macanese authorities to do forensic work for the police. And then, the same day, I took the ferry back to Macao to the casino and lost it all. It was a hundred and fifty thousand American dollars. I lost it all the same day in less than two hours." Gazing up at the sign, he wiped his fingertips across his mouth, "So, to start the business up and pay back the loan with nothing, I borrowed it all again. The same amount."

"From where?"

"From here. From Hong Kong. From Wanchai. From people I'd heard about when I did work for the courts." It was a disease, nothing logical or reasonable or explainable, and he could not think how to explain it. "From criminals. Then I went back to the casinos and I lost that, so I borrowed more"—he shrugged again—"from other criminals." He turned to face Feiffer head on. Tolliver said, "At first I thought you were one of them sent to kill me!"

There was nothing, no motive, no champagne, no reason—*nothing*. Feiffer said, suddenly convinced it was the truth, "You didn't leave here at all that day, did you? You didn't go to the bank at all. Did you?"

"For what? To kill everyone in there with poison? *For what?*"

He was a ruined, lost man waiting to die. All he was anymore was a shadow, uncorporeal, a shadow. He had nothing left and nowhere to go. Like the lowest coolie laborer, all he was was just one of the army of lost, ruined, hopeless souls with nowhere to go and no way to go there, waiting on a tiny rock in the South China Sea for the Communists to take over, or for death, whichever came first.

He was a man who, once, had taken up fifty lines in *Who's Who*.

With no pension left, no money, nothing, he was a man who could never go home to England, and when he died would take up only a single line on a cross in a potter's field somewhere and be forgotten.

Tolliver, Dr. E. G. A. (Edward George Arthur). All he was now was a man waiting through all the days and nights for someone to come to kill him.

There was nothing he could do for him. He was already a corpse. Gazing at the man, Feiffer asked, "Dr. Tolliver, have you any idea at all what a form with the logo of a hawk or an eagle wing called Form I–797–6–29–88 could be? Have you ever seen anything like that? Have you any idea what it could be?"

"No." His eyes were gone again to the No Smoking sign on the wall as they had gone to all the signs in all the rooms from the moment Feiffer had come in from the corridor.

"No." He shook his head. In the third room, turning to face Feiffer again, Tolliver at last said the thing that he had thought about to the exclusion of all else—even to the exclusion of the thought that maybe the man had come to kill him—"Please, for the love of God—" It was all he was anymore. "For God's sake! In the name of pity—please, *haven't you got just one cigarette you can spare me?*"

11.

On the phone from Headquarters, the commander said with his voice rising against the background noise of the pay phone on Empress of India Street Feiffer was calling him from, "Harry, are you telling me that you've eliminated this man Tolliver completely? That with everything you had—the unsecured loan, the appointment, the poison, *even the goddamned champagne-collecting thing!*—that what you've ended up with is *nothing?*"

The noise in the phone behind him was a Chinese funeral wending its way down the street towards the cemetery on Great Shanghai Street. It was the funeral of an old woman, judging from the tinted blown-up photograph held high by one of the white-robed professional mourners leading the procession, a woman of modest means with the lined and creased face of someone who had worked hard all her life. It was, befitting her station in life and the pocketbooks of her heirs, a modest affair with only three bands and a dozen mourners. The bands were composed almost entirely of drummers and cymbalists. What they lacked in musicology, they made up in volume.

Huddling in the pay-phone cubicle, jamming his finger in his ear to try to at least mute the sound, Feiffer shouted, "He didn't do it, Neal—there's no motive! All he's doing is waiting around to be chopped by one of the half-dozen triad gangs he borrowed money from as a warning to others that when you borrow you pay; or to just shrivel up and die of his own accord! In either event, there's no reason for him to have killed all those people in the bank! There's no reason for him to have even *been* in the bank!"

Behind him in the street, all three bands marked time, still playing. The noise of the cymbals and drums was so loud he could hardly hear himself think, "And even if he had had a reason to go there, the chances of him being still able to even plan something like that are nil! The man's about one step away from complete and total ruin! He's virtually little more than a walking goddamned vegetable!"

If the commander made any comment, he could not hear what it was for the bands. Feiffer shouted into the receiver, "Neal—? Are you still there?"

"So if there's no motive for Tolliver to have done it, who does have a motive to have done it?" The commander said, "Since nothing was removed from the bank, robbery wasn't the motive. So who else owed money they couldn't repay?"

"No one. Tolliver's was the only loan Lee was concerned about. All the others on his list are solid." Behind him, the three bands moved on, to be replaced in the procession by more white-robed mourners carrying paper replicas of houses and cars and all the things the departed might need in the next world that she had never earned enough to have in this one. Behind the mourners, the noise of the cymbals and drums was replaced by a cacophony of impatient honkings as cars on the street tried to get by.

"Killing nine people in a bank can't be motiveless! It isn't like some sort of drive-by shooting where the target is picked at random! Whoever entered that bank after closing time was *let in* by the staff! And then they all drank champagne with whoever it was to celebrate!" At the other end of the line, the commander demanded, "To celebrate what? Could it have been something as simple as someone's birthday? One of the teller's, or even Lee himself?"

"No." It had occurred to him too. "No, I checked all the ID cards in the bank when I did the preliminary identifications. The dates of birth are on them—no one had a birthday that

day or last week or this week, or even this month." Feiffer
said, "The only other possibility could be something like an
engagement celebration or maybe a birth, or something good
that happened that day to a member of one of the tellers'
families. The only way I can find that out is to talk to every
member of each of the nine families involved, and for that
I'm going to need you to assign me a special task force from
Headquarters. My own people are out on other cases. I've
got Spencer and Auden stuck on that job you gave them on
Wyang Street and my number-two man, O'Yee, wandering
around the streets on a God-knows-what job from Intelligence, and I just—"

The commander said, "I've already had Headquarters Uniformed look into the family angle. I've got their report in
front of me. There is no family angle. Lee and all his staff
were refugees from the mainland. All that Uniformed could
find of their families at the addresses from their identity
cards were framed photographs and letters from Canton and
Fukien provinces asking Lee and all the others, almost word-
for-word identically, when the hell they might be able to
sponsor them out of there. As for local boyfriends, fiancées,
or even friends, according to all the neighbors and people on
the street Uniformed spoke to, in every case they're nonexistent. If you want a task force, Harry, you can have one, but
the way things seem to be, God only knows what you're
going to be able to use them on!" He was down to nothing,
"So unless you've got some lead or method of approach I
don't know about—"

"All I've got is a torn scrap of paper from one of eighteen
copies of something with a fucking eagle wing on it from a
goddamned Xerox machine—the original and all copies of
which the killer evidently took away with him when he left!"
Feiffer said, "With a number or part of a number on it that
doesn't mean anything to anyone and may have absolutely
no bearing on this whole case at all."

"So what's your next move?"

He had thought about it all the way from Tolliver's office.
Behind him, the funeral must have gotten stuck on a cross
street and blocked traffic. From what seemed like every
street around, the cacophony of honking reached Babel level

and Feiffer yelled above the sound, "My next move—the only move I've got left—is to have another talk with the people in the mall. And then maybe plaster the place with Information Wanted posters on the off chance someone there saw something. You do know who the chief security officer is down there, don't you? It's George Shoemaker! I thought I'd go back and talk to him!"

He waited, but if the commander said anything in reply, Feiffer did not hear it. Shoemaker had been a detective chief superintendent. He had hobnobbed most of the time not with street cops from places like Feiffer's own Hong Bay district, but with the bosses in places like the Senior Officers' Club at Headquarters on Artillery Road. Feiffer asked, "You knew him well, didn't you, Neal?"

"Yes."

"How well did you know him?"

"Pretty well."

"He got canned, didn't he?"

"He resigned."

"Really? I heard that what happened was that he wanted a confession from someone he caught so desperately he stuck a fucking gun barrel in their mouth and it was only because someone stopped him at the last minute that he didn't pull the trigger and spread their brains all over the walls of an interview room."

There was a brief silence and then the commander said tightly, "He was burned out, Harry. He'd been on the case a long time. It was a kid who liked killing little girls—a serial. They brought the kid into the Headquarters Interrogation Unit one morning about 3:00 A.M. and because the place was pretty much deserted, apparently George got it into his head that he'd be able to scare a confession out of him without anyone knowing about it. So the stupid bugger took him to one of the main interview rooms and stuck his gun in his mouth without even remembering that the moment any of the doors in any of the interview rooms here are even opened an inch a video monitoring system comes on automatically and records everything that happens. Fifteen seconds after the kid took the first suck on the muzzle, six uniformed cops were on George hauling him off."

"What happened to the kid? To the serial?"

There was a silence.

Feiffer asked, "Did he got off?"

"We couldn't hold him. After his lawyer saw the tape all we could do was—" The commander, not wanting to remember it, said with an effort at brightness, "Oh, we got him again all right, a couple of months later. But not until after he'd killed two other little girls and left chopped-up bits and pieces of them in garbage bags all over Hong Kong." The commander said sadly, "I gave George a reference that got him the job at the mall, but it—"

"He doesn't make any secret of the fact that he was going to off the kid—"

"Then tell him to *make* it a secret!" The commander said tightly, "Tell him that it was only through the grace of God and his record and his friends at Headquarters that he didn't go to fucking jail!" He asked suddenly, "Why are you asking me all this anyway? What has George Shoemaker got to do with all this?"

"Maybe nothing." Behind him, the honking stopped, "But he knows more than he's telling."

"About what?"

"About the people in the bank. When I spoke to him, first he didn't want to even hear about what had happened, then, for no apparent reason, he wanted to know the names of the victims, and then when I told him, he suddenly clammed up and said he didn't know any of them." It was the longest of long shots. Feiffer asked, "Neal, to your knowledge, did George Shoemaker ever have a case involving poison?"

"Probably."

"And Dr. Tolliver, did he know him?"

"At one time Tolliver was an expert witness, so I guess he must have." The commander said, "Yes, probably. Yes, of course he did. He would have."

"He's got full access to the mall. He knows it. He knows the security there. He knows everyone who works there. And even though he claims his jurisdiction stops at the door of the bank, if he'd rung to get in after hours, because of who he is, Lee would have let him in."

He couldn't believe it. The commander said, remembering

not what Shoemaker had become because he did not want to remember that, but what Shoemaker had once been, "George? Are you saying that George—? George was one of the best cops we ever had! George was—" The commander said in protest, "George Shoemaker? No, I won't believe it. Not him." It was all senseless, pointless, leadless: someone, for no apparent reason or profit, had simply walked into a bank, offered nine people poison, and then, after he had watched them die, washed up the cups the poison had come in and *without taking anything or disturbing anything* simply walked away into oblivion as if nothing had happened. The commander said in horror, "Are you saying that George Shoemaker could have—?"

"The poison, if it didn't come from Tolliver, had to come from *somewhere!* And it had to be used by someone familiar with it!"

Everywhere in the background, the commander could hear the honking of cars. The commander said for the second time, unable to fully comprehend what the man was suggesting to him, *"George Shoemaker?* Ex–Detective Chief Superintendent George Shoemaker? Are you telling me that you think George Shoemaker had something to do with all this?" Once, Shoemaker had been his friend. Everywhere in the background to the call there was the honking and blaring of car horns, "Harry, George Shoemaker—? Are you completely fucking *crazy?*"

Out of respect, on the corner of Tiger Snake Road, O'Yee and Frank stopped what they were doing and stood to watch in silence as the funeral went by.

It was the funeral of an old woman on its way to the cemetery three blocks south on Great Shanghai Street—judging from the musical skill of the three second-rate bands and few white-clad professional mourners that accompanied it, bound for the poorest paupers' and coolies' section of the graveyard.

The big, blown-up memorial photograph of the old woman the lead mourner held above his head in a white-tasselled wooden frame looked like the family-album picture of an

old, worn-down woman O'Yee's father had once told him
was a photograph of his paternal grandmother in China.

It saddened him a little.

He glanced over to his new friend and saw, for the same,
or for some other reason, it saddened him too.

O'Yee said softly, "Well ... um? ..." He tried to remember the man's name.

He tried to remember it too. Frank said, "Um ..." He remembered, "Um—*Frank*." Frank said, " 'Frank'—right!"
Frank said, as if his mind was on something else much more
serious, "For a moment there, I almost forgot my own
name!"

Gazing at O'Yee, looking right through him, he smiled a
little wintry smile.

It was the smile of a man interested in death and funerals.

It was a smile that terrified. It was no smile at all. It was
the hungry, calculated smile of a spider.

By Hong Kong standards, it wasn't much of a funeral, but,
at the moment, it was the only one Frank had, and he turned
back quickly to the street to watch it with undisguised interest as it moved slowly by in procession, and behind it, trying
to get it to move a little faster, all the traffic from three
streets back honked and blared their horns at it in protest.

He listened to it all with a mounting disbelief that anyone
could have been taken in so easily by it.

On the phone from the security office in the mall, George
Shoemaker shrieked at him, "Jesus Christ, Feiffer, you've
got someone who owed the bank a ton of fucking money,
someone who could have made an appointment to be there at
the right time, someone who has access to literally gallons of
fucking poison, and someone who collects fucking champagne or whatever the poison came in—and you say it's not
him and that you've eliminated him from your enquiries?"
Shoemaker yelled, "You've got a number-one, watertight
suspect and he tells you he's old and sick and he owes some
fucking gambler a few dollars somewhere and what? You
pull out your fucking little hankie and weep along with him
and let him go?" Through the open door of the security office, he could see the fountain in the middle of the mall

atrium, and although it was back to working order again, he could not bring himself to order it turned back on. Shoemaker said in utter disgust, "Jesus Christ, *what sort of a detective are you anyway?*"

"I don't see what else I could have done." He was calling Shoemaker from the same pay phone on Empress of India Street he had used to call the commander, but the funeral and all the honking had moved on somewhere else and, except for the normal sounds of traffic and people in the street, it was quiet enough in the street for him to hold his voice at an even level, and Feiffer, sighing, said to prick the man, "And, quite frankly, ranting and raving about it notwithstanding, I don't think you would have done it any differently, George."

"Don't you?"

"No, I don't."

It got him. His voice rose an octave and then cracked. In the security office of the mall his hand must have been shaking on the phone. Shoemaker shrieked, "Don't you? Don't you think I would have done it any differently? I'd have done it fucking differently! I wouldn't have stood there being taken in by a man on his own territory where he could wander pathetically around the place showing me all the dust and telling me what a poor little fucking failure he is! I'd have done it differently all right! I'd have hauled his ass out of there in fucking handcuffs and put him in a fucking interrogation room with just him and me and a fucking bored-looking stenographer and wound him up so tight the poor little I'm-a-ruined-gambler routine would have disappeared faster than a fucking dollar bill down a whore's bra and he started telling me what I wanted to know!" His imitation of a burned-out, jaded cop seemed to have gone the same way. Ex–Detective Chief Superintendent Shoemaker roared down the line to Detective Chief Inspector Feiffer, two ranks and a lifetime of experience below him, "I'd have done it differently all right! I'd have got the fucking *truth* out of him!"

In the street, the traffic stopped for a moment and, far to the south, travelling somewhere down in the area of Canton Street and Tiger Snake Road, Feiffer heard the sound of the funeral as it wended its way down towards the cemetery on Great Shanghai Street. He heard the crash of cymbals and drums, and then the sound, a moment later, of honking as the traffic behind it continued to try to get past. He waited for a moment. Feiffer said into the phone, "There reaches a point, George, where, sometimes, you have to accept that the truth may just be exactly what it at first appears to be: namely, the truth."

"Oh, thank you for that little gem of wisdom. I didn't know that." Shoemaker said with heavy sarcasm, "My goodness me, I wish I'd known that when I was chasing serial killers whose idea of a good time was ripping up little girls. That would have saved me a lot of sleepless nights. And as for investigation costs and interviews and collation and computer searches and all the rest of it—not to mention manpower—*all we needed to have done was have you there with your crystal ball telling us who was telling the truth and who wasn't and we could have saved the fucking taxpayers a fucking fortune!*" There was a sharp sound on his end of the line as if he slapped hard at his forehead for not realizing it, "Jesus Christ, Harry, why the hell didn't you tell anyone you had this natural ability—*we could have put you to work right away on the fucking Jack the Ripper killings and the still-unsolved Cain and Abel investigation!*"

He stayed calm and pissed on him from a great height. With a bored tone in his voice, Feiffer said to explain it to him, "Circumstantial evidence isn't the same as conclusive evidence, George—not anywhere. The fact that this man had at what first appeared to have been a motive doesn't necessarily mean he—"

Shoemaker could do it too. He had pissed on more people than Feiffer could count. And when he pissed on them, they drowned. Shoemaker said, "Oh! Right! Right again! I just forgot for a moment, Harry. The fact that this guy had a motive doesn't count. And the fact that he had means: you know, that he collected wine or champagne or whatever it was the poison was delivered in, that doesn't count either. And the fact that he had opportunity: you know, that one of the victims had spent the whole day trying to get him to come in to see him—nothing. Just a coincidence. And the fact that he owed the bank a fortune he couldn't pay back—well, so what? And the fact that he's got gamblers after him who want their money back—pshaw. *And the fucking fact that he's got a whole room full of fucking poisons at his disposal and the cause of all of the nine victims was poison—!* Well, who cares?" Shoemaker said, "Yeah! Right! Now I can see the logic of it all! None of that counts and of course he was telling you the truth when he said he didn't do it!" Shoemaker asked, "Golly, why didn't I see it before?" He answered his own question, "Gee, goodness me—*I guess it must be because one of us is stupid!*" He paused for a moment, "And, I guess, considering your obvious psychic powers of seeing all and knowing all, it must be me. *Right?*"

"I don't think he was lying to me. If he was, then he's the best at it I've ever seen."

"Everybody lies! That's what people do!"

He pricked at him again. "Certainly, Tolliver has to appear at first glance to be the best suspect—Or, at least, that's what whoever set him up for it thought . . ."

"Oh, and whoever set him up hoped he'd just happen to be called into the bank that day and—"

"Either that or someone made sure he was going to be called into the bank that day by calling Lee first thing in the morning and telling him that Tolliver was no good for the loan."

"Oh, right! The conspiracy theory! I forgot that one!"

Feiffer said tightly, "Well, maybe you shouldn't forget it, George! Maybe you ought to stop and wonder why Lee's rush to get Tolliver in for an appointment certainly seemed to have come out of nowhere! Maybe you ought to stop and wonder where the information that Lee got that the loan was no good came from! There's absolutely no mention of it in any of his papers from the day before! Maybe you ought to consider that if nothing was taken from the bank then someone who owed the bank and everybody else in the Colony money may not therefore be the prime, shining, number-one likely suspect. Maybe you ought to consider another angle to the killings—like a family angle for a start!"

"The fucking victims didn't have any families! They're all refugees from China! All the families are still on the mainland waiting for the now-dead relatives to try to get them out!"

"How did you know that, George?"

"I knew that because I check up on the people who work here in the mall! I know that because I looked at their résumés which we've got on file here in the security office! I know that because it's my job to know who people are!"

"Anyone in particular?"

"What do you mean?"

"I mean, anyone in particular? Did you know any of the staff on a personal basis?"

"You asked me that the first time we talked!"

"And what did you say?"

"I said no!"

There was a silence. He was treading on dangerous ground. Feiffer asked, "And did I also ask you if you did business with the bank yourself? You know, have an account there or—"

"No, you didn't! And the answer is no, I didn't!"

"Did I ask you if you knew Dr. Tolliver? Or hadn't he surfaced as the prime suspect at that stage when we talked?"

On the other end of the line, Shoemaker said in a voice as cold as ice, "What are you getting at?"

"Do you know Dr. Tolliver, George? Did he ever give expert evidence in any of your cases when you were a cop?"

"No. Not to my recollection. No."

"But you had him on your list of experts in case you ever had a poisons job, didn't you?"

"I suppose so." His voice had gone defensive. "It would be a matter of Headquarters record if I did."

He lied to him. Feiffer said evenly, just as coldly, "It is a matter of Headquarters record. I've just spoken to the commander about it."

"Well, then you know the answer to your own question, don't you—?"

Feiffer said tightly, "And you. I've just spoken to the commander, at length, about you."

And suddenly, there was a silence on the other end of the line he could have cut with a knife.

"Let me ask you something, George: using the facilities you've got there in the security office or in the corporate headquarters of the mall, how hard would it be exactly for you to do a credit check about someone you wanted to find out about? Would it, say, show up gambling debts as the reason for a failing business—or would you maybe have to put in a call to an old friend in the Headquarters Gaming Squad for that part of it? How hard would it be?" Six streets away, there was a faint clash of cymbals as the bands readied themselves by the side of the old woman's grave for the ceremonial interment. "And how difficult would it be, George, to call up Mr. Lee as a personal favor and tell him the person he loaned a quarter of a million to was no good for it? How difficult would that be? How difficult would it be for someone like that to use all that information and power and experience he had to knock someone off in the bank he wanted to get rid off and make sure he got away with it by creating a perfect suspect all the way down the line?" He asked the question. Feiffer shouted down the line at the man, "How difficult would that be, George? In your professional, experienced opinion?"

It was a whisper. It was a whisper from somewhere so deep inside of him, Feiffer could barely differentiate the words. Shoemaker, talking not to him, but to someone else, something else, something from a long time ago, said softly, "You dirty bastard . . . You dirty, conniving . . . You dirty, cheap, sleazy, lying bastard . . ."

"You're divorced aren't you, George? After they caught you on videotape at Headquarters with your gun jammed down someone's throat and made you resign, your wife left you, didn't she? Are there children involved, George? And did she take them with her?"

He could not speak. On the other end of the line, Shoemaker made no sound at all. (He could not get his mind off the picture of the pudgy girl from the bank throwing her coin into the fountain for luck and jamming it, and he could not get it out of his mind how good it had felt to say nothing, but just to say it was a malfunction.)

"You knew one of those people at the bank, didn't you, George? You knew one of them well, didn't you? Which one of them was it?"

Shoemaker said in a rasp, "Go to hell!"

"Was it one of the girls? It was one of the girls, wasn't it, George?"

"You go to hell, Feiffer."

"Were you fucking one of them, George? Maybe, say, one of the younger ones who saw marrying you as her way out of the Colony and maybe the way to get her family out of China at the same time who—"

He could not speak. He could not reply. At his end of the conversation, sitting at his desk, he had become inanimate, turned into stone.

Shoemaker said in a whisper, all he could manage, "It's Tolliver! From everything you've told me, Chief Inspector, in my professional opinion, it's Tolliver!"

"Is it, George?"

"Yes."

"Is it, George?"

Shoemaker said, "Yes!"

"Is it, George?"

Shoemaker said, "Yes! Yes! *Yes!* You fucking moron, can't you see what he's done? Can't you see how he's trying to trick you? Can't you see that?"

"No, George, I can't. What I can see is—"

"It wasn't *me!* It wasn't me! I didn't report her! I didn't report the little pudgy girl from the bank for throwing the coin in the fountain for good luck and jamming it! I didn't get her into trouble for it! It wasn't *me!* I didn't do anything to her!" Shoemaker shouted at the top of his voice not to Feiffer but to someone else, "She was just a little kid! It wasn't *me!* I didn't do anything to hurt her! It wasn't *me!*"

"What the hell are you talking about?"

"It's Tolliver, Harry!" He was desperate, on the edge, "Harry, it's there, right in front of you: it's Tolliver! It has to be him! It's Tolliver. Can't you see it? He's tricked you! He's tricked you into letting him go so he can do it all again somewhere else!"

"Is it him, George? *Is it?*"

"Yes! Yes! *Yes!*"

With the door of the security office open, he was rigid, transfixed, unable to look away from the fountain where, one morning before work, he had seen the pudgy girl from the bank toss in a handful of coins for good luck and instantly and accidentally jam the mechanism.

Shoemaker shouted, "Yes! It's him! For God's sake, *don't let him get away!*"

He could not get it out of his mind that, around her neck, the girl had worn a little gold chain with an elephant on it for luck.

Shaken by a sudden tremor that seemed to rack his entire body, Shoemaker shouted down the line to the man at the top of his voice, "Harry! Don't you understand? If you don't get him now, right at the outset, *you won't ever be able to stop him and he'll just keep killing over and over again and you'll never, never be able to stop him!*"

12.

In the Great Wall Room, even with the door half open, Detective Inspector Bill Spencer did not see the surfboard carrier sneak across the corridor almost directly in front of him, glance out a window to check where Auden was on the catwalk, and then, reaching up, very quietly, open the window and, with a giggle, rest the point of his surfboard on the sill in readiness.

He was too busy. And also, staring up at the great wraparound four-sided full-blazing-color full-spectrum quadrophonic-sound invasion of the wall by the Barbarian Hordes with his mouth open like a small boy standing in the front row of a movie house seeing Cinemascope for the very first time, he was no longer Detective Inspector Bill Spencer, but someone quite different.

With the expression on his face inexorably changing to a sneer, as up on all the giant screens the hordes scrabbled up the Great Wall to do their evil deeds with the sound of their shrieks and war cries and clashing and clanging set to perfect mind-blowing level by the Brothers Yu in their control room at the end of the corridor, he was William, the young Lieutenant Lord Spencer, Lone British Officer at the Pass.

The Lone British Officer stiffened his upper lip. Gazing up, the Lone British Officer said with a lisp, "By George,

Wiffs! Wiffs everywhere!" (They weren't Riffs: they were Mongolians, but it was his fantasy). The Lone British Officer, fixing them with a smirk of surpassing superciliousness, said in a simper, "Wather a lot of them—but not a particulawly perplexwing pwoblem for a fellow fwom *my* wegiment!"

He was happy. The door to the corridor was still open, but concentrating hard on the pwoblem of the Wiffs and getting the accent right, he did not notice the Hawaiian-shirted surfboard rider, very gently, raise the tail fin of his surfboard and, a little at a time, begin to push it through the open corridor window.

Neither did he notice, three windows away, someone from the next room down the corridor—an ice-hockey goalie in full mask and pads—open another window and begin to climb out, nor, two windows down from that, a Zulu warrior click open the catch on his window with an assegai and clamber up onto the sill on all fours.

He had more than a corridor—he had an empire to protect.

Spencer, deep in his joy, gazing up at the hordes on the screens, suddenly near deafened by their screams of conquest as in the control room the Brothers Yu turned the sound up to *Unbearable*, yelled, "Praise the Lord! And pass the ammunition!"

He didn't have any. All he had against them were his bare hands.

He used those hands in a flash. Full of delight, Lieutenant the Honorable Sir William Spencer of the Hussars, ready for the battle of Rorke's Drift and a V.C. or two from the velvet commendation cushion of good Queen Victoria herself, God bless her, laid them quickly flat against the door to the corridor and pushed it shut to be alone.

There was a single clash of cymbals from Valhalla just over the horizon from Auden's catwalk (actually, it was from the funeral of the old woman in the Great Shanghai Street cemetery, but no matter), and there he was circling alone above him in all his hateful magnificence: the Odin of Ornithology, the Price of Perfidious Piracy, the Scourge of the South China Seas, the One, the Only, the Undisputed, horri-

ble, disgusting, beat-up, Authentic and Original nadir of horrible, disgusting, beat-up, fish-market seagulls: *Attila the
Seadog Seagull!*

He had come to do battle alone. He had come, where all
his minions had failed, to fight the Mighty Auden *mano a
mano,* face to face, man to man. Beak to baseball bat.

As both Auden and Auden's mind balanced together on
the barely two-foot-wide catwalk, the very thought of it
was—

It was mind-blowing. It was Auden's greatest moment.

Raising his bat in salute as the filthy, moth-eaten, half-
blind creature whirled and soared above him taking his measure, Auden yelled as another Wagnerian clash of cymbals
from somewhere in heaven echoed and rang in his ears,
"Aaggrrrah!"

He understood. Circling high up the sky, Attila, squinting
his one good eye hard and making it glint, squawked back,
"Cawwww!"

It was on, the clash of Titans. It was a done deal.

With, everywhere, people with surfboards and hockey
sticks and Zulu assegais and shields starting to crawl out of
windows above the catwalk in droves to hurl themselves out,
it was a fight to the finish.

Reprising the world according to RTG–68:

ITEM: 4. *Final Instructions.*

> *Whatever may occur, you will take no direct,
> self-motivated action or actions in this matter, un-
> less*
> *(i) circumstances suddenly and unexpectedly war-
> rant it*
> *(ii) a situation presents itself;—or*
> *(iii) —in other events.*

From behind him, O'Yee looked hard at Frank.

ITEM: 3. *Nature of Crime or Potential Crime.*

Staring at his back, it occurred to him suddenly that—

> *This, at your level of involvement, is information
> deemed unnecessary to the successful completion or
> otherwise of the operation.*

O'Yee said in sudden horror, "Frank? Frank, it isn't you,
is it? You're not the one I—"

ITEM: 2. *Disguise.*

> *You will appear to all who come into contact with
> you to be a hopeless, ill-used and mistreated,
> unloved bum.*

That was how he appeared to Frank. That was why Frank
had befriended him. That was why—O'Yee said in horror to
the man's back, "Frank—?" A moment ago, the man
couldn't even remember his own name. O'Yee, reaching
down to his pants leg to touch the PPK to make sure it was
still there, said in a strangled voice to make the man turn
around, "Frank? *Frank?*"

But he didn't turn around. He merely stood there listening.
He listened as, from the cemetery, there was a single drum-
beat and then a clash of cymbals.

O'Yee, going forward, said gently to the man so as not to
alarm and turn him suddenly from mild-mannered Mahatma
Gandhi into mad-as-a-meat-axe Mohamar Gaddaffi, "Ah—
Frank—?" Everywhere around them there were shoppers and
harridans rushing home to serve up a member of their family.
O'Yee, drifting fast into a scenario that made the *Texas
Chainsaw Massacre* look like an ecological antilogging
movie, said, going forward to the man to touch him, "Um . . .
F-Frank—?"

He turned. He had soft brown eyes. So did Charles Man-
son. Frank said as if he had just remembered why he was
there, "Ah, Christopher . . ." He looked him up and down,
and smiled.

He thought about it. Frank said slowly, with supreme

irony, "Ah, Christopher, you are really not what you try to pretend you are at all, are you?"

Yes, he was, yes, he was, yes, he was. He was *a hopeless, ill-used and mistreated, unloved bum*. He was, he was. Yes, he was. O'Yee said nodding, "Yes, I am—"

"Ah, no." He looked up at the sky to where, presumably, the soul of the poor, dead, buried woman from the funeral had gone. Frank said, "It's getting late. Maybe we should now think of somewhere for you to spend—"

He was still thinking. He looked down at the pavement and read the single word.

Frank said, still smiling, "*Eternity*."

Frank said, deep in thought, as if all the answers one by one were becoming clear to him, "Yes."

He nodded.

He put his hand against his side and patted at the pocket of his ragged pants.

Like a cat waiting outside a mouse hole, he narrowed his eyes and smiled.

God, it worked! One Yu and you were one. The scenes on all the walls of the Great Wall were interactive, just like the street-combat shooting course in the police pistol range. You hit the bad guy on the screen with a bullet and the bad guy stopped, staggered, and fell down.

The Great Wall Warrior Room was just like that.

It was better.

You got up right next to the screen and as the hordes came over the wall screaming and yelling and waving knives, you reached out and grabbed them by their two-dimensional throats and squeezed until they went red in the face and fell screaming as you hurled them off the wall with superhuman strength.

In the Great Wall Room, the Lone British Officer, with superhuman strength, hurled them one after another.

He hurled off a horrible little armored creature waving a vicious six-foot-long sword and screaming things in low Chinese that suggested everyone's mother, including his own, had mated with a dwarf.

He hurled off another, a foot behind the creature, wearing

warts and a leather helmet who didn't even have the cultural evolution to make comments about anyone's mother because he wasn't even too sure he had one himself.

Then he turned, and behind him on the other wall of the room a cannoneer dragging a huge bronze cannon had one foot over the wall and was swinging up and over like a monkey, making roaring noises.

As the mighty hands of Lone British Officer Lieutenant the Honorable William Spencer of the Hussars caught him around the throat he made a croaking sound and went back over the wall with his cannon flying after him.

Spencer shrieked, "Woe to Wiffs!" He hurled back another Wiff. And then another. And then six of them, then eight.

His Yu was in full flight. He was Spencer of England, the last of the poet-warriors, a good chap, a fine fellow, a great loss to the regiment—but, oh, how he had covered himself in glory for the empire!

He wasn't afraid to die. He sneered at death. Spencer, rushing to another wall in the room to hurl back a particularly nasty-looking customer wearing what looked like a distorted teapot with dragon flames coming from his horrid heathen head, yelled,

> We have fed our sea for a thousand years
> And she calls to us, still unfed,
> Though there's never a wave of all her waves
> *But marks our English dead!*

Spencer yelled in his ecstasy, "Ah—Hah!"

He wasn't afraid to die.

Neither were the people on the screen. They were all actors, extras from a thousand Chinese epic movies shot in the New Territories and on sound stages all over Asia.

As if it was the finest role of their careers—an Oscar performance every time—gasping, yelling, shrieking, fighting, falling—for the first time in their careers at the forefront of any screen anywhere—in full wrap-around picture and ear-splitting quadrophonic sound, they fought and died—all of them—*magnificently*.

*   *   *

In the staff records room of Headquarters on Artillery Road, sitting alone at a desk in the secure document reviewing room, Feiffer punched up the first page of Shoemaker's file onto the computer screen in front of him.

It was a standard bio form listing the man's date and place of birth, education, places of service, and a list of all his promotions and postings over all the years he had been with the force.

At the top of the page there was a standard rubber-stamp impression that read, THIS PAGE: INFORMATION MAY/MAY NOT BE RELEASED. (Tick Option.)

It was nothing, just standard stuff, and above the word, the reviewing clerk had ticked MAY.

At the desk, Feiffer touched at Page Down button on the computer keyboard to bring up the second page in the file. It was a confidential-document warning.

The warning read:

WHAT FOLLOWS MAY INCLUDE OPERATIONAL NOTES AND AIDES-MÉMOIRES OF SUBSE-QUENTLY UNSUBSTANTIATED OR UNPROVEN ALLEGATIONS AGAINST LEGALLY INNOCENT INDIVIDUALS ARISING FROM VARIOUS INVES-TIGATIONS AND/OR ENQUIRIES THIS OFFICER MAY HAVE BEEN INVOLVED IN IN THE COURSE OF HIS OR HER CAREER.

THIS INFORMATION IS HIGHLY SENSITIVE AND MAY NOT BE RELEASED, COPIED, OR COMMUNICATED IN ANY FORM WHATSOEVER, WITHOUT THE SPECIFIC WRITTEN APPROVAL OF THE COMMISSIONER OF POLICE.

WHAT FOLLOWS MAY ALSO INCLUDE DETAILS OF ALLEGATIONS AND/OR INVESTIGATIONS CONCERNING THE OFFICER WHOSE FILE THIS IS AND MAY THEREFORE CONTAIN MATERIAL OF A LIBELLOUS, DEFAMATORY, OR CRIMINAL NATURE AGAINST THAT OFFICER.

*THE ABOVE WARNING APPLIES IN PARTICULAR
TO THIS MATERIAL!*

At the desk, Feiffer steepled his fingers together for a moment and touched at his chin.
He tapped the Page Down button for the next page.
The next page read:

Subject: Shoemaker, George.
Rank: Detective Chief Superintendent, Headquarters.
Present Status: Retired.

PAGE ENDS.
ENTER SECURITY CODE TO CONTINUE TO
NEXT PAGE.

He entered it.
Carefully, line by line, looking for something—*anything*—
Feiffer began reading Shoemaker's file.

No point in the restraint of social inhibitions now. At the moment of death you were entitled to say a few words of your own.
On the catwalk, taking a mighty swipe at Attila as he came in with his Wilkinson-sword-quality beak glinting in the dying light of the day, Auden screamed in a few words of his own, "*Aaaarrrggghhhhh!*"
Attila screamed back, "*Caawww!*" came down like a winged razor, and with a sound like a Vulcan minigun firing on full auto, swept over Auden's cork hat at zero feet to tear it and the head under it to pieces.
And missed.
Auden screamed, "You missed! You *missed!*"
The scream was a little too loud for the few molecules the razor-sharp beak had left intact, and the cork hat exploded into pea-sized pieces on his head and blasted down around his face like shrapnel.
Oh, he was the worst—he was the worst that had ever lived to ruin the lives of men. He was the worst that— Up there in the sky, wheeling and turning, Attila took a quick

peek from his glinting eye at the treasure galleon *Auden* on the catwalk laden down with the big silver fish, set his for'd cannons on point-blank fire, and with a sound like a dive bomber at Mach 2, hurtled straight down at Auden's naked head with his wings folded back against his body like a bullet.

The bullet missed. It hit the point of the surfboard on the catwalk where the surfer in his Hawaiian shirt was about to hang five over eighteen stories of nothingness and, with a crash, chopped the entire fiberglass board to splinters.

Auden screamed, "Ah-hah!"

The surfboard rider, toppling, starting to go over the edge in a surf full of glass, yelled, "Ohh-*oh!*"

Auden screamed, "Hah-*hah!*"

Attila squawked, *"Caw!"*

It was a very basic conversation. Moving down the catwalk after the retreating Attila, Auden smashed the surfboard rider across the side of the head with the bat and blasted him back inside the window.

Auden said, "Hmm-hah!"

The surfboard rider, bludgeoned into a coma, fell back inside the window like a fish.

But it wasn't the fish the greatest of all birds wanted.

The greatest of all birds wheeled once, then flashing down like a lightning bolt, Attila, the cunning devil he was, seemed to come in straight for the tip of Auden's raised silver bat, and then—and then at the very last moment—*and God! how you had to admire the brilliance of it!*—turned and hit the Zulu's assegai flat on, ricocheted off it, and, like a torpedo bomber, got in a single hit with his talons an inch from Auden's ear that blew the tip of the giant baseball-fish bat to shreds and turned it into a school of airborne minnows.

The Zulu, with his lion's-claw-decorated naked leg halfway out the window, yelled in Chinese, "Goddess of heaven! What was that?" He got his head out the window to look, saw a deranged person carrying the remnants of a baseball bat charging down the catwalk at him like a maddened hippo, and, twirling his assegai to fight his way out, yelled in basso profundo English, "I Zulu warrior!"

He Auden. There was a single crash of Taiwanese bat on

Zulu side of head and the Zulu, like a crab at the moment of death throwing all his pinchers, threw all his lions' claws and fell back inside the window.

Goddammit, now there was someone else clambering out of a window trying to get into the act. It looked like Gary Cooper in *High Noon*. It wasn't. It was a Chinese person dressed like Gary Cooper in *High Noon*. The Chinese person, getting one booted leg over the windowsill, cocked his long-barreled Colt to get a shot in at the bad guy on the catwalk.

The Colt's hammer went . . . *click* . . .

The bad guy's bat went *Thump!*

Gary Cooper, flying back into the corridor in a brained heap, went *thud*.

Ah-ha. Now, all that was left was just Auden and the gull, man and beast, good and evil, yin and yang—all that. Auden, dancing along the catwalk, yelled, "Come and get it, you *bastard!*" He knew who Attila was all right. He was evil. He was as evil as— Auden, swinging the bat in the air as Attila rounded in the sky for another shot at him, screamed at the top of his voice, "*Death! Death!* Death to *dentists!*" then suddenly there was someone else halfway out on the catwalk from a window in front of him and for a moment he thought it was the dentist from his childhood come back to get him with a long needle-sharp hypodermic in his hand.

It wasn't. It was the warrior from the Great Wall Room come to get him with a long Chinese executioner's sword in his hand.

The warrior, getting out onto the sill and balancing on his armored shoes, yelled, "I want to die! I want to die!"

He was in luck. Pounding down the catwalk to get a hit at the bird as it came barreling down out of the sun for another run, there was someone who wanted to kill him.

The warrior looked in the other direction, and in the wanting-to-die stakes his luck doubled. Coming down a foot above the catwalk like a spear with wings there was a moth-eaten bird moving towards him at the speed of sound.

With his shoulders and head and sword poking out the window on the edge of eternity, the warrior was in the way of both of them.

Auden screamed, "Gar-*raagh!*" and with a mighty sweep

of his bat got the warrior out of the way by the simple expedient of clobbering him full force on the face mask and blowing him back against the Institute of Yu wall and pulverizing him to Crazy Goo.

He never hit a woman. On the next windowsill, there was someone dressed like Scarlett O'Hara in *Gone with the Wind*.

It was a guy.

He hit him.

Auden shrieked to all evil dentists everywhere, "You hurt me! You hurt my mouth and you made me go home all alone crying with the pain!"

He lifted his bat, and as Attila roared by at Warp 10 with all his phasers on Kill, he raised his bat and swiped a mighty swipe of revenge.

There was a swish as the bat flashed through the air and then a sort of tinkling sound as the end of it got phaser-razored into sawdust. Auden screamed, "Come on! I'm big now. *I'm a man!*" He heard a pounding, a thumping from somewhere and turned for an instant and saw, smashing on the glass of the closed windows behind him, the Brothers Yu. He looked back and saw Spencer pounding at the window in front.

He saw Doctors, Psychiatrists—

He saw . . . *Dentists!*

Auden shrieked, "No! *This time I won't just sit there and let him drill!* This time, the dentist is going to *die!*"

There was a rush of air as something tore by him and then a rush of rags as whatever it was that had torn by him tore the shoulder pad, shoulder, and lining of his suit to pieces.

At the half-open window in front of him, Spencer screamed, "Phil—!"

The bird came down for the final assault. He was a mess, a mongrel, a guttersnipe, the ragged, moth-eaten remnant of a life gone wrong. He had no fear or finer feelings at all: all he could do well was fight.

Him too. Auden, raising the chewed toothpick of his bat, yelled, ready for him, "Here I am! Come and get it! Scumbags!"

They were two of a kind. Two warriors with fucked-up childhoods full of pain.

It was the end. It was the true Yu of Auden. It was who he really was. With everywhere around him people pounding on the windows and everywhere behind them people unconscious in the corridor, it was his essence, his soul, the sum of everything he ever was.

He waited. He saw the bird come.

He raised the bat. Auden shrieked, "Now! At last! *Now!* And this—this is for my *pain!*"

He readied the bat.

He did not see Spencer push open the window ahead of him and start to climb out to save him. He saw only Attila coming at him head-on for the final battle.

Attila saw only him. He didn't see Spencer or the window either.

Auden, deep in his lizard brain, bereft of id and ego and superego and even the ability to see five feet ahead of him, roared, "*Aaaarrggghhh!*"

Attila, deep in his tiny chick's recollection of always being the last one in the next to be fed, seeing only Auden, cawed, "*Caaawwww!*"

Spencer, trying to get out, said with one leg over the sill, "Phil! . . . *Phil!*" and then the bird hit the glass of the open window head-on and everything around him exploded into a snowstorm of detonating seagull, blasted him back inside, spun him around like a top, and laid him and the two Yu brothers just behind him flat on the corridor floor like nine pins.

And hast thou slain the Dentist-wock?

Ah, come to my arms, my beamish boy . . .

On the catwalk, it came back to Auden from his childhood.

He hadn't. He hadn't slain him at all. It had been the window. Auden shrieked, "No! No! No! *No!*"

Foiled again. Auden yelled, "Oh, no!" Racing for the open, cracked, seagull-splattered window, Auden yelled in horror, in protest, in the sudden, terrible, deep pain of grief of being thwarted at the last minute, "Oh, no! I waited all my life for that! *I waited all my life for one great final battle with that dentist!*"

There was nothing in Shoemaker's file he did not know already or the commander had not already told him.

All there was at the end of it in the Investigations section was the case of the serial-killer kid who had ripped up five girls before Shoemaker had caught him, and then two more after Shoemaker had screwed up and the kid had been let go.

At the end of the computer-copied file there was a final notation that read:

PRESS PIX AND PIXPRINT TO VIEW AND/OR HARD-COPY NUMBERED-CODED PHO-TOGRAPHS WHERE WANTED. DO NOT REMOVE HARD COPIES FROM RECORDS SECTION WITH-OUT PERMISSION. SHRED AFTER USE.

Kneading at his forehead with his free hand, Feiffer pressed the button to bring up the photographs of the first five dead girls.

They were all schoolgirls, all in their summer uniforms, all dead, two Chinese, and two Malays, and one Eurasian.

PIXPRINT. HARD COPY?

Feiffer pressed *N* for *No*.

PIXVIEW CONTINUE? ENTER NUMBER CODE OF PIX.

He pressed *6*.

The photo that came up on the screen was a Morgue photo of a sixteen- or seventeen-year-old Chinese girl with her stomach laid open and her dead eyes staring out into nothingness.

PIXPRINT CONTINUE?

He pressed *7*.

And it was a photograph of the seventh victim, another young girl in uniform, chopped to pieces, the stuff of nightmares.

She was about nineteen or twenty, maybe in her last year of school, still with baby fat on her face and hands, wearing around her neck—

At the work station, Feiffer said in a gasp, "Oh, my God—!"

Around her neck, like so many Chinese girls on the brink of adulthood, as a gift or as merely something they had bought themselves for luck and prosperity, she wore a little gold elephant charm on a chain.

She was the stuff, not of nightmares, but of Shoemaker's nightmares.

She looked almost exactly like the dead girl in the bank, the girl Shoemaker, moving around the mall on his rounds, must have seen over and over.

Feiffer said in a whisper, "God in heaven, George! . . . God in heaven!"

He could not even begin to understand what seeing her day after day must have done to the man, what it must have reminded him of, what it had shown him of himself, what it had brought back, what it had—

A voice behind him said, "Mr. Feiffer!"

He turned. It was a Chinese uniformed sergeant from the commander's office.

He had not even heard him come into the room behind him. Feiffer said in Cantonese, "Yes. Yes, Sergeant, what is it?"

He didn't answer in Cantonese. He answered in English.

Something had happened.

The Chinese sergeant, relaying the message in English so there would be no mistake as to what its source had been, said urgently, reaching down to the back of Feiffer's chair to get him up, "A radio message from the commander. The commander says for you to come quick. The commander says for you to come now. The commander says there's a siege situation in progress now at the offices of the Hong Kong Analysis Laboratories in the Cathay Pearl Building on Aberdeen Road involving a man called Dr. Tolliver and he needs you to meet him there now!"

They were inconsolable. Surrounded by unconscious warriors and Zulus and surfers and someone dressed in a hooped skirt like Scarlett O'Hara inter alia, Aaron Yu howled in unison with his brother Douglas's sobbing noises, "We're ruined! Everything is ruined! The work of our father's lifetime and ours now amounts to nothing! Our father's dream—our continuing dream—of being a haven to the soul-torn has been turned by you two morons into—into—" He couldn't think of a word.

Douglas sobbed, "Into *nothing!* Into *dust!*"

"Into nothing! Into dust!" He looked at Spencer standing there gazing down at the deeply unconscious Warrior and Surfer and Zulu and Scarlett O'Hara and Gary Cooper all laid out in a line on the floor like a row of wine bottles. "You cretins! You oafs! You incompetents! You—you—you—" He couldn't think of a word.

Douglas said, "Imbeciles!"

"You imbeciles!" He couldn't believe it had happened. In his starched white doctor's coat he began howling and hopping up and down at the same time. Aaron wailed, "Look at them! They're all unconscious! Comatose! When they all come to—if they ever come to—they probably won't remember a thing that happened! They won't remember why they wanted to jump! They won't remember why all the Rooms of Yu failed! *All they'll remember is that they got mashed by two madmen!*" He hopped even higher. "Single-handedly, you two have managed to do in one day what a thousand years of ignorance and superstition and the combined power of all the churches in Asia and Europe and even the Inquisition and mass murder never managed to do: *in one day you've destroyed not only the entire modern twentieth-century concept of psychiatric therapy for the desperate and deranged, you've propelled the entire pursuit of Science back five centuries into the Dark Ages!*" He was hopping mad. He went on hopping. He looked at the Chief Madman sitting against a wall cradling a battered, moth-eaten seagull in his arms and could have killed him. Aaron shrieked, "You've destroyed the entire reputation of the Institute of Yu as surely as if you'd put a bomb under it! We may as well close down and rent the entire place out to a bank!" Aaron shrieked, "This will kill our father! After this, if he ever recovers from the shock of the publicity, all he'll be able to do with his once-shining life is sell matches on the street!"

Douglas said, "Or pencils!"

Aaron said, "Or *pencils!*"

Attila was still alive. Hanging limp in Auden's arms, he was broken-winged and battered—his one good eye wandering from the brain-bludgeoning against the window—but still alive. Cradling him in his arms, Auden, afraid to look up to Spencer's face, said in an undertone to Spencer, "I'm sorry, Bill, I guess I just got a little carried away and I . . ."

Spencer said softly, "That's okay." He looked down at the man holding the seagull in his arms. Both the seagull and the man were hurting. Spencer said gently, going forward and leaning down to stroke Attila on the head to console them both, "We all have things left over from somewhere we have to work out somehow . . ." He touched the bird gently on the head, "It'll be okay."

What the Brothers Yu had left over to work out was what they were going to do with the rest of their lives. He looked down, with them, at the line of clobbered costumed characters in the corridor. For a moment, he thought their faces all looked familiar, but he couldn't place where he had seen them before. Spencer said as a confession, "When I—when I was in the Great Wall Room, I have to confess a lot of things I thought were hidden came out in me too."

"Can we get the bird to a vet, Bill?"

Spencer said, "Sure."

"Please! Can we do it now?"

Spencer said, "Sure." He looked at the Brothers Yu not at all. He looked down at the Warrior and the Zulu and the Surfer and Gary Cooper and Scarlett O'Hara and the Hockey Goalie.

Spencer said softly, "Sure. Of course we can. We'll do it now." He looked up and saw the two Yus glaring at him in hatred.

Spencer, going forward and taking Auden gently under the arm to help him up, said with a sudden lightbulb of total comprehension lighting up his face, "Oh, my God," Spencer said, "Yes! Yes! Yes! Let's do it now! Let's get out of here and do it really urgently now!"

Maybe he wouldn't have made such a good psychiatrist after all, but boy! he made one hell of a brilliant *detective!*

Spencer, hauling Auden and the seagull up and practically

launching them in the direction of the elevator to get out, said with only a cursory glance at the Mystery of the Demented Defenestrators laid out for his inspection in a line on the floor, "Leave now, of course, is exactly what we *must* do, the only thing we *can* do!" Spencer said in triumph, "Leave! Of course! *Leave now!*"

He knew it all. He had found his true Yu at last. He was not, never would be, Spencer of the Hussars—he was, and always had been—Sherlock Holmes of Baker Street.

And now, Watson, time to leave. But not first without a word to the peasantry.

Spencer, raising a single finger to show it was but a single-pipe problem, said as Great Detectives always did, smiling and nodding, "Ah, Aaron, Douglas, so glad to have been of help to you along your chosen little path of life. Happy to have been of assistance." He smiled again.

Aaron said, *"What?"* He stopped hopping. His mouth fell open. Aaron said, unable to believe his own ears, *"WHAT—?"* He began hopping again. Aaron screamed, "Help in *what?* Be of assistance in—*what?* Along our chosen little path of—*WHAT?"*

He was surrounded by the debris of his life, talking to a man talking to a man carrying a seagull in his arms.

Aaron shrieked, *"Are you—Are you—"*

He didn't need Douglas this time. He thought of the word all by himself.

Aaron yelled so loud it made all the windows all along the corridor rattle, "Are you people both completely, completely, *insane?"*

The sergeant said with his hand a fist on the back of Feiffer's chair, "Mr. Feiffer, the Emergency Unit's already on the way. The situation, apparently, is very desperate. The commander says there's a man holding Dr. T. in his office threatening to kill him at any moment!"

13.

The man holding Tolliver hostage inside the Hong Kong Analysis Laboratories poison room was George Shoemaker.

He was insane.

He had been insane ever since the kid he had let go had killed again.

The first thing he had done the moment Tolliver opened the door to let him into the reception room of the laboratories was take a single step back from him, quickly measure the distance between them, and then, stiffening his arms like pistons, drive both his thumbs simultaneously high up into the arterial axillary pressure points under Tolliver's armpits and paralyze both the man's arms, then, a second later as he staggered back and went over, kick him hard dead-center in the genitals.

The screaming from that kick was what had alerted the other occupants of the building all along the corridor of the third floor to call the police.

Once he had managed to get his breath back, Tolliver, rolling on the floor with his arms flapping like a puppet's, had screamed for help and he had let him do that to make doubly sure the other occupants heard, then as the man tried to stagger to his knees, Shoemaker reached into his pocket, took out the set of hard rubber knuckle-dusters he had brought with him, slipped them over the fingers of his left hand, and with a blow that left no mark at all, smashed the man back down to the floor and stunned him into silence.

He had brought a little zip-up airline overnight bag with him.

The bag contained six twelve-fluid-ounce screw-top bottles of Coca-Cola, his hand-tuned fifteen-shot Heckler and Koch P7 automatic pistol, and two rolled-up, best-quality white-leather chef's aprons from Le Bon Cuisinier gourmet kitchen-supplies shop in the mall.

Then he waited.

He waited until some idiot or self-styled hero braver or more curious that anyone else came running down to the open door of the reception room to see what was happening.

As he waited, he used the time to take the pistol out of the bag, check the magazine, and then, with a snap, pull back the slide and chamber a round.

On the floor, Tolliver was on his hands and knees gasping for breath.

He waited. He waited until the idiot came. The idiot was a young Chinese man of athletic build wearing a suit and tie: a salesman in at the end of the day to report his figures to the head office.

He looked educated—the sort of career-climber who had made learning English his first priority on the road to success—but Shoemaker, to be sure, standing facing him with the gun in his hand, spoke to him in Chinese.

His face as he said the words to the man was rigid, without expression. Shoemaker said in Cantonese to the goggle-eyed salesman, with no tone in his voice at all, "Don't try to be a hero. If you try to be a hero you'll die and your family—if you're their sole support—will suffer financial hardship and grief for the rest of their lives because of your pointless heroism."

He saw the salesman's eyes goggle even more. He saw him see the muzzle of the gun. Shoemaker said, "If you haven't already done it, call the police. If you have already called them, call them again. Tell them what you've seen. Tell them it's an armed-siege situation and they need the Emergency Unit with their listening devices and their fiber-

optic TV cameras. Tell them the siege is in the Hong Kong
Analysis Laboratories on the third floor of the Cathay Pearl
Building on Aberdeen Road, Hong Bay. Then repeat the address and make them read it back to you to make sure
they've got it right."

The muzzle of the gun was freezing the man's mind: he
could see it in his eyes.

Shoemaker asked in Cantonese, "Do you understand?"

At the open door, the salesman opened his mouth to speak,
but no sound came out.

"*Do you understand?*"

The salesman said, "*Yes!*" He looked down at the man
rolling on the floor in agony scrabbling to get up and all he
wanted to do was run. The salesman, nodding hard, said in
English to make sure the man with the gun knew he understood, "Yes! Yes! *Yes!*"

"Good." He lowered the muzzle of the gun so the salesman could see what was about to happen and be in good
enough mental shape to report it clearly and precisely. Shoemaker said calmly, "You're in no personal danger if you just
stay there for another brief moment or two and watch what
happens."

The salesman said in a gasp, "*Yes!*"

"Good." On the floor beside him, Tolliver, almost on his
hands and knees, convulsed through the full length of his
body and threw up, and Shoemaker, looking down at him,
waited until the convulsion finished.

Looking down at him, with the salesman frozen in horror
at the door, he waited until Tolliver, gasping and panting, got
his feet together behind him to try to push himself up, then,
aiming carefully, with no pause between the two reports,
shot the man twice through the soles of his leather shoes and
crippled him.

Working alone, it was the only way he could be sure Tolliver would not try to break free when the interrogation
began.

Shoemaker said to the salesman, "Okay. Now you can
go."

He reached down with his free hand and, taking Tolliver
by the hair, began dragging him a little at a time towards the

still-closed door of the poison room of the laboratory complex.

Shoemaker said again to the salesman, "Go," but the screaming from the stricken man in his grasp was so loud the salesman did not hear it, and to move him, Shoemaker, pausing for a moment with his load, aimed the gun in the general direction of the salesman and squeezed off a round that blew away the doorjamb above his head and sent him fleeing.

He was insane. He had become insane the moment he had looked down at the first of the two dead girls the kid serial had ripped up after the courts had let him go because of the botched interrogation.

The first moment he had seen the little pudgy girl from the bank in the mall with the lucky elephant charm around her neck he had thought she was the harbinger of the spirits of all the dead girls the kid had killed and she had come back to accuse him.

He was insane, but he thought, as he stopped dragging the man for a moment and paused to pick up his bag of torture instruments with his free hand, that he had never seen things clearer in his life than he did at that moment.

He giggled. Shoemaker said with a little grin, "The Coke bottles—now that'll confuse the first uniformed mutt on the scene just a little . . ."

Still grinning at the thought of it, he got Tolliver to the door of the poison room, pulled the door open with the hand holding the bag and gun, pulled him in, and then kicked the door shut after them.

He had thought of everything. He knew exactly—probably for the very first time in his life—exactly what he was doing.

There was a long trail of blood running under the bottom of the closed door from where Shoemaker had towed him in from the reception room, and, letting go of Tolliver's hair and dumping the still-vomiting, ruined man like a sack onto the floor, he looked back at it carefully, then, raising up his gun, blew two holes in the door exactly seven and a half inches above the floor so the fiber-optic TV camera and listening microphone the Emergency Unit would bring with them would have predrilled holes available to them at exactly the right spots for optimum reception.

There was no reason in his plan for what he did next.

It was strictly for his own pleasure, strictly something personal, something done out of old habit from when he had been a cop.

Stepping back from the howling, bleeding man as he convulsed and vomited blood and froth and tissue from somewhere deep in his lungs and throat, Shoemaker put the rubber knucks back on his hand for a second time, and, squatting down beside him, drew back his arm like a piston and smashed the man full in the right eye and exploded his eyeball in a fountain of liquid and albumen and blood all down the side of his face.

Suddenly, with darkness starting to fall, O'Yee was so frightened out there alone with him that at first he did not understand what it was Frank said to him.

Frank said in a strange soft voice with his eyes still narrowed, "Well, 'Christopher,' after we have found somewhere for you to spend the night, maybe we should find out who you really are . . ."

They were on the corner of Wyang Street where the fish markets were. They were on the corner of Wyang Street not where the fish markets were, but where the deserted, empty, darkened, totally uninhabited fish markets were. They were in the worst part of town. They were in the worst part of town with night falling.

Frank said with his voice like the edge of a razor, "And discover why you are that person and what it is that person is here to do."

What was he here to do? He was here to die. What RTG–68 had sent him out to be was a victim. He hadn't bothered to give him any more details about how to do it because there was no need for a victim to know what the hell anything was about because all he was going to be in the great plan was dead. O'Yee said in a strangled voice, "Me? Oh, I'm just—"

Once, he had thought Frank had a nice face. He didn't have a nice face. He had a face like a skull, like arid, dry death. He had hands like claws. He laid one of the claws gently on O'Yee's shoulders and death seeped in through the bones into O'Yee's chest and froze his heart from a beating, warm living organ into two and a half pounds of frozen meat. O'Yee said desperately, "I am—a—" but he couldn't get the word *cop* out in case Frank the serial killer or mass murderer or whatever he was took offense and decided to kill him on the spot. O'Yee said, "I'm a—I'm a—" O'Yee said in his terror, "Ima, Ima, Ima—"

He couldn't get to his gun. RTG–68 had seen to that by making him wear chains around his chest so there was nowhere under his rags to hide it except in an ankle holster. O'Yee said in a gasp, looking around on the street for help, "No, I'm not—Ima, Ima, Ima—"

He saw no one on the street. It was growing dark, and suddenly, between the end of late afternoon and the beginning of night, he was caught in the brief, eerie, deserted few moments of the day when everybody was somewhere else.

He sounded like a tired, bored grandfather talking to a small frightened child. Frank said with a sigh, "Ah, 'Christopher,' what are we to do with you? You who pretend to be someone else? You dressed in rags and chains with your chalk and your *Eternity* and your coat hanger whose purpose you do not even know?" His voice became hard, "You who pretend to be crazed and schizophrenic—*but clearly are not!* What are we to do with you? Where are we to take you?"

Home? Home would be nice. Home where he could live like a cockroach and weep. Home where he could— O'Yee said in a gasp to try to think of somewhere nice, "Um . . ."

With his face an inch from O'Yee's, Frank asked in a voice like a razor, "What's the coat hanger for, Christopher?"

"I don't know! *I don't know!*"

"Who are you? Why are you here?"

He didn't know. RTG–68 had never bothered to tell him.

"Who are you trying to *trick?*"

"No one! No one!" Digging deep into his shoulder, Frank's claw was like a pincer, crushing him, drawing the life out of him, terrifying him. O'Yee said, "No one! *I don't know!*"

Frank said, "Then—" (With the pain from Frank's grip

making his ears ring O'Yee could not make out the next two words Frank said.)

He was Death. He turned O'Yee a little with the strength of his claw. Frank said, "Then . . . you must come with me."

It was where RTG–68 had brought him—to the end.

O'Yee said in a whisper for his own life and the lives of his wife and children and the grandchildren and great-grand-children and great-great-grandchildren he would never live to see again, "Oh, my God! . . ."

As they began to walk, he looked around for someone to help, but there was no one, only the shadows everywhere of falling night.

One of those shadows across the street in an alley moved, but O'Yee did not see it and, if he had, would not have been consoled by it.

It was the shadow of a well-dressed, tight-faced southern Chinese male in his thirties.

In the alley, the shadow watched with unblinking eyes as "Frank," still holding "Christopher" by the shoulder, slowly turned the man and began to lead him away with him up the street.

He watched, timing it on his watch, for exactly one minute and five seconds as, unkempt, ragged, unwanted by society, both shambling a little, they began to walk north up Wyang Street, then, pausing only long enough to slip his hand under his coat to check the huge stainless-steel gun he carried was still there, he came out of the shadows and went after them.

Outside the Cathay Pearl Building, the entire width of Aberdeen Road was full of ambulances and fire trucks and police cars, blocking the stalled traffic in the street, lighting it up in the first darkness of evening in a myriad of turning blue and red and yellow roof lights.

Everywhere there were Hazchem trucks from the fire brigade, foam wagons, fire marshals' cars and trucks and emergency-rescue and ladder units, and parked between them and around them, rapid-response trucks from the Emergency Unit with their back doors open, police cars and trucks from Headquarters, and, up on the sidewalk, almost at the twin glass entrance doors of the building itself, marked with decals of rank and importance above the standard police crest on their doors, the official cars of the commander and his staff and aides and subcommanders.

As he went all the way up to the third floor in the elevator, Feiffer's jaw clamped tight of its own accord, and even though he closed his eyes and tried to settle his breathing, he could not get the muscles in his jaw to loosen and let go.

He knew, up there, what he was going to see and hear.

"*Motive! Means! Opportunity! Confession!*" He heard Shoemaker screaming at the top of his lungs before the elevator doors even opened.

They opened into a chaos of silver Hazchem fire-suited firemen and uniformed cops in bulletproof vests and ambulancemen and emergency medical technicians with stretchers and oxygen tanks, and everywhere, crowded down the full length of the third-floor corridor at the door to the stairs, people from all the offices screaming in panic to get out.

"*Motive! Means! Opportunity! Confession!*" Somewhere in the crush of all the cops and entry teams, the voice was being amplified electronically like the voice of God above all the sounds of the crouched people in the corridor at their equipment, counterpointing it, focusing it, terrifying the people fighting to get away down the corridor and making them cringe and whimper in fear.

In the exact center of the corridor, one of the technicians from the Emergency Unit—Sergeant Tack from the bank— had the sound and scene of what was happening in the laboratory on video and audio linkup.

On the flickering black-and-white audio-and-visual surveillance thirteen-inch television monitor with its leads running back across the floor into the reception room to where Winter and his black-clad entry team crouched ready at the closed door to the laboratory with their guns out, he had sounds and pictures from hell.

"*Motive! Means! Opportunity! Confession!*" It was Shoemaker. On the flickering screen, dressed in his white-leather apron with his face twisted as he shrieked at the bloodied, mutilated, horror-film victim he held on his knees in front of him, he looked not like a man at all, but something mutated, less than human, a figure from a nightmare.

On the screen, as he jabbed the muzzle of his gun over and over into the back of the man's neck, arranged in lines everywhere behind him on shelves and in cabinets and on benches, there were poisons, lines and rows of chemicals and acids and things that if released would fill the room and all the other rooms around it, in a moment, with enough toxins and gas and fumes to kill everybody in the building and in all the buildings and streets for three blocks around it.

The man he held in his grasp on his knees in front of him—what was left of Dr. Tolliver—also no longer looked human. He looked, with his mouth open in a silent scream, with his eye gone and his face bloated and swollen and running blood, like something already dead. Sagging in Shoemaker's grasp, he looked like a bloated, long-immersed corpse dragged from the harbor with nothing left of its face and hands but formless, melted, stark-white fatty tissue.

In the room and on the screen, Shoemaker shrieked like Satan at the Inquisition, *"Motive! Means! Opportunity!— CONFESSION!"*

He had the six twelve-ounce screw-top bottles of Coca-Cola laid out in a line on the floor, ready, and, reaching down with the hand holding the gun, he took the first one up, spun off the top, and with his thumb over the neck, began shaking it to make it fizz.

"Motive! Means! Opportunity! Confession!"

Standing over the wretch of a man in his grip, he shook the bottle over and over, harder and harder, until, starting to froth white under his thumb, all the dark liquid in the bottle turned into boiling, high-pressure foam.

In the car outside the twenty-four-hour vet's office on Cuttlefish Lane, Auden, still cradling the wounded sea-gull in his arms, said in a whisper, "I'm sorry, Bill. I didn't mean to ruin it all for you." In his embrace, Attila lay limp as if he were asleep, his one good eye closed, his breathing easy and deep. "I know how important things like that are to you: you know, psychology, and solving mysteries, and—and all that." He looked down at Attila and gently ran the fingers of his huge hand across the bird's head and neck feathers to smooth them, "It was just that it wasn't—"

The vet's office was the only light on in the darkened lane. Auden said with real feeling, "It just wasn't a fair fight after he hit the open window like that! It just wasn't a battle between two equally matched enemies anymore! It was just a trick!" With his eyes staring absently out the windshield, he stroked gently at the bird and smoothed its feathers. Next to him, Spencer lit a cigarette, and for a moment, Auden watched him smoke it. Auden said softly, "It wasn't noble anymore." Auden said in his own defense as if Spencer had accused him of something, "I'm not an unfair, unfeeling brute like a dentist enjoying hurting a kid stuck in his goddamned chair like a pinned goddamned butterfly! I'm a person with a sense of fairness and a heart—I give my enemies an equal chance to fight back!" His eyes were full of tears. Auden said, "I'm sorry about the case, Bill! I'm sorry you're never going to find out why a whole lot of people might want to commit suicide on a catwalk, but it all came back to me in that place and I—" He looked down at the gull and wiped at his eyes.

"That's okay, Phil." He reached out and patted Auden gently on the shoulder to console him.

Auden said, "They said back there in the institute that I was the hero type. I am the hero type. Any little kid who can live through what I lived through in that fucking dentist's office is a hero!" Auden, looking down at the gull, said against anyone who might say otherwise, "And so is he! So is this poor goddamned bird! He fought fair too and it wasn't his goddamned fault that someone tricked him and smashed him into defeat with a goddamned window! And it's my duty, one hero to another, to take him into the vet's and get him seen to so he can have the strength to fight another day!" He was a noble bird. They both were. Auden said, "It wasn't his fault he hit the window. That was something out of his control. That wasn't fair!" Auden said fiercely, "That was something underhand and low he didn't even know about while he was being brave and someone has to make it right for him!"

Clearly whatever it was that had happened at the dentist's office all those years before had never been made right for him. Auden said, brooking no opposition, "Okay? Is that okay with you?"

"Sure." He looked hard at Auden's face and wondered what it was he wasn't telling him. He had the wounded sea-gull cradled gently in his arms like a protector. Spencer said, again, "Sure. Of course it is. If it's important to you, Phil."

"It is."

"Okay then."

"I'm sorry about the case, Bill."

"Don't be." Gazing out into the darkness in front of the windshield of the car, the Great Deductor permitted himself a little momentary grin of satisfaction. The Great Deductor said lightly, as if it were nothing at all, "As a matter of fact, if it puts your mind at rest, the case is already solved, and, except for the final assembling of the entire cast of players in it and the denouement, there remain in it only details to be cleared up."

He was talking funny. He sounded like Basil Rathbone in one of the old Sherlock Holmes movies. Spencer said to put the man's mind even more at rest, "My dear fellow, the entire affair was but a revamping by poor imitators of the plot of one of my most celebrated triumphs: *The Mystery of the Barking Dog in the Night.*"

Auden said, "What barking dog in the night?"

Spencer said, "Precisely!"

Auden said, "There wasn't any barking dog in the night! All there were were a lot of people trying to commit suicide by jumping out of windows!"

"Put, as usual, old friend, to a tee!" He gazed at him deeply. He put his hands around his invisible meerschaum. Spencer asked sweetly, "Ah. But were there?"

Auden said, "Were there what?"

Holmes said in that funny old Dorset beekeeper's drawl of his, "A lot of people trying to commit suicide by jumping out of windows."

"Weren't there?"

Spencer said in triumph, "Ah, that is the question!" All the time he had stood there being abused by the Brothers Yu he could not get over the feeling that he had seen the Warrior, the Surfer, the Hockey Goalie, the Zulu and Gary Cooper, and even Scarlett O'Hara somewhere before.

He had seen them before.

Spencer said easily, confidently, but with an urgency starting in his voice, "No, there were no people trying to commit suicide by jumping out of windows. Not one. What there was, was not real at all in its own terms but merely a rehearsal for something else. And that something else, I believe, is a *murder!*" God, he loved this stuff! Spencer said, still grinning, "And the more I consider it, the more I believe I know the exact moment of its commission!"

"When?"

Spencer said, "Ah, do I hear you enquire when the game's afoot?" He was in heaven. He could solve two mysteries at once if he wanted to. The second mystery was the mystery of the seagull and the dentist and what Auden was not telling him about it, but he thought he might leave that till later. Spencer said in his glory, so sure of himself and who he was that it hurt, "Tonight! Soon! When all the cast is reassembled and the play reaches its inevitable, planned, and pre-arranged final act, the murder is planned to take place *now! Tonight!*"

Oh, the joy! The ecstasy! The pure, simple, logical, wonderful, elementariness of it all!

Reaching past the man and gull and flicking down the door handle to open the door for him to get out with the gull to take it to the vet, Spencer calooed in his joy a moment before he started the car to go, "God, Phil! And to think I actually get paid *money* for doing all this stuff! . . ."

In the corridor, the commander yelled, "He's completely over the edge, Harry! We can't treat this as a standard negotiable hostage situation with his state of mind and all that goddamned stuff lying around in the lab—we have to go in and chop him before he fires a shot off and turns half-a-dozen city blocks of the Colony into another fucking Chernobyl disaster!" In the lab on the screen, Shoemaker, still screaming at the man, got his arm across Tolliver's mouth from behind, and, with his free hand, jammed the neck of the fizzing Coke bottle hard against his nose and jerked away his thumb.

It was a technique the Thai police had invented. There was an eruption of foam as the entire contents of the bottle, held under unbearable pressure by the shaking, exploded into Tolliver's nose. The commander shrieked, "Oh, *Jesus!*" He, like Feiffer, had seen it done before and what it did. It was said by those who survived it that it was like simultaneously drowning and having your brain blown apart. The commander, in full uniform and braid and ribbons and badges of rank, roared as an order to everyone jammed into the corridor, but especially Winter and his team by the door, "I want him chopped! I want him chopped now!" The commander demanded, stabbing his finger in Winter's direction to get it set up, "You there! Senior Inspector! Have you got any subsonics with you or do you have to—"

Crouched down hard against the closed door with his team, Winter could hear what was happening on the screen. Dressed in a heavy black flak jacket with his bulletproof vest on under it against his chest, he was covered in sweat and he could not stop himself trembling. But it was the commander and he got his voice to work. Reaching down for something in a pouch on his belt and holding it up, Winter snapped back with his voice as professional as he could make it, held it up, "One clip, sir!" It was a twelve-shot clip full of the subsonic hollow-point nine-millimeter close-kill rounds the Israelis had invented in the terrorist-filled seventies—bullets that went through an airliner hijacker's flesh and bone and body and destroyed them instantly but did not pass out again to pierce the fragile skin of an airplane. Winter snapped, "One clip only, sir! In possession of antiterrorist-trained officer, sir!" From the monitor out in the corridor the sounds of Tolliver in suffocation and terror were so awful all he wanted to do was jam his hands flat against his ears to shut them out. Winter shouted, "Shaped door charge already in position! Team in position! Ready to initiate entry, sir!"

On the screen, hauling his drowning, gagging victim back up against him so he could drown him again with the next bottle, Shoemaker screamed again, "*Motive! Means! Opportunity! CONFESSION!*"

If Shoemaker was over the edge, he was the one who had put him there. Grasping at the commander's sleeve to turn him away from giving the order to blast in the door, Feiffer yelled above the sounds of Shoemaker's voice, "Neal, he won't kill him! If he kills him he won't get anything out of

him and he'll have failed! He's used this sort of stuff on people before! He knows how it works! It's a torture technique!
The psychology of it isn't that it's going to kill the victim!
The psychology of it is that it isn't going to kill the victim
and it's going to keep on happening to the victim forever!"

On the screen, Shoemaker wrenched Tolliver's head up
and back and, as the vomit and foam and blood poured out
from his nose and mouth in a wave, reached down for the
second bottle on the floor and uncapped it.

Feiffer, holding the commander's arm in a grip of steel,
roared at the commander to convince him, "Neal, Shoemaker
thinks Tolliver murdered all those people in the bank! He
thinks he's going to get away with it because when I talked
to him I didn't push him hard enough to get it out of him! He
thinks—" Feiffer said desperately as the commander tried to
pull away to give Winter the order to blast the door down
and go in, "He thinks everything that was ever wrong or
fucked up or unfair in his life hinges on getting the truth out
of the man! He won't kill Tolliver because he needs him to
stay alive to confess! He won't fire a shot anywhere near any
of the poison bottles to spoil it! He won't do anything but
scientifically, carefully, one step at a time, torture the poor
bastard until he gets what he thinks is the *truth* out of him!"

"What truth? The truth about what happened in that bank?
Tolliver hasn't got any truth to give! He didn't do anything
in the bank! You told me that yourself!" The commander,
pulling away, making a decision, said as an order, "No! We
do it my way! The safe way!" The commander said as an accusation, "The last thing you told me on the phone was that
you'd eliminated Tolliver from your enquiries and your enquiries were heading in the direction of Shoemaker! Look at
them! How the hell does that make any sense now to anyone?"

"I don't know!" There was nothing. Everything was darkness. Feiffer said desperately, "Neal, I don't know how anything makes sense! Tolliver and Shoemaker are all we've got
and if we lose one of them or both of them now in a fucking
shoot-out, we may never know what the hell happened in
that bank! We may never know why someone—" He saw the
commander's face. He knew whose fault it was. Feiffer said

in desperation, "Goddammit! Neal, I'm doing the best I can with the case, but I can't work fucking *miracles* overnight! For God's sake, give me a chance to at least talk to Shoemaker before you decide to send the fucking cavalry in to kill him!"

On the screen, Shoemaker, shaking the second bottle to near detonation point, shrieked at the sagging dying man in his grip, "*Motive! Means! Opportunity! Confession!*"

In the corridor the commander ordered Winter, "Lock and load! Stand by to initiate entry charge on my order!" The commander ordered everyone in the corridor, "Clear the area! Clear the area now!"

"*Motive! Means! Opportunity! Confession!*" In the lab, he was killing him, drowning him.

Everywhere in the corridor people began running for the stairs. Standing his ground, Feiffer saw Winter at the door covered in sweat and fear. Reaching out to yank at the commander's sleeve but being shoved and pushed away and lost in the crush of fire fighters and cops fleeing, Feiffer yelled desperately, "Neal, I know that man at the door! You can't send him in first! He's—"

"*Motive—!*"

Winter screamed to drown out Feiffer's words, "Sir! Charge ready! Team ready! Sir!"

It was an order, a command. The commander, without pausing, yelled, "Now! Hit the door! *Now!*"

He had no words and his eyes felt dry, like sand, and twenty minutes later, as Feiffer sat in his car a little way down Aberdeen Road from the Cathay Pearl Building and watched without seeing them as one by one all the trucks and vehicles went away, he listened to the radio and heard for the second time how the killings at the bank had been resolved in a brief exchange of gunfire between the police and the perp in the office of a well-known scientist-doctor, someone the newscaster called, not having quite gotten it right on the phone from police public relations, Dr. "Oliver."

It had been a very brief gun battle: two shots only, and only after the person believed responsible for the bank poisonings had shot Dr. Oliver point-blank in the temple did the

Emergency Unit police officer involved in the confrontation fire back and kill him with a single shot to the head.

The name of the perpetrator, believed to be an ex-policeman employed somewhere in Hong Bay as some sort of shop security guard or janitor, had not been released pending notification of the next of kin.

The name of the Emergency Unit officer, however, had been released by authorities.

It was Police Senior Inspector James Arthur Winter.

On the radio, as Feiffer sat silently and alone in the darkness, the newscaster reminded everyone listening of how that same Senior Inspector Winter had been a hero once before . . .

14.

Walking three feet in front of O'Yee all the way, halfway down Wyang Street, Frank turned into the eastern end of Stamford Street, then, halfway down that again, went back south again into Taipei Lane, then, a quarter of the way down that, made a left through the pitch darkness of an unmarked passageway between the walls of two three-story stone buildings, and suddenly he was moving southeast along an unlit lane full of trash and blowing papers, and O'Yee, a street cop in the immediate area for over fifteen years, had absolutely no idea where he was at all.

His voice came out as a strangled rasp. He looked up and all he could see was the moon. O'Yee asked politely, "Um . . . where are we, Frank?"

He was musing and did not turn around. When he spoke, he spoke over his shoulder. Frank said, "Ah, 'Christopher' . . ." He said the name the way you said the name of a dog that had disappointed you a moment before, with a touch of regret, you took it down to the pound to have it put down. Frank said sadly, "Ah, 'Christopher,' how sad it is that so often those we think we know well are not what they appear to be at all . . ."

True. He thought he was Frank. He was really regretful that he had turned out to be Death.

O'Yee said with an urge to screw his coat hanger up into a little ball and sink down against a wall and cry into it, "Um . . ." He looked up into the darkness of the night and had absolutely no idea where he was. Oh, yes, he did: he was on the banks of the River Styx with old Charon the boatman. O'Yee said with his whole being concentrated on the thought of keeping Old Death on the Installment Plan and not turning him on the spot into Instant Cash on the Barrel Head Death, "Um, yes, Frank . . . um, people can be very, um, misleading sometimes, can't they?" He was going to die. RTG–68 had set him up with the greatest mass murderer since Vlad the Impaler impaled a mass of people and he was going to die. O'Yee said to apologize, "I didn't mean to mislead you though, Frank—"

Frank asked without turning around, "What are you without your rags and chalk and coat hanger, Christopher? Are you, perhaps—" He thought about it for a moment—"A *hunter?* And if so, who do you hunt?"

He knew! He knew he was a cop. Something in O'Yee's throat fell through his entire body and landed at his feet with a clang. It was his heart.

He shook his head without turning around. Frank asked, "Is that what you are? A hunter?" Then he turned and, although O'Yee could not see his eyes in the darkness, stopped and stared at him full in the face, "Is that who you are? A hunter? Or are you, instead, merely the *prey* of a hunter?"

Okay, that did it. That was it, okay, out with the PPK and up with your hands and they call me Mr. O'Yee time! That was—

That was rooted to the spot in terror time with your throat too paralyzed to make a sound time.

In the darkness, Death took a step forward. Death asked as a mild enquiry, "Are you truly in charge of your own fate, 'Christopher'?" He took a step forward, "Or not?"

O'Yee said, "Yes!"

"Hmm. We shall see." He turned back again and, only a shadow in the darkness, began walking again. Frank said sadly over his shoulder, "Tell me, do you even know where you are?"

Did he mean geographically or spiritually? Or did he mean—

ITEM: 1. *Description of immediate area.*

> *The immediate area of operations consists of a grid of from five to fifteen various arteries and capillaries of pedestrian and vehicular movement, depending on their size, importance, volume of activities, toponomically termed "Streets," "Roads," "Lanes," or "Alleys." (The last two occasionally used interchangeably and, in several instances, for example Ladder Alley—which, having only pedestrian traffic for the rear entrances of one or two large businesses on Wyang Street should be, in fact, termed "Rear of Wyang Street Access" or similar—quite incorrectly.)*

He was on Ladder Alley! O'Yee said in a burst, "Yes! Yes, I do! I do know where I am— I'm on Ladder Alley, which, as a matter of fact, having only pedestrian traffic for one or two businesses on Wyang Street, really isn't an alley at all and should be termed, in my opinion, more correctly 'Rear of Wyang Street Access' or similar."

Good old RTG–68! His hands were clammy with sweat and he wished he had something to soak it up and get his hands dry in case he had to reach quickly for the gun.

ITEM: 3. . . .

He had chalk! Chalk was good for sweat. Chalk was what goddamned Olympic wrestlers put on their hands before they wrestled Death to the ground and punched his lights out! Chalk was it. Chalk was the greatest thing for hands since fingers! Chalk! Glorious chalk! He got a stick out and rubbed it hard across his palms. God bless RTG–68!

ITEM: 4. *(iv) Above all, you will not misplace, vary, or otherwise lose physical possession of any of the above items aforementioned and listed in Item 3—especially, and in particular—the metal coat hanger.*

Frank said softly, still musing, still looking for somewhere to stop and tear his victim to pieces and then eat him, "We all, each of us, suffer in our own way the slings and arrows of outrageous fortune, Christopher . . ."

Not him! He had three layers of unseasonable, thick-padded clothing wrapped around his vitals to be an ill-used and mistreated, unloved bum. Slings and arrows just bounced off! O'Yee, gaining in confidence, walking a little faster, said happily, confidently, "Oh, yeah? Well, maybe some of us are going to suffer just a little more than others, 'Frank!' " He stopped for a moment, thanks to the foresight of the Great and Good RTG–68, armored, ready, thanks to the foresight and tuition of the Greatest Mind in The East, the Fastest and Driest Draw in the West. O'Yee, spoiling for a fight, said with his eyes narrowed, "Where to now, Frank?" He looked up at the building in front of him, "In here?" He watched as Frank took out a key and unlocked a door. It was a door to a private elevator. "Into the elevator next to the rear service entrance here of the—" His mind raced with maps, "Of the *Hop Sing Wa Investment and Insurance*— 'Frank?' "

He had it all. He had chalk, he had charts, he had cuirasses. He also had seen and had seen not at all, a shadowy figure tracking him step by step, every step of the way.

O'Yee demanded, full of confidence, "Well, 'Frank'? What now?"

He found out in a hurry. As the door of the elevator suddenly opened in complete darkness, two sets of hands instantly reached out for both him and Frank and hauled them both in, and before he even knew what was happening, something swished through the air like a baseball bat, hit him dead center in the chest, and exploded into splinters around him.

Whoever had hit him wasn't wearing chains.

As the other hands—the ones not wielding the baseball bat—pushed at the Up button in the elevator and propelled everything and everyone in the car upward like a rocket, the splinters, exploding back at him in a storm, strafed him from head to foot like shrapnel.

In the rapidly ascending car, O'Yee heard the strafed man

shriek, "Aaah!" then there was a ping as the elevator opened onto the eighteenth floor into more darkness, and then as O'Yee, full of splinter-shrapnel himself, crashed into someone and pierced them like a pincushion, there was another scream and then another, and, a moment before someone somewhere hit him with a blow on the chains that made them ring, there was the sound of a window suddenly being pulled open and crashing back against its metal frame.

Parking his car outside the garage entrance to the Hop Sing Wa Building and getting out to look up at it, Spencer, still grinning, thought he had all the time in the world.

He didn't. Far up on the darkened eighteenth floor of the building, he heard a scream of pain. Far up, as it caught the moonlight and flashed, he saw a single window fly open, and, slamming the car door shut, he raced to the basement garage area and pounded at the elevator button panel to get the elevator down.

There was a small, handwritten card taped to the elevator doors that read in both English and Chinese, Out of Service, and, drawing his gun, Spencer ran at top speed for the stairwell, ripped the metal stairwell door open and, going hard, took the stairs towards the eighteenth floor at top speed, two at a time.

He had heard the scream too.

He had his own key for the rear service elevator, and, racing down Ladder Alley, the shadowy figure who had been tracking Frank and O'Yee all day got to the service elevator door and tried the lock.

The elevator was still up on the eighteenth floor and all he got was a single electronic ping from somewhere inside the empty elevator well on the other side of the door to signal him to wait.

He heard another ping, and then another, and then as the elevator must have moved and begun to come down to him, a single buzzing sound.

In the lane, the shadowy figure, fighting to keep calm, drew his revolver from its heavy leather custom Berns-

Martin shoulder holster under his coat and checked to see whether it was loaded.

It was loaded. It was a laser-sighted stainless-steel Dan Wesson .445 Super Mag six-shot with a ten-inch barrel—a hand-built weapon designed for Dangerous Game loaded to kill anything on the planet.

As he slipped his thumb behind the customed-widened and extended combat-style hammer and cocked it, in the silence and darkness of the alley, the huge gun, glinting dully in the moonlight, made a single, well-oiled, urgent—*click!*

Fighting and kicking and punching and gouging against the open window on the eighteenth floor of the Institute of Yu, they weren't ignorant armies clashing by night—they were a melee of bodies and fists and smashed baseball clubs and rags fighting a battle to the death in a darkened corridor three inches from a drop of eighteen stories above the ground.

Whoever they all were, they were everywhere. In the darkness, O'Yee hit someone hard—there was a crash as whoever it was bounced off a wall and screamed in pain—and then, as he reached down for his gun to shoot whoever it was, someone else flew through the air and crashed into him with a shriek of blood lust and he went over, and then, as two feet and twenty-five feet of half-inch chest chain met the thin-shod feet of someone leaping on him with both feet, he heard a terrible shriek of shattered arches as the chains won and the kicker went down an amputee.

It was what the chains were for.

Somewhere in the darkness, Frank screamed, "Christopher!" and then there was a thud as someone else got hold of him around the throat and made him gurgle, and then, as whoever it was tried to drag him towards the open window and throw him out, a series of grunts and gasps of exertion.

On the floor in front of him, the kicker was a shadow halfway up on his knees. The shadow seemed to be wearing a white coat. The shadow screamed in English to the other shadow busily getting Frank up onto the windowsill to eternity, "*Kill him! Kill this one first!*" and then, as O'Yee tried a little kick of his own, the kneeling shadow stopped kneeling and skidded across the floor shrieking in pain.

They weren't after just him: they were after both Frank *and* him.

In the darkness, O'Yee yelled, "Frank! Frank! Over here!" then as the skidding figure stopped skidding and came back flailing, there was a crash at the window and as O'Yee, reaching down for his ankle to get his gun, ran to get to it, there was a sound like a swish and the flailing man stopped flailing and executed a karate leg-scissors to his knees that scythed him to the floor and sent the gun spinning away into the darkness.

Without the gun he was bereft of the necessary machinery to satisfy his heart's fondest desire: to launch a lethal projectile six inches into the bad guy's head at just under the speed of sound.

But he had chalk!

He had chalk to ram into his ear at the speed of ram.

He rammed it.

The bad guy—whoever the hell he was—his face full of baseball-bat shrapnel, both his feet mangled from the collision with an armored chest circled with twenty-five feet of chain, and now with six inches of best-quality yellow shoved deep in his ear, shrieked at the top of his voice, "*Aaaarggghhhh!*" and as O'Yee, trying to get past him to the window, tripped over him and fell, reached out to kill O'Yee with his bare hands.

He wanted . . . throat.

He got . . . rags and unseasonable heavy clothing.

There was a ripping sound and he got nothing, then a grunt and, as O'Yee pulled free, he got a punch square in the chest that made him gasp.

The bad guy shrieked, "Ooofff!"

At the window, Frank shrieked, "*No—!*" and then there was a series of thumps and crashes and as the other bad guy got Frank further up onto the windowsill to hurl him out, then another shriek as the bad guy on the floor got up again and took a swipe at O'Yee that made the chains ring.

Rags, chain, chalk, coat hanger . . .

There was a shriek as the ear-speared man got really mad at him and, coming at him like a bull, rammed him hard against the back wall and tried to beat the chains around his chest to death with his bare hands.

There was a second, instantaneous shriek as the chain-beater's brain suddenly learned the maxim in basic physics that human flesh and bone were at least two gradations lower on the Rockwell Scale of Hardness than heat-tempered steel chain link, and then as his second ear got four inches of chalk rammed into it, the message that four inches of chalk rammed at full strength into the human cochlea felt like it penetrated all the way down to the toes.

Rags, chain, chalk, coat hanger, RTG–68—

There was a crash at the window as Frank must have somehow pulled himself back in, and another, louder crash as whoever it was who was trying to push him out got him back up on the sill to push him out again.

Frank screamed, "Christopher—*help!*" and then as O'Yee got over the fallen body of the chain beater to get to the window, there was a thump as Frank's flailing feet caught the window-frame edge, and, with a terrific crash, slammed the window shut.

There was another crash as the man trying to hurl Frank out flailed at the window with his fist and got it open again.

There was another crash as Frank must have kicked it closed, then there was a crash as the hurler, with a snarl, smashed it open again, and then, as O'Yee leapt over the fallen ear-speared chain beater and got to the window, there was another crash as Frank, held horizontally in the window hurler's arms like a body about to be buried at sea, kicked at the window and slammed it closed again.

There was a thump as the window opener, grunting and staggering to get one hand free, reached out from under Frank's rigid body and crashed it open again.

Rags, chain, chalk, coat hanger . . .

O'Yee yelled, "Frank—!" and then the window opener, spinning Frank like a plank, swivelled around and hit him with Frank's feet and spun him backwards into the stagger-ing, still-ear-speared chain beater and sent the chain beater sprawling.

The chain beater had a white coat on, like a doctor's.

Framed in the open moonlit window, the window opener,

holding Frank up like a sacrifice, yelled to Frank to let him know just what was about to happen, "Now . . . *You die!*"

O'Yee shrieked, "*No!*" and, as the man drew Frank back two feet from the window to get a good throw going to propel him out into the open abyss of eternity, got his hand to the very edge of the window frame and slammed it shut.

Eternity.

Rags.

Chains.

Chalk.

Coat hanger.

O'Yee shrieked in triumph, "Ah-Ha!" and, as the hurler, spinning Frank hard to get to the window to open it again, reached out to get him, with the simplest thing that God and RTG–68 had wrought, with a click, slipped the hook of the coat hanger through the matching latches on window frame and window and, with a click, jammed it shut.

O'Yee thought he screamed, "*Coat hanger!*" but if he got it out, in the sudden blast of gunfire as Spencer at the open stairwell door fired his .38 twice in the air and lit up the corridor with the flashes, he didn't hear it.

He wasn't even sure he heard the .38.

What he was sure he heard was the earthquake detonation of a .445 Super Mag revolver as the shadowy figure who had been tracking him all day let go all six shots in a volley at the other end of the corridor, and then, in the moment suddenly all the lights in the corridor went on, a single word of recognition from Frank to the man crushing him in his arms to kill him.

That word was—said in a tone of horror and shock and disbelief—"*—Aaron!*"

It was a frozen-frame moment that seemed to go on forever.

Openmouthed in tableau against the jammed-shut window with Frank rigid in the arms of the white-coated man who had tried to throw him out, O'Yee, gazing wide-eyed down at the stairwell door, said to make sure it was who he thought it was, "*—Bill?*"

The man at the stairwell gazed wide-eyed back at the

unloved, unwanted bum standing in rags by the window next to another bum standing in rags by the window. Spencer said, "—*Christopher?*"

Still in Aaron's arms, Frank gazed at the fallen creature on the floor of the corridor still trying to remove sticks of chalk from his ears. Frank said, "—*Douglas?*"

Douglas said in shame, wanting someone else to explain why it had been necessary to hurl the old fellow from a window on the eighteenth floor to certain death, "*Aaron*—?"

He looked too. Frank said, "—*Aaron?*"

He was contrite. He looked away.

Aaron said, "*Father* . . ."

Spencer said, staring at him, "*Mr. Yu?*"

The man at the end of the corridor, holstering his gun, said, coming forward with tears of relief in his eyes, "*Daddy*—"

He looked at him. Frank said in joy, "*Son!*"

He had awe written all over his face. Spencer, gazing at the approaching man, said with his mouth open, "*You! . . .*"

The approaching man said with a nod, "*Yes.*" He glanced for just a moment and smiled at him. The approaching man said with a nod, "*Christopher!*"

Spencer said in his awe, "*You! . . .*"

O'Yee said to Spencer, "*Who*—?" He saw the approaching man glance just for a moment at the twisted coat hanger jamming the window shut. He saw the look and the nod.

O'Yee said with his mouth open and his eyes like saucers, suddenly making everything in the corridor absolutely shiningly crystal clear to everyone, "RT—?"

It was a whisper, "RTG—?"

It was a gasp.

O'Yee said with his eyes the size of dinner plates, "*RTG–68?*"

15.

After Uniformed had taken Aaron and Douglas away, none of the others were ready to leave, and they all sat together on the floor in the corridor under the coat-hangered window, the four of them—two bums, one master detective, and one very well-dressed son and secret cipher—lit up under the fluorescent lights on the corridor ceiling like Boy Scouts around a campfire under the moonlight.

The secret cipher—RTG–68, Frank's oldest son Willard—gently held Frank's—Father Yu's—hand in his and stroked it.

RTG–68 said softly, but firmly, "They wanted to kill you, Father. They wanted you to die so they could sell the institute property and set up their own institute in America." He was a smooth-faced, fine-boned man with soft brown eyes. RTG–68/Willard said, "They wanted it to seem that you were so depressed by all your patients attempting suicide after your Yu treatment had failed on them that you threw yourself out of a window in despair and died." He looked down at Frank's old, lined, fatherly hand. RTG–68 said, "When they approached the commander and specified the names of two detectives they wanted to investigate the so-called suicide attempts, the request passed through my hands and immediately aroused my suspicions." He was, in his own way, apologizing for being greater than his father. RTG–68 said, "My younger twin brothers believe themselves great judges of character. They believed the two detectives they specified would fail miserably to even come close to seeing what their real purpose was." He looked suddenly at Spencer.

Spencer said in protest, "But I did see it! I saw it when I realized that I'd seen all the attempted-suicide people before on the screen in the Great Wall Room! I solved it when I realized they were actors brought in to play parts!" Spencer said, "I came back here because I knew they were setting up a pattern of play-acted suicide attempts in order to set the scene for a real one—for a murder made to look like suicide!" He had only ever seen RTG–68 once before in the flesh. It was at an international police medal ceremony in Macao hosted by the head of Interpol from Paris. In the course of the ceremony RTG–68 had referred to the head of Interpol twice as "Jean-Pierre." In the course of the ceremony, the head of Interpol had referred to RTG–68 four times as "sir." Spencer said on the brink of signal triumph or dismal failure, "I saw it! I solved it! I worked it out! They didn't fool me!"

RTG–68 said firmly, "Yes. In their insulting assessment of your deductive powers they could not have been more wrong." He looked at the unloved, unwashed, unwanted, beaten-up bum who was O'Yee.

O'Yee looked away.

RTG–68 said to Spencer as a high fellow Hawkshaw, "Of course, Bill, the moment the request came through, I realized that things were not as they appeared to be. I assumed, like you, that the mine, as it were, was salted." He was probably the greatest detective in the universe. RTG–68 said kindly, "But it was clever of you to realize exactly who the mine—as it were—was so diabolically and clandestinely salted with."

It was the same way—as it were—he talked in his Written Orders to Offal when he sent them out in the streets to die. O'Yee said in a grunt, "Huh!"

Spencer said, "Thank you, RTG–68."

RTG–68 said, "Call me Willard, Bill." He stroked his father's hand.

Spencer said, "Gosh! Thanks!"

Frank—Mr. Yu—said contritely, "And to think, my son, that I sometimes had my doubts about the merits of your chosen course in life. To think that sometimes, secretly, I wished my oldest offspring had taken the road of psychotherapy and not police work . . ."

Willard said with a smile, "Ah . . ."

In the glow, Spencer had forgotten about Auden. Spencer said to rectify the omission, "Phil Auden helped too, Willard. We mustn't forget about him—there's a lot of credit due to him in this too, you know."

"Exactly." Willard said with a nod, "Quite right. My brothers, having studied him, knew that he would behave as an unfeeling brute and render each of the attempted suicide victims useless for interrogation before their plot was brought to fruition, and that was exactly, I gather, what he did." He didn't want his father to think his brothers were all bad, "There, at last Aaron and Douglas showed they knew what they were about."

He was his friend. Spencer said in protest, "Phil's a good cop. It's just that he's—"

He liked him. He was made. RTG–68 said to Spencer in admiration, "And so are you."

They had all forgotten O'Yee. Only Frank of the kind face remembered he even lived. Frank said to his son to encourage him to maybe find a little word of praise for O'Yee along the way, "And so is he—Christopher—he's a good cop too."

RTG–68 said with a start, "*Cop? Him? A good cop? Him?*"

Maybe he had got the wrong word. Frank said, "Detective." Frank said, "In his own way, he led me back here and saved my life with the coat hanger."

O'Yee said tightly, "That was your son's coat hanger. It was your son's directions, and your son's chains, and your son's chalk, and your son's coat hanger." He hated RTG–68. O'Yee said, "All I did was just sit on the sidewalk scribbling until you came up and found me."

RTG–68 said, "Exactly." He looked at his new friend Spencer, "My father every day trolls the streets on the look-out for ruined souls suitable to lead to self-revelation." He turned and looked at O'Yee with a strange look. RTG–68 said as if O'Yee already knew it himself, "Mr. O'Yee's role in this as a detective was nil! Aaron and Douglas chose Mr. Auden and Mr. Spencer. I chose Mr. O'Yee not to deduct or solve, but merely to sit on a street in rags and *be!*" He looked at his father, "Father, I hardly chose him as a *detective!*"

O'Yee said, "Thank you." He thought he'd stand up now and get the coat hanger off the window and sail away.

RTG–68 said, almost unable to control his laughter at the thought, "You thought I chose Mr. O'Yee because he was a good *detective?*"

No, he chose him because he was a fucking bum, a cock-roach, a nothingburger, a mere coat-hanger holder on the rack of bespoke-tailored triumphs for the Headquarters world firm of RTG–68 and Ego. O'Yee said to Frank, so the poor, kind old fellow wouldn't be too disappointed all at once, "No, he didn't choose me because I was a good detective!"

RTG–68 said in despair at his father's obvious waning powers of perception and intelligence, "Father! And you the great Senior Yu, the inventor and founder of the greatest soul-probing system since the invention of the Catholic con-fessional!" He sniggered. It was a hee-hee snigger. "A good detective? I didn't chose him as a good detective! All a de-tective would have done was find you. I chose him because I knew you would find *him!* I merely armed him with the few necessary props for the battle with Aaron and Douglas and I knew you would lead him here to the Institute!" He looked over at O'Yee with a strange look on his face. The strange look on RTG–68's face was admiration. RTG–68 said, point-ing at the man, "Just a good detective? Him? Look at him! Father, don't you see the great, gentle soul shining out from his eyes! Don't you see that noble face full of intelligence and deep, deep nobility? Didn't you speak with him, Father? Didn't his soul draw you like a magnet? I chose him not as a mere detective who would be able to find you—but as a man *you* would find! Because I knew on your street trolling you would never have passed up a man such as he, and, in the end, if you had to, *beg* him to accompany you back here to the seat of all your life's work if you had to!" RTG–68 said, scorning the thought, "Detective? *I* am merely a *detective!* What Mr. O'Yee—and I dare not call him by his first name because I, like all the rest of mankind, am so unworthy—is, is not a *detective!* What Mr. O'Yee is—and I am certain he saw through my little ambiguous set of instructions to him the instant he set his eyes upon it—is a man of true nobility and kindness, of deep, deep scholarship and learning, of abiding, shining humanity!"

He stood up and, looking down at O'Yee, gently lowered his head to him in humility. RTG–68 said to the world, "*Detective? Mr. O'Yee? A mere detective?* No, what Mr. O'Yee is—and see even now his great spirit glitters there in his eyes like water—is the Perfected Man, the embodiment of all those finer, kinder feelings all men strive for—*and I, for one, never cease from thanking my good fortune that I have the honor and the joy of, however briefly, sharing the earth of the same world with him!*"

He was overcome.

He had exhausted his vocabulary of superlatives. He had no words left to say about the man's glory and greatness.

With love and tears everywhere on his face, a mere mortal before the altar of true greatness, he could only gaze down at O'Yee sitting on the floor looking up at him in silent, awed, humble admiration.

They were all right about Auden—all of them: Aaron, Douglas, RTG–68.

He was an unfeeling brute.

He cared for no one, understood nothing. He was, like the unconscious seagull lying on the vet's examination table with its wings spread back and its head fallen to one side, a blunt instrument with no feelings of care or concern or mercy or pity at all.

He belonged to no one. He was, like Attila, like the great lone seagull itself, the brute who belonged to himself.

Leaning down over Attila, moving his stomach and neck feathers aside with his fingers to check for wounds, the vet asked the brute without looking up, "Is he your pet? The bird?"

The brute said in a snarl, "What?" The vet was one of those no-shouldered, wimpy-looking Chinese with horn-rimmed glasses who always won all the prizes for math and geometry and everything at school, and then when they grew up became vets, and, instantly, Auden didn't like him. Auden said, "No, he's not my fucking pet! Who the fuck has a fucking seagull for a pet? He's a fucking fighting bird! He's a fucking *warrior!* He's a fucking warrior brought into the forward aid station by his enemy before he goes back out into fucking battle again! Okay? Got that? He's nobody's *pet!* He doesn't give a damn about anyone and nobody gives a damn about him! *Okay?*"

He was an unfeeling brute. That was how unfeeling brutes reacted to wimps.

It worked again. The vet, starting backwards, said with his little wimpish eyes wide behind his glasses, "Yes! Sure! Whatever you say!" The vet said in terror, "I'm really sorry I asked! It was a mistake! I didn't mean to say it! It was a stupid thing to say!"

Brutes fought. In order to survive through each day that was what brutes had learned to do. No more fucking dentists' chairs for them once they'd got the message about real life, just toe-to-toe, face-to-face, tell me the truth and die for it unfeeling brutishness brought to the brutish level of perfection where never, never again were you going to put yourself in the position of giving a damn about anyone and being hurt.

Auden demanded brutishly, "Well? Is he going to make it or not? And don't hand me a load of soft soap and bullshit! I want it straight: is the fucking bird going to die or not?"

The vet said straight, "The fucking bird is going to die."

Auden said, "What?"

At school, all the tough kids had beaten the crap out of him every day because he studied when they thought he should be out with them breaking things. That was why he liked animals and birds better than people. The vet said, "The bird is dead mutton. The bird is all chopped up inside and, any second now, unless you're prepared to pay for a major operation that'll cost about the same as open-heart surgery on a human, the fucking bird is going to throw up, flap its wings about, have a few convulsions, and then, crapping itself as it goes, croak its way off to bird heaven." Every day of his life when he'd been a kid he'd been the victim of bullies. Every day, a little at a time, it took away all his dignity. The vet said, "You want my advice? Take your fucking seagull off to fucking Soup Street and have him minced up and sautéed with a little sauce and fucking eat him—because at the moment he's no fucking good for anything else." For a long while, every night, he'd cried himself to sleep in shame and humiliation. But not anymore. The vet said, "Okay? Straight enough for you?"

Auden said, "*What—?*" Every night, after he'd learned that the reason his mother had left him there in the dentist's office alone was that she was having an affair with the man's brother, he'd cried himself to sleep. But not anymore. Auden said, "What—?" It had destroyed him, ruined his life, and then, after the divorce when his father accused him of knowing about the affair all along, something inside him had shattered like glass. Auden said to the vet as if he had not taken in the words, "What? What do you mean?"

Auden said, "Oh, no!" He wanted to reach out and very gently touch at the bird's wing and console it in its last few moments, but he could not. He had no finer feelings at all. After the divorce, he had trained himself out of them. He had trained himself to be a brute. He had trained himself by fighting people and hurting people and hating people a little more each day, until finally, at last, years later when he had the brute business finally perfected, he was safe and all the other feelings were gone.

Auden said, "No! He can't die! That isn't right! He wasn't even hurt in a fair fight—he was cheated! He was betrayed! He fought fair all by himself through all the pain because he thought he could trust other people to treat him fairly too! But they didn't! They cheated him and lied to him!"

He never cried, not anymore. He never cried again after his parents' divorce all those years ago.

Reaching out and putting his hand on the vet's shoulder to bring him into the deepest, most secret part of his soul and understand what was there and why he did the things he did, Auden, begging the man, hoping that all his years of study and studiousness might pay off this one time, said from his heart, "Oh, please, Doc, oh, please, you must have studied so long and hard to be where you are— Please, please, can't you just reach out and save him?"

He didn't have a normal sex life. He was incapable of love or trust.

Auden, begging the man, for some reason totally unable to read the strange, surprised look on the vet's face and not understanding at all why the man's shoulders suddenly sagged as if they had been tensed for a very long time, said, begging him, "Please! Oh, please. Whatever it costs, please save him! He's the only other creature on earth who's ever understood what it's like to be me!"

He was an unfeeling brute and as a brute he did not understand at all why the vet suddenly reached up and put his hand comfortingly on top of his, or why the man's eyes, behind his thick glasses, were full of tears.

Auden said, defenseless, trusting, full of love for the ragged, moth-eaten, bruised and beaten one-eyed warrior bird lying unconscious on the table in front of him, "Please! Please! Please make it right for him again! Please! *All he ever wanted was for his goddamned, rotten family to just love him a little!*"

In the deserted detectives' room at the station, as Feiffer sat at his desk under a single desk lamp and rubbed at his eyes, the phone rang.

It was Mansor calling from his office in the Association of Small Banking Businesses and General Commerce Accountants, 52 Great Shanghai Street.

In a nervous voice, Mansor said respectfully and politely, "Sir, Mr. Feiffer, I am extremely loathe to intrude myself upon you at this late hour, but at the bank you asked me to continue to do my best on this matter, and I, in turn, continue to take you at your word."

He was a man who always gave excellent service, even when sometimes it was neither welcomed nor required. Mansor said carefully, "I hesitate in case the news reports I have

just heard on my little office television set about the death of
Mr. Shoemaker and Dr. Tolliver—although I believe they
said 'Oliver'—may mean that as far as the police are concerned the matter is concluded, but—"

On the other end of the line he could almost hear the man
wringing his hands. Feiffer said, "Yes, Mr. Mansor?"

It was his life. It was what he did. Mansor said, "But, sir, I
am by profession an auditor and I simply cannot find it in
myself to permit the final sealing and stamping of the ledger
Closed without at least making some reservation of mine
known for the record." He was a man who always dotted all
the *i*'s and crossed all the *t*'s. Mansor said suddenly force-
fully, "And, Mr. Feiffer, sir, I have spent all day rechecking
the manager's papers from the bank and confirming all the
entries and I have to tell you that I have discovered that certain things I have found there are not—are not exactly as
they should be."

A lot of things were not exactly as they should be. That
Tolliver and Shoemaker were dead was not exactly as it
should be. That there was no one else left—no suspects, no
one—was also not exactly as it should be.

Outside the window of the detectives' room, the night was
dark and still and silent, and, leaning forward under the yellow light from the lamp with his hands still to his eyes, Feiffer, with a dry, gritty feeling in his eyes, said, "Mr. Mansor,
what certain things are you referring to?"

"I regret it deeply, sir, if I have intruded upon your busy
schedule at an inconvenient moment—"

He was doing his best. As he had said, at the bank, Feiffer
had asked him to do his best, and even in the middle of the
night, still at his office on Great Shanghai Street, he was still
trying to do it.

Feiffer said, "It's not an inconvenient moment." The man
needed to think he was important. "I appreciate everything
you've done. What things are you referring to that aren't exactly as they should be? Can you itemize them for me?"

The few words of client satisfaction were all he lived for. In
the background behind him there was a rustling sound as he
seemed to shuffle papers to get them ready. Mr. Mansor said
brightly, "Yes, sir." The rustling sound stopped as he finished

laying out the papers to read from them or, able to quote their contents from memory, laid them aside. Mr. Mansor said, "The things that are not exactly as they should be are you will find on the list of outstanding loans I gave you when we spoke at the bank." He was quoting from memory: at his end of the phone as he went down the list there was no sound of paper moving at all. "One: the loan by Mr. Lee of one million five hundred twenty-three thousand American dollars to the Industrial Electrical Supplies Company of Hong Kong and Singapore listed as loan number one on the outstanding-loans list daily breakdown; two: the loan to the Mercantile Credit Company of Hong Kong and Macao of one million three hundred and fifty thousand American dollars; three: the loan of US one million four hundred thousand dollars to the Cavite Import-Export Company of Manila and Hong Kong; and, four: the loan of US two hundred fifty thousand dollars to the late Dr. Tolliver of the Hong Kong Analysis Laboratories of Hong Kong—"

He paused. It was, in his epic, exciting life as a bank auditor, perhaps his greatest moment.

Mr. Mansor said, "Mr. Feiffer, I spent all of the afternoon and evening going over the details of each of the loans so the board members and shareholders of the Asia–America–Hong Kong Bank may continue to earn their interest profits on the loans and, eventually, recover their principal, and, except for the loan made to Dr. Tolliver, I have discovered that each of the other loans was no loan at all!" He put it simply. Mansor said, "Each of the loans was paid out in one lump payment in the form of a single bank check, not to the local so-called borrowers, but, in every case, to what appears to be the parent company of each of the so-called borrowers: the Industrial Electrical Supplies Limited one-point-five million dollars to Singapore, the Mercantile Credit one-point-three million to Macao, and, finally, the one point four million for the Cavite Import-Export Company to Manila."

"So?"

"So it should not have been done that way at all! Each of the loans was taken out for the *Hong Kong* operation of each of the businesses! The loan should have stayed here in the Colony to be used in the Colony for that local business!"

"So it was some sort of tax scam to avoid paying local tax on the loan by routing it through a bank overseas? Is that it?" If that was it, it was nothing. It was just some sort of barely legal tax-avoidance scheme for the directors of the various companies to line their pockets by skimming a percentage off the top that happened all the time, "The overseas firm borrows money on a local bank here, then reroutes it back as investment capital in order to—"

Mansor said, "No, sir." Mr. Mansor said tightly, "No, that is not what happened at all." It was his greatest moment and he paused on the phone for a moment to savor it, "It did not happen that way for the simple reason that, according to all the business directories and even telephone books I have consulted, not one of the overseas head offices of the firms has any sort of operation *in* Hong Kong! The businesses to whom the loans were officially made by Mr. Lee of the Asia–America–Hong Kong Bank, Lotus Flower Mall, Hong Bay, Mr. Feiffer, simply do not *exist!*"

"But according to the loans breakdown you gave me in the manager's office at the bank the loans were being paid back! Weren't they?"

"Yes, so it would appear—"

It was an adventure in accounting, nothing more. "So what you're saying is that for some reason several overseas companies wanted to borrow money here and give the impression it was for local use when it wasn't, and instead of paying it back locally they were paying it back from overseas. Is that it? Is that what you're saying?"

"Yes, so it would probably appear to the mind of the average accounting practitioner who might happen on it in the unlikely event of a full-scale audit of the bank's long-term transactions. That would probably appear to be the situation, yes."

What he wanted known was that he was not an average accounting practitioner. Feiffer asked tersely, "Well, is that the situation or isn't it?"

"In my professional opinion, no, that is not the situation. In my professional opinion, I believe that somewhere far back in the bank's papers—although I have not yet located it in the papers—there exists evidence of another totally fictitious loan made to a totally fictitious client with perhaps a very long grace before first repayment period, and I believe *that money* was being used to pay back each of the loans."

"You're saying that each of the loans was phoney? Except for Tolliver's?" Outside all the windows of the detectives' room the night was pitch dark, and to Feiffer, hunched forward under the circle of yellow light from the desk lamp, it was as if it was the last faint light in the last tiny, safe, lit place in the world, and even that was receding into darkness. "But how can you know that? You say you haven't located the other loan—if it even exists! So how can you know that it was being used to pay back all the other loans?" He was at the end, all his patience gone. Feiffer shouted at the man, "You're just guessing! You're saying that all the big company loans on Lee's list were phonies, but you haven't got any evidence to back it up at all! You haven't got any evidence to back it up until you locate the earlier loan!" He didn't need any more twists and turns. He didn't need anything else hidden and secret beyond penetrating. Feiffer demanded, "How can you be so sure you're right? If you haven't located the earlier loan all you're doing is just starting up something that could turn out to go nowhere! For all you know, there isn't any dummy loan and the overseas firms were each paying back the money from overseas—and it's still nothing more than a tax scam! For all you know—"

He was an auditor. He was not some sort of mere adder-up or accountant, he was an investigator, probably, he thought, the best there ever was. He gave, always, not merely good or barely adequate, but excellent service.

He gave it now.

Mr. Mansor said with just the slightest pique in his voice at being doubted, "Sir, in the profession of bank auditing there are more ways than one to verify the truth of everything. I do not have to physically *locate* a dummy Peter-to-Paul repayment loan to know all the other loans were false and were being paid back by the Peter-and-Paul loan! I merely have to, as I have done, telephone all the overseas banks to whom payment was made to each of the firms in each of the foreign cities and discover that in each case the money for each loan was not lodged in long-term deposit in favor of the drawer, but, instead, in each case instantly re-transferred by the drawer out of the country concerned to various banks in the Cayman Islands and Bermuda for paying out into anonymous, numbered accounts!"

He was giving a lecture. Mansor said with his voice hard, "I then merely have to pick up the telephone again and telephone each of the contact numbers in each of the overseas cities for each of the so-called parent firms and get, not the representative of a firm worth and borrowing millions—not a Chief Executive Officer Mr. T. W. Kwan or an Executive Vice-President Mr. A. S. Singh, or a President Mr. A. J. Alvarez—but instead a Mr. Kan, a Mrs. Patel and a Miss Martinez—*each and every one of them representatives not of a business of international proportions, but of three separate, sleazy, barely legal mail-forwarding and telephone-answering services in three countries with, between them, assets worth perhaps less than a few hundred dollars in forward, paid-up office-space rental—if that!*"

Mansor said, hurt by the doubt, "I am sorry to inconvenience you when, clearly to the mind of the police, having killed people in a blaze of gunfire, the case may appear to you to be solved, but in my professional opinion, someone in that bank stole over four and a quarter million dollars in the name of loans to overseas companies and businesses that did not exist and then transferred it via dummy bank accounts in the names of those companies and businesses directly into other accounts in banks in the Caymans and in Bermuda where, because of those countries' laws, it can never be traced or recovered!"

"Do you know who did it?"

He was a professional. There was nothing personal in it. Mansor said evenly, "It would have, of course, to have been done and directed by someone in the bank."

"Do you know who?"

"Yes, from the technical expertise required and the procedure required at any bank to transfer such large amounts over a long period of time, I believe I do." He gave facts. He checked, computed, calculated, and finally came up with the only true answer.

He paused a moment and gave that answer.

Mr. Mansor said, "In order to continue such a deception for such a long time through all the major and minor transactions and cross-checks and balances it would have required, I believe, that each and every one of the nine members of staff of the Asia–America–Hong Kong Bank had to have known about it and conspired in it." He made it simple, "All of them. They all did it. Every last one of them, the full nine members of the staff. In my opinion, they all did it."

"Then who the hell killed them? And if it had been going on for such a long time, why that day? And what the hell were they celebrating before they died?"

Outside the window by his desk, the night was pitch black and silent and, suddenly, terrifying beyond bearing.

For a long time there was a silence, and then Mr. Mansor said softly, "I don't know. I shall be at the bank all day tomorrow to commence a full, in-depth audit, but I fear that any answers I find will not answer any of those questions . . ."

Mr. Mansor said to make it clear, "The answers to those questions, I fear, sir, are beyond my simple powers."

If he wanted to say something to comfort the man, in his auditor's mind, he did not know how to say it.

He merely said a respectful good night, and then, as if he was suddenly embarrassed at some lack in himself, abruptly hung up and was gone.

16.

At eight the next morning, Feiffer was still at his desk in the detectives' room. During the night he had transferred everything he had onto a long incident board at the back of the room behind his desk. Surrounded by all the photos from the bank and by cut-out and torn-out pages from telephone directories and business directories from all over Asia, leafing through a mound of printouts and CRO requests and faxes from the Fraud Squad, in the morning light he looked tired and unshaven and old, as if he had not slept at all.

Sitting on the corner of the desk opposite him, O'Yee on the other hand looked as if he had had the best night's rest of his entire life. He had come in at six with Auden and Spencer, but after two hours of staring at the incident board and trying to make sense of what had happened in the bank, all the benefits to his brain of the good-night's sleep were fading fast.

Written up in chalk on a blackboard to one side of the incident board, the sum total of all the phoney loans the bank staff had stolen was over four and a quarter million American dollars. Even divided equally by nine, that still came to over four hundred and seventy thousand dollars per person. O'Yee asked, "But, Harry, if they all lived like monks, what was the money for?" According to all the reports from Uniformed also pinned up there, not one of the people in the bank had any family in the Colony, any friends, or even any social life, "What the hell were they going to do with it all?"

He didn't know. He had no idea at all. Feiffer said, "I don't know."

"Is that all of it?"

"I don't know that either."

"Well, they must have used some of it for something. If it all went to Bermuda or the Caymans, didn't at least one of them fly over there once or twice to *enjoy* some of it?"

Feiffer said, "No, apparently not." He had checked with the night-duty officer at Immigration. From the various times over the last four and a half years each of them had entered the Colony and been granted ID papers, not one of them had left the Colony to go anywhere. Feiffer said, "No."

He looked almost at the end. Spencer asked gently, "Harry, do you know if any of the banks in the Caymans and Bermuda received instructions to forward the money on somewhere else?"

"No."

"Do you know if, maybe somehow, it was sent back to the families in China?"

"No, I don't."

Auden asked, looking up for a moment, "How about the poison? If it didn't come from this character Tolliver, where did it come from?"

"I don't know that either."

"Where did the champagne come from?"

"I don't know that either." He had gone over and over it in his mind all night. Feiffer said before anyone could ask, "And I don't know why they all drank it together! I don't know what they were celebrating or why! And I don't know why whoever it was who came into the bank that night wanted them all dead! According to Mansor, if someone hadn't killed them en masse for no apparent reason, no one would ever have known what they were doing! According to Mansor, they could have gone on stealing probably forever and it wouldn't have been picked up until there was a major long-term audit—which there probably wouldn't have been because they were doing it so well nobody would have had cause to suspect anything and order a major long-term audit!"

Maybe the man in the bank with the poison was the one who had set the whole thing up from the beginning. Maybe the weak spot in his plan was the use of the three mail-forwarding links as business addresses for the accounts in Manila and Macao and Singapore. O'Yee asked, "What about the forwarding offices? Who set them up? The bank manager Lee and his staff, or someone else?"

They were each twenty-four-hour numbers for crooks and embezzlers all over the world. At 5:00 A.M., on a conference line first with the head of the Fraud Squad in Manila, and then with the assistant commissioner of police in Singapore, and then, finally, with a detective captain from the Macao Police, he had spoken to each of the three forwarding businesses and asked the same question. Feiffer said, "The bank staff did. Mr. Lee did, one time for the Singapore connection; one of the tellers, Mr. Mok, did another time for the Macao one; and the Manila setup was handled by one of the senior female tellers, Miss Wong." His mouth was trembling. Feiffer, turning to the horror gallery of the photographs of the dead from the bank and from the Morgue, said to O'Yee with sudden violence, "You can't miss her—she's one of the last two who crawled away towards the rest room while the killer watched! She's the one in the blouse lying next to the goddamned water cooler with vomit and blood all over her face and chest!" Feiffer said with his voice suddenly shaking, "And as for who did it to her and why it happened, I don't know! I have no idea what happened in the bank after closing time or how it happened or why it happened! And I have no idea on the face of the entire fucking planet who it was who *made* it happen! *None at all!*" He was on the point of exhaustion. He felt as if his body was covered in a sea of tiny biting, crawling insects, "All I know is—all I know is I thought Tolliver did it and I was wrong! And then I thought maybe Shoemaker, and I was wrong there too!" He was shaking, rocking back and forth in his chair, "And I—and now they're both dead, and I—"

He could not look at any of them.

Feiffer said in a whisper, "And I can't help thinking—"

In the long, lonely, empty night as he had checked and called and checked again and gotten nowhere, all there had been in his head were demons.

Feiffer said so softly that in the room they all had to strain to hear what it was he said, "And I can't—I just can't stop thinking that it was all my fault for being so fucking stupid and quick to jump to conclusions and that I was the one who got them both *killed!*"

Maybe he did have a shining soul. Maybe everything RTG–68 had said about him was true. In the detectives' room, standing to one side of him and laying his hand gently on Feiffer's shoulder to comfort him, O'Yee, taking command, said gently, "Look, Harry, try taking it from the center. Forget who the people in the bank were or where they might have come from or what they might have been planning to do—or if they were even involved in it—ask yourself, 'Why the hell, apart from anything else, did they even drink the champagne in the first place? What were they celebrating? They can't have drunk it just because they felt like it—they drank it for a reason. And they drank it with someone they let in after hours. So they knew whoever it was who brought the champagne in there and they at least drank a toast with him or her to salute something or commemorate it." O'Yee said with his fist clenched on Feiffer's shoulder to encourage him, "Ask yourself *what?* What was it they wanted to toast?" He turned to Spencer and nodded hard at him to get him started, "Bill?"

Spencer said helpfully, "All I can think of is, say, a fiancé of one of the women celebrating their engagement, or—" He looked over to the Morgue photographs and the papers accompanying them, "Were any of the women wearing brand-new engagement rings when you found then, Harry?"

He was finished, useless. He could no longer think of it as a connected series of events with meaning, but only as a series of isolated moments and events and sights and sounds with no meaning at all. The flashes were pictures of the dead, and the smell of the dead and the sound of Tolliver suffocating as Shoemaker tortured him for a confession he did not have to give, and the pushing and crushing of people running as the commander ordered the corridor in the Cathay Pearl Building cleared so Winter could blast the door down and kill Shoemaker. Even the dead girl in the bank merged in his mind with the dead girl on the computer at Headquarters that had sent Shoemaker crazy. Feiffer said, "I don't know," and his mind became stuck on a picture of the pudgy girl on the Morgue table with the top of her head cut off and all her hair lying wet and matted with blood.

Feiffer said, "I can't remember." He did not want to turn around and look at the photographs to find out.

O'Yee said to Spencer as the man went to the incident board and peered hard at all the pictures, "Bill?"

Spencer said, "No. No rings visible in the photos." He looked over the copies of the Morgue admission records pinned up next to each of the photos, "The Morgue personal-property list doesn't list any removed before PM."

Auden said, "Uniformed would have surfaced a fiancé if there was one." He had thought a lot about families in the last twelve hours. "What about something unexpected? Say, a family member coming in from China, or a—"

Spencer said as a fact, "Family members don't normally tend to carry poison as standard equipment."

One of his had. Auden said, trying hard, "How about— how about a *lottery win?* How about that? How about they'd all taken out a joint ticket and it'd hit and they—"

O'Yee said, "Taken it out with who? According to Uniformed, they didn't *know* anyone else!"

Feiffer said, "They knew whoever it was who came in there and killed them!" He was coming back. Little by little, he was coming back. Feiffer said tightly, "And so what if they did win? What would it represent to them? *Another mound of money they were apparently never going to use?*" Feiffer demanded, "And if they did win something like that, where's the money and ticket now? In the hands of the last living member of a syndicate of ten people who's going to be only too happy to explain that the other nine members were murdered but he didn't have anything to do with it, and could he please have all the money, thank you?" Feiffer said, "No, whatever it is, it's nothing even remotely like that. It's nothing to do with money."

He tried again. Auden said, "Maybe they were celebrating the final success of getting the money across to the Caymans or wherever it was."

Feiffer demanded, "With who? It was a bank staff fraud! They were the bank staff! They didn't get someone else to do it, they did it themselves! And they'd been doing it consistently over a period of time, for *years!*"

O'Yee said, "They had to be celebrating something—and they had to be celebrating it with someone else."

"*Who?*"

"I don't know." O'Yee said, to try to reestablish the unestablishable yet again, "The only other possibility is that everything was just going fine for them and nothing was going wrong, so they all drank a shot of poison and then—"

Feiffer said, "And then washed up the fucking poison cups, vaporized the champagne bottle into thin air, and died."

O'Yee said desperately, "Bill?"

Spencer shook his head.

O'Yee said, "Phil—?"

Auden said, shaking his head, "I don't know."

In the detectives' room, there was a silence.

With his hand still on Feiffer's shoulder, suddenly, he understood. O'Yee said softly, "Oh, my God, Harry, is what we're talking about here—with no suspect, no motive, no leads, is it possible—is what we're talking about here the proverbial—" O'Yee said in horror at the thought of it, "Are we talking here about a *Perfect Crime?*"

"Yes!" His voice was a rasp. Leaning forward and touching his fingertips to his forehead to somehow hide his face, Feiffer said desperately, "Yes! Yes! Yes, I think that's exactly what we're talking about here!"

As a Great Detective it offended him. No criminal could commit a crime without leaving some trace or part of himself at the crime scene. Every Great Detective knew that. Spencer said, "There must have been something left at the bank from whoever it was who came in! There can't have been nothing! Every creature on earth leaves a trail to show where they've been, and someone coming into a bank to kill nine people has to have left a trail a mile wide! Fingerprints, clothing particles—something!" He looked hard at Feiffer.

He hadn't. He hadn't left anything. If he had left anything it had been destroyed when Winter and his team had blasted down the door with explosives and filled the place with stun and flash grenades. As for fingerprints, Forensic had found so many from the staff and from customers they would be still searching and cross-referencing them until the next Ice Age.

Feiffer said, "No, he left nothing! Whatever he may have brought in with him he took away again, and if he used anything that was there in the bank, like the cups he put the poison in, he washed it up neatly like a well-trained little housewife and put it back again where he had found it!" They weren't going to find anything by reviewing what they already knew; the only possibility, and that was a slim one, was that Mansor was going to surface someone from the original Peter-to-Paul bank loan he wasn't even sure existed—and then, even if that had the name of the poisoner listed on it for some reason—and it wouldn't—it was going to be the name of someone so far out of left field he was going to be totally unreachable. Feiffer said, "What I found in the bank was all that was there to be found: Lee's outstanding loans record, his telephone log and appointments diary—*and the poisoned bodies of nine dead people, men and women, who were apparently all carefully and systematically engaged in a criminal conspiracy to take millions of dollars from the bank and never use even one single dollar of it!*" Feiffer said, "They were ciphers, zeros—they had nowhere to spend their money so they spent it on nothing!" It made no sense at all. It always came back to the same brick wall. He tried, but he could not think it through. Always, there was the wall. Feiffer demanded, "Where were they ever going to use it? Apparently, from the way they lived, not here. Not in the Caymans and Bermuda, because they never went there. Not in China because they weren't going to go back there either!"

O'Yee asked, "But, Harry, if they were never going to use the money they stole, what were they celebrating?"

"*I don't know!*"

"*Something* must have happened before they celebrated!" He looked at Spencer, but Spencer only shook his head. "Nobody just walks into a bank and says, 'Hey, let all get smashed on champagne because it's fucking Tuesday,' and nine people say, 'Oh, okay, why not?' and then drink fucking poisoned champagne and die!"

"Apparently, these people did!"

He tried again. He was still fixated on the things of childhood. Auden asked, "What about someone's birthday, Harry? Say, one of the staff, or the manager, Mr. Lee, or—"

"No."

Spencer said, "A national day of some sort? Say, some sort of Chinese holiday or—"

Feiffer said, "No."

"How do you know?"

"Because I *checked!*"

He was reaching. O'Yee asked, "Harry, you said you checked that none of them had ever been to Bermuda or the Caymans in the past to spend their money. You did check, didn't you, that they didn't have plane tickets to go sometime in the future?"

Feiffer said, "Yes, I checked. I checked at three in the morning first with Immigration for exit visas and then, just in case, over the next hour and a half I checked with every airline and shipping company that had anyone working at that hour I could raise." Feiffer said, "They weren't going anywhere. They were staying here. Apparently, they had no reason to stay on here, they had no reason to celebrate, they had no reason to steal four million dollars, and, for all I can see, they didn't seem to have a continuing reason to even go on living! Whoever killed them, killed them for what they were—ciphers! And he left nothing behind!" He turned and reached up to the incident board and wrenched down a scrap of paper in a glassine envelope from next to one of Photographic's crime-scene photos of the interior of the bank, "The only thing I found in the bank that anyone left was this! And all this is is just a torn corner of a photostat with a line of fucking letters and numbers on it and the wing of sort sort of fucking bird that probably doesn't mean anything! I thought when I found that someone had made eighteen

copies of it at 5:45 P.M., that it could have been done the day
of the killings, but for all I know it could have been done a
week before and all it represents is the ripped corner of eighteen copies of a document someone in the bank made for a
customer as a favor or at five cents a copy!" He shoved it
into Spencer's outstretched hand, "That's the only trace of
anything I found in the bank that shouldn't have been there.
That's it! Any ideas what that is? Any great shining motive
or revelation of a motive spring to mind from *that?*"

Maybe he wasn't the Great Detective he thought he was.
He looked down at it and had no idea what it was. Spencer
said, "No. Nothing." He handed it to O'Yee.

It was the ripped left-hand corner of a sheet of copying
paper with the letters and numbers I–797-6-29-88 printed on
it in black and, next to it, what looked like part of the wing
of a bird.

O'Yee asked, "Is it part of some sort of banking form?"

"No, it isn't some sort of banking form!"

"What's the bird wing for?"

"I don't know."

"Is it some sort of logo or trademark?"

"I don't know."

He was at the brick wall. O'Yee, shrugging, said, "Well, is
it a—" Auden was suddenly on his feet behind him, and he
turned back briefly out of courtesy to hand it over to him to
look at, then almost instantly reached out for it again to take
it back. O'Yee said, "I don't know—" He felt nothing put in
his outstretched hand and looked back to Auden to see why
he hadn't given it back. O'Yee said, "Phil, can I have it back,
please?"

He had never thought that writing an enormous check to
cover the repair of some scruffy bird nobody gave a damn
about would feel like the best thing he had ever done in his
life. He had never thought it would make him feel this good.
Auden said, "It's part of a notification from the state-department section of the US Embassy here in Hong Kong that the
person or persons listed herein have been granted permanent
resident alien status in the United States of America. The letter *I* and numbers *797* identify it as Immigration Approval
Form number *797* and the date represents the date the con-

gress of the United States and president signed the bill it's issued under into law."

O'Yee said, with his hand still outstretched to the huge smiling brute standing there looking at him, "What? Are you *serious?*"

He was serious. Standing there like a barn door left open in the wind, Auden said easily, not even looking down at the scrap, "It's notification of the approval and issuance of an American green card. It's a notification that if you happened over the years to have stashed a few million away in banks in the Caymans or in Bermuda, just a few miles offshore from the continental United States, by God, at last—finally—you were going to get the chance to go and spend it all where you could enjoy it most: out of here, safe and permanent, *in America.*"

Spencer said in a gasp, "What—?"

Auden said easily, "Sure." He looked in a kindly helping way to Spencer and spelled it out for him line by line. Auden said, "They probably all applied for the green cards years back when they realized, even after they had escaped from China, there was still no long-term future for them in Hong Kong. They knew, when they finally got the green cards, they were going to need money for their new lives in America—so they stole it. They knew they couldn't risk getting caught spending any of the money before the green cards came through—so they hid it. And then when, finally, the green-card notifications came through and they made their photostats of the original document—eighteen copies: two for each lucky winner—they celebrated."

His seagull was going to be well. He was going to be well with him. Auden said with his heart full to bursting at his own brilliance, "Motive: getting out of Hong Kong before the Communists come. Method: steal money from the bank where you work and put the money close offshore to the United States where you intend to spend the rest of your life. Means: collude with every other member of the place where you work and maybe one other person from outside to make sure nobody finds out until you're long gone and the place itself has been taken over by a foreign government and is in complete and utter turmoil."

He looked over to his friend Spencer. He didn't want to make the man unhappy, but, in the long run, disappointment and hurt and pain was what made you the man you always wanted to be.

He tried to say it gently, but could not.

Auden said, to explain it to the poor dumbstruck fellow, "Bill, *it was the reason the Yus wanted to bump their father off and close the whole Institute of Yu down*. They told you. They told you they'd been granted green cards, but they were so noble they didn't intend to take them up. *They told you that*. They even showed you the Form I–797–6–29–88 with the American Eagle seal on it at the bottom so you could *know* how noble they were being!"

It was his culmination, his catharsis. It was, at last, his own ultimate, fully developed, wonderful true Yu. It was his final metamorphosis into all he was meant to be all his life: the gentle, caring, Prince of the City with only love and concern and help in his heart for all the living creatures he so benignly and kindly shared the planet with.

Auden said as everyone in the entire room stared at him, "My God, Bill, you're supposed to be the intelligent one, not me. Are you some sort of unfeeling brute? *Don't you take any notice of what people put there right under your nose for you to see?*"

17.

At 8:53 A.M. the embassy of the United States in Hong Kong wasn't open for business. At the other end of the phone at his home number in the Leighton Hill apartments near Happy Valley, it sounded like Ben Voigt, the local police liaison officer for the US Federal Drug Enforcement Administration, wasn't either.

In the background, there was the sound of Voigt's horde of children discussing volubly with Voigt's wife whether or not a mild sniffle one of them had caught was cause enough for them all to stay out of school as a quarantine measure and spend the day recuperating with video games, and he had to get Feiffer to repeat the form number three times before he had all the numbers straight.

Finally, shouting above the racket, Voigt said, "Yes, it's the identifying series number for an INS form—Immigration and Naturalization. It's the form they send out to tell you they've either approved or denied an application for US permanent residence—and you've either been granted or denied what's popularly known as a green card." He had to think, "But it's not handled by INS overseas in embassies: it comes from State."

"Can you access their computers through the DEA office?" At the other end of the line there were a series of moaning sounds as the procession of small Walking Dead must have congregated around the altar of their father and pleaded with him for mercy. "I've got a list of the names of nine people I need run. I need to verify that they were each sent out a form granting them permanent residence, together with all the information and circumstances surrounding their applications."

"Okay." He asked someone named Katherine to stop begging and please either go back to the breakfast table or leave the planet. Voigt said, "I can check the names for you on the basis of a standard DEA background-check inquiry. As for the circumstances of the applications, they'd be with the original application packages in Washington and since the usual waiting time from application to approval is about three years—"

"Is it that long?"

"Sure." Voigt said with a trace of pride, "Everybody wants to live in America." (Including him. Preferably alone. Voigt said in desperation, "*Please, Katherine—!*") "It's a very complicated process in a very complicated legal context and, even if everything is done exactly right, one that still has a very low rate of success." He paused for a moment to check that his daughter was going in the direction he wanted her to go. "That's why people who are serious about it don't try to do it themselves and use lawyers or third parties who are expert in it to make sure it's all done right."

"If an application is granted, who gets the letter granting it—the Form I–797–6–29–88—the applicant?"

"No, the third party who prepared the application would normally get it and pass it along." He wasn't sure. "Well, he or she would certainly get it first. Whether a second form would go out to the applicants themselves at a later date, I just don't know." Voigt said, not only to pinpoint his exact occupation in life, but also to justify his apparent failure to get anyone in his family to do anything, "I'm a cop, not a diplomat. I only know as much as I do because with Hong Kong due to go in the next three or four years, once people realize I even work at the embassy everybody and his brother asks me about getting a green card so they can get out before the Communists come." Voigt said suddenly as from somewhere behind him there was a wail of disappointment from one of his children that was instantly and deafeningly taken up by all of them, "What I can do I'll do. Give me the names of the nine people and I'll check them. And the third party—whoever prepared the applications—give me his name too if you've got it."

He paused just for a moment, then, touching each of them on his list with a pencil as he went carefully down them, spelling them out for the man, Feiffer gave him the nine names.

Somehow in the melee, Voigt managed to get every one of the names written down.

Voigt asked, "And the name of the third party?"

He could not keep his voice from trembling and he wondered if Voigt noticed. Feiffer said, "I don't have the name of the third party."

He was a cop. He noticed everything. Voigt said quickly, "Okay. Leave it to me."

He was no diplomat. Out of patience, he threatened to do something to Katherine that made her shriek at the top of her voice for her mother.

Voigt said, a moment before he hung up, "I'll get back to you."

There had been ten people in the bank that evening: the nine staff members of the Asia–America–Hong Kong Bank, and one other: the one who had brought the letters of green-card approval with him—the third party.

At his desk, Feiffer said, with it all suddenly beginning to make sense, "Whoever it was who handled the green-card applications for them and oversaw the whole process over what, evidently, could have been as much as three years, got the notice or notices of approval that day and he took in a bottle of champagne to celebrate it with them because it was everything they'd waited for for years, and why they'd done nothing with all the money they'd stolen, and why they hadn't formed any personal lives here in the Colony—*because they'd all—each of them—directed their entire lives and hopes and dreams towards one single aim: getting out of Hong Kong to America with over four and quarter million dollars to spend!"* Feiffer said, so close he could taste it, "The tenth person in the bank that evening—the poisoner—was the person who arranged their green cards for them—a lawyer or agent of some kind who shepherded them through the whole process to success!" Feiffer said, "And then he killed them."

Auden said, "Why?"

Spencer said, "For the money! What else?"

He'd always believed no one could follow something better than Spencer. Maybe it was because he always believed he couldn't follow anything at all. Auden said, "But the money hadn't been stolen by him or her, it had been stolen by the bank staff. And sent out through banks and forwarding agencies and numbered accounts they themselves had set up. So if the third party in all this bumped off all the people who'd sent it out—" He looked hard at Spencer "—*and presumably were the only ones who could draw on it when they finally got where they wanted to be*—how was the third party ever going to get his hands on it?"

It was there, so close, with just one tiny thing missing. Feiffer said, "Unless he was one of them—one of the applicants for the green card himself!" It would explain Tolliver. It would explain why the moment the letters had arrived from the embassy someone had called Lee and told him Tolliver's loan was no good and that he should be called in urgently that day. "And the third party had full access to the money even without the other nine people!"

O'Yee said incredulously, "And what? Tolliver just happened along out of nowhere to borrow money from the bank, and just happened to be a man with access to poisons who just happened to also be a champagne and wine collector and just happened to be in trouble with his loan that morning?"

"No, Tolliver didn't come later in the plan, he came first. The waiting period between application and approval of a green card can run out to as much as three years. Tolliver didn't apply for his original loan from the bank in the last three weeks: he applied for it three years ago! He came even before the staff started stealing the money! He was set up as the patsy with all the right background and knowledge to kill *years ago* as part of the third party's whole plan!"

Spencer asked, "But where did the third party come from, Harry? This expert in American green cards? There were nine people stealing from their own bank—they're not going to just cast around for a friendly lawyer or immigration agent and inform him that they're stealing millions of dollars from a bank and would he care to represent them in their applications for green cards for a cut of some of the stolen loot!" He shot a quick look at Auden to remind him he knew how to ask hard questions too, "How did they pick out someone like that? From the fucking phone book listing under *Scumbags?*"

Feiffer said tightly, "They didn't pick him. He picked them. He came first. He had the whole idea clear in his mind probably before the idea of green cards even occurred to anyone in the bank."

"How do you know that?"

"I know that because, from the beginning, he had to have been the one in charge—because he was the only one who knew how to go about applying for green cards! Because the whole thing goes too far back and it's too tight for the other people involved in it—" Feiffer said to make the logic of it obvious, "For God's sake, when the embezzling started in the bank, at least one of the girls involved in it was only seventeen years old! The whole idea of embezzling and green cards wasn't invented by someone like her or by someone she just picked out of a telephone book—it was invented by someone in authority she looked up to and trusted—*someone who laid out the whole plan for her with the final glittering prize of a green card and a new life in America at the end of it!*"

"But after he'd killed them all, what the hell did he expect was going to happen?" As far as it went, it was fine, but it went no distance after that. O'Yee, shaking his head, said definitely, "If he was the person who got them their green cards and suddenly they're all dead, there's going to be an investigation, the embezzlement's going to be found—"

It had been found. Mansor had found it. And he had found it easily.

O'Yee said, "And then, just like the lottery-win idea, the third party's going to have a great old time explaining first to the US Embassy, and then to us, why all his fellow nine green-card applicants seem to be suddenly dead on the same day the green cards were granted!" O'Yee said, "No." He shook his head hard to dismiss the idea. "If the third party's a lawyer and that's his or her idea of legalistic, long-term, three-year planning, remind me never to use him in court!"

His brain was deducing as it had never deduced before. Spencer said slowly, "Unless, of course, the moment he gets into America, he instantly changes his identity and just disappears and no one can find him to ask him anything!"

Auden said with disdain, "Yeah! Right!"

He just hadn't been the same after the seagull. It miffed him. Spencer, turning to the man, demanded, "Why not? People get lost in America all the time!"

He had grown up in America. He shook his head. O'Yee said, "Native-born Americans do. Foreigners do rarely. Especially foreigners granted green cards. Foreigners granted green cards have records. They're on file. They're on file with everyone. They're on file with Immigration, with State, with Social Services, everyone. Their fingerprints are on file with the FBI, and, for all I know, the CIA and the National Security Agency. And as for a foreigner who happens to have four and a quarter million dollars or so available to him, forget about the FBI or the CIA or even the NSA—he's on file with the Internal Revenue Service!" O'Yee said definitely to scotch the idea, "No. Get-um green card, bump-um off bank staff, enter US tepee with heap too much wampum equal—equals one very quick IRS investigation, equals even quicker federal deportation hearing, equals very quick-quick great-silver-bird flight in sky back to where you came from, and—in this case—equals quick putting of two and two together equals conviction on nine counts of murder, God knows how many on embezzlement and aiding and abetting and whatever else, and ten thousand years in the pokey!"

Suddenly, it was all going nowhere again. Suddenly, as if it was all collapsing in front of him and meant nothing. Suddenly—

The phone on his desk rang, and, wrenching it up, Feiffer said urgently, "Feiffer."

It was Voigt calling back with his information about the

applications and approvals of nine green cards to nine members of the bank.

His information was simple and straightforward.

On the state-department computer there was no record of any such approvals, but the consular clerk Voigt had spoken to had suggested that might not necessarily mean anything because the paperwork might not have been transferred to the computer yet and was still sitting in hard-copy form on someone's desk.

Helpfully, the clerk had offered to punch up the original applications made in the names of all the nine people and get the name or names of the embassy clerk or clerks handling them so Voigt could speak to them directly.

The information there on the original green-card applications in the names of T. M. Lee, and Jessie Fan and Jennifer Wong and Henry Lin and Martin Mok and Louise Chiang and Mary Sun and Louis Wing and George Chan, in each and every instance, was equally simple and straightforward.

There were and never had been any applications whatsoever in any of the names and, although the clerk, at Voigt's request, had grudgingly checked all the records for not merely three, but five then seven, then ten years back, no mention as far as the state department or the immigration and naturalization service or any arm of the United States government was concerned of any of the names in any context whatsoever.

If there was no third party who had handled all the green-card applications for the bank staff, then there had been no tenth man at the bank.

There had been a tenth man! The tenth man was the one who had watched as they all died in front of him or crawled away in agony to die in the washrooms.

Maybe it had been Tolliver after all. Maybe he had been wrong about him from the start. Maybe, as a cop, he could no longer tell the truth from fiction, or even when a man—

At his desk, putting his hand to his head, Feiffer said, "Goddammit! Nothing about any of it makes sense! It's all back to nothing! All the paper was was a scrap of Xerox of a fucking green card someone in the bank copied for someone else as a favor, or for a payment over the counter of five fucking cents a copy!"

Maybe it was Tolliver. Maybe it had been him all along. Maybe the killings and the embezzled money and the Caymans and Bermuda and all the rest of it weren't even related.

Feiffer said at the end, "Maybe the two things haven't got anything to do with each other at all! Maybe they're completely separate! Maybe everyone else was right and Tolliver did go to that bank to kill everyone with his last fucking bottle of champagne so he wouldn't have to pay back the loan Lee was dunning him for—and maybe the fact that Lee and every other member of the bank was stealing had nothing to do with him at all! Maybe they had some other idea in mind for the four million dollars we haven't even thought of! Maybe they had a fucking plan to take it to fucking Mars with them on a fucking spaceship!"

He felt so sorry for him. O'Yee said softly, "Maybe Tolliver didn't even kill them to save himself paying back the loan. Maybe he just killed them all out of revenge for turning his life into a nightmare by demanding he do something about it that day . . ." It was the simplest, the easiest answer.

"The least of Tolliver's problems was the bank loan! He didn't spend his days and nights cowering in his office afraid that some bank was going to have him made bankrupt for nonpayment of a loan, he was fucking terrified that a troop of goddamned triad gangsters was going to come in and hack him into mincemeat for gambling debts! He was so fucking terrified he was barely in enough shape to shamble from one room to another! If he could barely do that, how the hell could he have been in good enough shape to go to a bank and kill nine people?"

O'Yee said carefully, "Shoemaker thought he was a solid suspect—"

He had. And now he was dead. And because of him, so was Tolliver. But he didn't want to think of that, and getting up from the desk Feiffer turned to stab his finger at all the photographs of the dead pinned to the incident board.

Feiffer said to convince anyone, himself, "Look at them! Look at what he did to them! Look at the way he did it! He poisoned them! He poisoned them with a concoction of cyanide and champagne, and they drank it all at once! For what? For a celebration! For who? For Tolliver? To celebrate what with Tolliver? That he couldn't pay back the loan and the bank was going to have to call in the loan?"

He shook his head hard to forestall anyone else saying anything, "No! No. Tolliver was part of it all right, but the part he played was worked out and planned and carefully choreographed by someone else: the person who really did kill everyone in the bank, not out of desperation that they might call in Tolliver's quarter-of-a-million-dollar loan that had already been spent anyway, but out of a plan to get hold of the four and a quarter million dollars the bank staff had stolen and was sitting somewhere in the fucking Caribbean just waiting to be spent!"

It was almost there, almost within reach, Feiffer said tightly, "I think Tolliver was supposed to turn up at exactly the moment the killings were going on and Tolliver was going to be found there dead, surrounded by all his victims, but he simply didn't turn up!" Feiffer said with his eyes narrowed, "Like all banks in the Colony, there's a gun there in the vault. I think, in theory, in his death throes Lee was supposed to knock off Tolliver with it, or Tolliver, somehow, was supposed to put it to his head and blow his brains out so we could close the case without ever finding out anything about the embezzled money!"

He could follow things. He followed this and it didn't follow. Spencer, standing at his desk with his back to Auden, said gently, "No. It doesn't work. Harry, you say that (1) the whole embezzlement thing was set up by a third party on the promise of green cards—and there are no green cards; (2) that Tolliver was part of the three-year plan and that he was supposed to go into the bank a financial failure to kill everyone when he couldn't pay back his loan—when there's no way anyone on earth would know three years later he *was* going to fail; and (3) that if Tolliver was found there dead we'd close the case and never discover the embezzled money—when, in fact, the accountant checking the financial state of the bank so he could make a report to the stockholders found it all almost straight away." Spencer said, sorry to be the one to say it, "Harry, no. It doesn't work—any of it."

He was his friend and he went over to stand next to him, but as O'Yee put out his hand to console the man, Feiffer was not to be consoled and pulled away.

Feiffer, still hanging onto it, demanded, "If Tolliver was there to tell Lee that he couldn't pay back the loan somebody has to tell me why it was a cause for celebration! And why would he even think to put the poison in the champagne in the first place? Why go to all that trouble? If all he wanted to do was slaughter everyone in the bank he had enough fucking fuming prussic acid in his lab to wipe out the entire bank and himself three seconds after he just uncorked it in air! The cynanide was used in champagne because someone wanted us to think it was Tolliver and they'd had the cyanide for years, not because it's as effective as, say, prussic, but because it's easier to keep!"

It wasn't right and he wasn't going to let go of it. It was crazy. Spencer, still on the time problem, said in protest, trying to sound as convincing about it as O'Yee had about the American connection, "But, Harry, if this was all planned three years ago when Tolliver got the loan, it means that someone not only had to know he was going to fail and be unable to pay back the loan, he also had to know, exactly to the day, *when* he was going to fail! He had to know exactly to the day when all the bank staff were celebrating something—whatever it was. So how did he do that? Did he do something to *make* him fail?"

An inch ahead all was darkness. Feiffer said sadly, "No. When Tolliver took out the loan, with his gambling problem, he was already a failure."

"Then how could he predict the two events occurring simultaneously? The green cards—which don't exist—or whatever the cause for celebration was going to be three years in the future, and his patsy Tolliver's complete and final financial failure *on the exact same day?*"

Suddenly, again, something in Auden's postbrute mind worked again. Auden said, "Wait a minute." He went over to the incident board and looked at it for a moment, then reached up and laid his finger on the first entry Mr. Lee had written on his telephone-log page. Auden, running his finger carefully down the listings, said, reading them off, "Wait a minute. According to this, the first time Lee tried to call Tolliver about his loan was nine o'clock in the morning. How come it appears out of nowhere? How come—am I right, Harry?—there's no mention of it the day before? What did Lee do—think of it on his way in for breakfast out of thin air?"

Feiffer said softly, "No. He was phoned at home or somewhere by someone. Someone told him the loan was bad, someone who—"

Spencer said in total exasperation, "Had done *what?* Made sure Tolliver's business was going to fail on that exact day? Someone who, *somehow*—God knows how!—had spent three years, a little at a time, somehow making sure he was going to fail on that exact day?" Spencer said angrily, "Harry—!"

It was all it took. Feiffer said suddenly, "Oh, my God!"

He had it. At last, he had the one missing piece. Feiffer said in triumph, "No, not someone who spent three years making sure he'd fail on that exact day, but someone who spent three years keeping him from failing *until* that exact day! Someone who had access to his poisons, someone who knew, day by day, exactly the state of Tolliver's business and exactly day by day the state of the bank embezzlements, and someone who knew, after Lee and his staff had sent the money to the Caymans and the Bahamas, exactly how to move it one step on into another account the bank people didn't even know about and someone who—"

He stopped in midsentence.

Feiffer said suddenly, with it all so clear, "The phones in the bank! Tolliver told me when he tried to get through to the bank after five all the lines were busy! Someone else told me when he tried to get through the lines were all down. The reason the second person who said it made the simple mistake of saying they'd gone down instead of that they were just off the hook was because he never *heard* the busy signal because he never made the call! He was in the bank with, probably, the main phone switch off and he just assumed that if anyone called what they'd get would be a sound like the lines were broken when, in fact, exactly the way Tolliver described it, what they'd get would be the *busy* signal!"

He had it. He had it all. Feiffer said, "There *was* a notification of a green-card approval on the exact day everyone died in that bank, and the scrap of paper I found in the bank is a copy of it—but it isn't a copy of one of the nonexistent green-card notifications issued to any of the nine people in the bank, it's a copy of the notification of the third party's green card! All he had to do was make a copy of it and alter it to list all their names on it along with his and take it in to show them after closing time and they would have drunk champagne with him until it came out of their goddamned ears—and still asked for more!" It all fitted together. It was perfect, without fault. Feiffer said, "They made copies of it for themselves on the Xerox machine because there was only one original, and that was the one he had!"

Spencer said, "But how could he keep Tolliver's business going day after day till the exact right moment? How could anyone know that much about anyone else's business dealings? How could anyone—"

He saw it too. Spencer said in a gasp, "Oh, my God—! It has to be him, doesn't it? Everything fits. It has to be him, doesn't it?"

Feiffer said, "Yes!"

Feiffer ordered O'Yee, "Call Ben Voigt. Tell him to get his embassy computer clerk back on the phone on a conference line. Tell him there's one more green-card name to check. Tell him after that you want him to accompany you to the embassy so you can get a copy of all the information the embassy's prepared to give you about it." He turned to Spencer and saw him staring at all the photographs of the dead in the back with a look of new horror on his face, "Bill, I want you and Phil to get around to Headquarters and get the commander to set up a no-knock unspecified-evidence search warrant for two premises, one business and the other residential at exact rooms and addresses to be specified—and the moment you've got them, I want both places turned over by a search team!"

He was already dialing another number himself. Feiffer said to the room, with a sudden shiver running up the entire length of his back, "My God, he arranged it all right from

the beginning! He probably even got Tolliver the loan!
Right from the very beginning, he nurtured it piece by tiny
piece, entry by minute entry, all aimed at the one single
moment when all the players would come together and it all
blossomed, all the time being so helpful and humble
and—"

Hunched over his desk, O'Yee, holding up the phone,
said, "I've got Ben. He's patched in the conference line to
the embassy. They've got the list of recent green-card approvals up on screen. What name do you want them to
check?"

The name was Mansor.

Waiting for the party at the other end of his line to pick
up, Feiffer said in a gasp, "My God, he even planned to be
the one to discover the missing money to throw suspicion
even further off himself because he knew once he'd moved it
from the accounts in the Caymans and in Bermuda no one
would ever be able to trace it to him!"

They picked up. The party at the other end of the line said
in English, "Association of Small Banking Businesses and
General Commerce Accountants. Mr. Lai speaking. How
may I help you?"

On the phone, Feiffer told them who he was and, watching
O'Yee as he waited for the embassy to search for the name
on their screen, asked the man at the other end of the line a
single question.

He asked whether Mr. Mansor was listed in their records
as the accountant of record for a Dr. Tolliver of the Hong
Kong Analysis Laboratories on Aberdeen Road.

The man he was speaking to, Mr. Lai, was the chief accountant and vice-president of the company and, like Mansor, he carried everything he needed in his head and did not
even have to look it up.

Mr. Lai said, "Yes."

Feiffer asked the man if he knew where Mansor was now.

Mr. Lai said, "Yes." He told him where he was.

At the computer terminal in the embassy, the clerk typed
in the query: Green-card approval? . . . Mansor? . . .

It was an easy one, no long-term search or cross-referencing or hard copy—to—data delay involved in it at all.

At his computer terminal inside the embassy, transmitted over the conference line, first to Voigt and then to O'Yee, and then in the silent, waiting detectives' room by O'Yee to Feiffer, the clerk said, "—*Yes!*"

18.

He was not an accountant or a poisoner: that was not what he was at all. That was only part of his identity. What he was was a fully developed, one-hundred-percent perfect, exceptionally dangerous and unremitting psychopath.

Standing at the sink in the washroom of the Asia–America–Hong Kong Bank, carefully and thoroughly washing his hands, Mansor also had an incident board and blackboard covering every twist and turn in the events of the last three years, but it was not on open display on a wall for anyone else to read, it was in his head.

And it was not confused and out of order and searching like the one in the detectives' room that Feiffer and O'Yee and Auden and Spencer had worked through—it was exact and precise and accurate, divided neatly into two columns down the center with what was for him on one side and, on the other, what was against.

It listed on the left, in chronological order, each of the careful, calculated actions required in his plan, and on the right, the estimated degree of difficulty and risk involved in it and the odds in percentage form of bringing it to fruition.

As each step had been completed, he had erased each of the estimated-risk percentages and replaced it with a tick.

The percentages had all been in the eight-percent range,

so there had never been any luck involved in it, only calculated risk, and even what began it all—the fact that he had lucked onto Lee embezzling money from his own bank on the very first audit he did for him—was not luck at all, but merely opportunity favoring a prepared mind.

The first item, long, long ago ticked, read, *Cover funds shortfall and lock in Lee,* the second, also long, long ago ticked, *Replace staff one at a time,* and the third, *Ascertain motivation for staff*—he had starred at the bottom of the column where he did his notes, **US residence offer?*—and the fourth, *Ascertain method of killing Lee and staff and locate and lock in hundred-percent motivated suspect.*

He was an auditor, privy to people's deepest secrets. He knew, sooner or later, he would find exactly the man he wanted.

The first day he had been employed by the Hong Kong Analysis Laboratories to do the books he had written in alongside the fourth item: *Tolliver.*

He had written in as the man's little thumbnail biography to set his mind working on the problem, *Chemist. Poisons. Wine collector.* And then, as things progressed and he learned more about the man, *Gambler. Poor businessman. Chances of company surviving in present form: zero percent. Arrange loan from Lee. Sum: Plus or minus $250,000.*

Then it all came together. He wrote in the column after Tolliver's name: *Motive. Means. Method. Opportunity.*—and, one by one, ticked each one as he set it up.

It was all flawless, perfect.

The next item read, *Bring all parties together in bank on pretext of (1) [Bank Staff] green-card issuances, and (2) [Tolliver] urgent repayment of loan, and kill.*

Just in case he might have missed someone, he had the names listed in alphabetical order.

The names were:

> *Chan*
> *Chiang*
> *Fan*
> *Lee*
> *Lin*

Mok
Sun
Wong
Wing
and last, *Tolliver.*

He had made his only mistake there. He thought after he had told Lee that Tolliver's loan was no good that Tolliver would come in for his appointment, but, in the long run, it was of no consequence, and he had merely taken Tolliver's name off the list of people to be killed in the bank and put it into a secondary list of loose ends to be tidied up with the notation *Kill at appropriate time in lab. Poison? Apparent suicide?* and moved on to the last, final, prime entry.

The last entry read, *Sabotage police investigation by suggesting existence of two apparently unrelated crimes happening simultaneously: (1) Lee and bank staff embezzlement without apparent motive, and (2) Mass murder of staff by Tolliver motivated by imminent financial ruin at hands of bank staff, and (3) Throw any suspicion off self.*

Because it had involved him, he had calculated the odds of success on that one too. The chances of success in that, especially when he was the one who would discover the bank embezzlement and report it to the police, was one hundred percent.

It was his credit and debit account, his list.

Because he was thorough and always gave excellent service, it was thorough and excellent.

Because he was a psychopath without any normal human feelings, and only mimicked human feelings to make his way through the world in a manner acceptable to the normal people he came into contact with, his list took into account nowhere anything human—no extraneous concerns of pity, or mercy, or any feelings or emotion at all.

It was unique. As he was.

He was not like other people. The only people he was like, not because he knew any, but because he had read about them in the papers occasionally, were other psychopaths: serial killers and assassins and, here and there, giving themselves away by something they said or did that shocked

ordinary people and they later tried to amend to make acceptable, self-made men who ran great corporations or specu-
lated in city-wide land deals or, here and there, politicians
and dictators who let nothing deter them in their single-
minded rise to the top.

Other people—normal people—from what little he could
learn of them in his efforts to pass himself off as one of them
in public life, he thought of as merely stupid.

He could not understand why Shoemaker had done what
he had done at all.

Usually, if he set his face into the same expression as the
expression he saw on the faces of people around him, he
could understand a little what that expression represented in
their minds and say appropriate things to mimic it, but what
expression Shoemaker must have had on his face when he
killed Tolliver and was himself killed defeated him entirely,
and, gazing into the mirror above the washbasin, he could
not make any sort of face that even gave him the remotest
clue to the man at all.

It didn't matter. He had a last important item on his list to
be dealt with that read, *On pretext of continuing bank audit,
retrieve eighteen green-card photostats, wash champagne
bottle and cork from hiding place in vault,* and, pausing only
long enough to glance one more time at his face in the mirror and patting at his slicked-down hair, he folded the washroom hand towel neatly, put it back where it should be on its
rack, and went out of the washroom down the corridor into
the main section of the bank to go into the vault to do it.

At 9:15 A.M. the mall was still closed and he had to hold
up his police ID card against the main glass doors and then
identify himself for a second time as a police officer to persuade the single security guard on the ground floor to open
the door and let him in.

Feiffer yelled, "Police! Detective Chief Inspector Feiffer,
Yellowthread Street!" The man was one of Shoemaker's
rent-a-cops, a young, nervous-looking Chinese wearing a
Sam Browne belt with handcuffs and a baton, and once he
got the door open Feiffer gave the man no time to think or

contact his superiors to check to see if what he was doing was right.

Feiffer yelled, "Mansor. The auditor for the Asia–America–Hong Kong Bank—is he still here or not?"

He was. The man said in Chinese, forgetting for a moment that as an employee however humble of the Lotus Flower Mall he was supposed to be sophisticated, international, and polygot, "*Hai!* Yes!"

All the escalators and elevators in the giant place were off, and immediately taking the man with him in his wake, Feiffer ordered him, "Take up a position at the bottom of the center escalator and stay there after I go up!" Like Shoemaker, the man had no keys to the bank. "And if I yell down to you to do it, call the police dispatch number and tell them I need the Emergency Unit in here with explosives to take the door down!" Feiffer demanded, "Got it? Do you understand?"

"*Hai!*" He was about twenty-three or -four with an athletic build, a cop manqué. "Yes!"

"Good!" He was already climbing the stairs of the center escalator. Up there, three floors away, Mansor was in the bank destroying evidence, or changing it or amending it, or hiding it, or God only knew what.

He was a man who had poisoned nine people and stood over them for as long as it took for the last of them to crawl away and die.

He was the man responsible for the deaths of Tolliver and Shoemaker.

He was up there only three floors away, up there.

Mansor . . .

Feiffer said, "Good!"

He said it again, for no reason at all, in a whisper, "*Good!*"

Mansor.

With his face tight, taking the steps two at a time, Feiffer went urgently up the stilled and frozen escalator—*at last! At last!*—to bring him in.

On one of the photostats of the green-card notification the bank staff had made, there was a piece torn off: a corner with the type and number of the form on it, and, in the vault,

Mansor, his mind racing with the possibility that it might have caught in the machine when one of the bank staff had copied it, ran to the machine and ripped the lid open to check.

It was not in there, and he went back quickly into the vault and overturned the big resealed cardboard box of obsolete deposit and withdrawal forms in the corner where he had hidden the photostats under the big padded envelope he had smashed the champagne bottle to powder in to check that maybe he himself hadn't accidentally torn it off when he had put it in there.

He hadn't, and, standing in the vault still holding the box, he looked straight ahead and set his mind to working out what the loss of the little scrap of paper from the photostat might mean to him.

First, he calculated the odds against the chances (1) that the corner had ripped off and he had not noticed, and (2) that if it had, the police had found it and (3) knew what it was, and (4)—

In the vault, Mansor said aloud, "No."

He stopped calculating.

No, the odds against it were too great, heading for astronomical, and when his mind reached the total percentage possibility of less than one half of one percent that the police had found the corner, worked out what it was, and then extrapolated from it what it had been used for, he turned his mind off and stopped thinking about it.

He decided the copy paper had been faulty before the teller who had made the copy had even inserted it into the machine.

And he had other things to think about that were more important, and, putting the forms neatly back in the box and setting the box high up on the vault shelf, he checked that he had the phoney Peter-to-Paul loan form from Lee's files, gathered up the eighteen photostats and the envelope containing the powdered remains of the champagne bottle, and put everything neatly in his briefcase.

Perfect. All perfect.

On his way back to his office, the remains of the bottle

would go into the harbor, and at his office he could shred the eighteen photostats to confetti.

Then, his last duty as a good, honest, innocent citizen, as an auditor who gave excellent service, would be to hand over the Peter-to-Paul papers to Feiffer, say he had found them hidden in Lee's desk—and he was out of it completely.

All he had to do then was just go on doing his work at the Small Banking Association for another year or so before suddenly telling them he had to leave to go home to Pakistan or somewhere on family business and he was out of it completely with a green card and a new life in America and a total of four point two-seven million dollars available as interest-free, nonrepayable loans from three different straw business accounts in Bermuda and the Cayman Islands he himself owned with no questions asked.

It was all perfect.

Snapping his briefcase closed, he nodded at the pure, perfect mathematical elegance of it all.

He had no human feelings and he did not smile out of personal pride or triumph or surprise that he had succeeded at it because he had always known he would be able to do it and there was no pride or joy or triumph or surprise to it.

He made his face smile a little smile. As he moved among them, watching them and mimicking them to appear to be like them, he had seen sometimes the little smile-look people got on their faces when something good happened, and he thought if he was going to succeed in America as well as he had succeeded in Hong Kong, he had better practice a smile; and as he unlocked the main bank door and stepped out onto the third-floor gallery to leave the mall, he smiled again.

He glanced over for a moment to the center escalator and saw Feiffer coming up the escalator steps two at a time and the smile-look froze.

He saw the hard, determined look on the man's face and, because all his life he had copied and mimicked all the looks people got on their faces, knew instantly what it meant.

It meant he had to think fast and cleanly and with careful, clear mathematical logic.

It meant—

His mind clicked through the problem so rapidly he only

stood there for the merest part of a moment looking at the man, and then before Feiffer even saw him there gazing at him as he came, he had the solution to the problem and turned instantly back towards the bank and went inside to take the first step towards its execution.

He had him. He had everything, at last, clear and worked out and, at last, he had him.

He had the man who had stood there and watched as nine people had died in front of him. He had the man responsible for the deaths of Tolliver and Shoemaker.

At the closed replacement bank door, steeling himself to sound normal, Feiffer called out to rouse him, "Mr. Mansor? . . ."

The big plate-glass windows on the bank were heavily curtained and he could not see if the man was still in there or not.

He knew he was still in there.

Feiffer called, "Mr. Mansor? . . ."

He rapped at the door hard with his knuckles and it moved open a fraction.

Feiffer called out, "Mr. Mansor? . . ."

He pushed the door gently and it gave and swung open into silence and darkness.

Taking a single step inside, Feiffer called, "Are you there? Mr. Mansor? . . . Are you still in here? . . ."

He saw, across the main customer area of the bank, a single glow from a light somewhere in the vault area, and he thought the man was in there, and crossing quickly over the carpeted main floor he went towards the swinging door at the end of the bank of glassed-in tellers' cages to—

He saw, from out of nowhere, a shadow suddenly appear behind him.

He saw Mansor.

He saw his face and it was a face that was not human.

He saw something black in his hand. He saw it come up. He heard a single click, and then in the same instant as his brain ordered him in a panic to reach down for his own pistol, Mansor, holding the bank's Webley out in two hands like a target shooter, shot him once dead center in the heart and dropped him like a stone where he stood.

He was on him the instant he fell. Wrenching Feiffer's revolver out of his holster and leaping back quickly again from the shot, dying man, Mansor yelled at the pure mathematical elegance of it all, *"Yes!"*

He yelled it to steel himself.

Getting to the open door, without pause, he put the muzzle of Feiffer's gun exactly where his computations had told him it should be put—against the fleshy part of his left arm just below the bicep—and pulled the trigger.

He knew the security guard down on the ground floor would hear him.

Shrieking in terror and pain and panic—the mimickry done perfectly—Mansor screamed down at the top of his voice to get the man to come up and save him, "Help! *Help!* Help me! He was part of it! He was in it with Shoemaker and Tolliver and all the rest of them from the start! Help me! *Please!* Help me! *I've been shot!"*

19.

When Feiffer came to, he came to in a wave of pain. When the shot had hit him it had hit so hard he thought it had blasted his heart out, and as he lay facedown on the carpet with both his hands caught flat against his chest, he could not understand why he could still feel beating against his palms.

He thought he should be dead, and he could not understand why he could still hear his heart beating in the blood vessels around his neck and in the canals of his ears.

Then the pain ebbed away and his body became numb and he thought then he was on the point of death.

Then, waxing and waning between life and death, the pain came back and then ebbed again, and he could no longer hear his heart and, like a man floating on a raft on a limitless, empty, silent sea, he drifted away again into stillness and vastness and darkness and silence.

It was not the green card that had brought the man to the bank with that look on his face. The chances of the single torn corner of paper leading to the green-card applications and the entire plan were so slight that as he stood stock still in the bank perfecting his plan, Mansor dismissed it from his mind and did not think of it again.

No, it was the Tolliver connection: he had found out that

he had worked on Tolliver's accounts, and he put the green-card question from his mind and worked only on that problem.

The man on the floor was still moving, but he was only moving in some sort of near-death coma, and he wasn't a problem anymore and by the time the problem was solved would be dead.

The guard was still a living problem, but he would not come up to the bank until he had called the police, so he did not have to deal with him straight away and could concentrate on more immediate things.

Standing absolutely still in the center of the bank with his briefcase in one hand and the two revolvers in the other, Mansor said aloud to get it right, "*Item: Cover eighty-percent possibility that connection between Tolliver and self has been discovered.*"

He glanced over at Feiffer.

"*Action: Do not deny connection. Inform next police investigator that such information was given to his predecessor and ignored.*"

That would do it.

Simple was best. He was bleeding from a gunshot wound from Feiffer's gun and that would be enough to start the next investigator searching for Feiffer's part in the whole embezzlement and murder scheme, and the suggestion by an innocent party that vital information he had given had been ignored would only make him search harder.

So that was settled, and he moved on cleanly and easily to the next consideration.

Standing there, watching the open doorway where, in due course, the guard from downstairs would appear, his face had no expression on it at all.

He was stone cold, calculating, a psychopath.

On the next consideration to be dealt with, Mansor said aloud, "*Item: Security guard. Likelihood of understanding inference that Detective Chief Inspector Feiffer was the first to fire*"—he calculated it quickly—"*plus or minus seventy percent. Likelihood of passing on clear inference to police emergency number, plus or minus*"—he paused just a moment and let his mind work clearly and cleanly on all the permutations—"*the same. Plus or minus seventy percent.*"

Unmoving, thinking it through, he stood still in the center of the bank like a statue. Heavy drops of blood from the bullet wound in his left arm were beginning to drop down over his wrist onto to the floor, but he had calculated the placement of the shot to exactly the right place in his arm where it would do no permanent injury or interfere with any of the full movement he needed from it, and he did not move to look at it.

He was in pain from the shot, but the pain was merely a side issue that had no direct bearing on the final outcome of his calculations, and he ignored it.

He moved smoothly back to the things that did have a direct bearing on the final outcome.

He glanced at Feiffer momentarily to check the progress of his dying.

Mansor said, "*Item: Create motive for first investigating police officer's attack on self in bank.*"

He thought it through. "*Manufacture forged memo of deposit from Cayman bank account for substantial sum in joint names of Lee, Feiffer*"—he thought for an instant—"*Shoemaker and Tolliver. And back date.*"

He needed to appear totally and completely at a loss about the whole business when the next investigating officer interviewed him: a poor, stupid, unworldly little Pakistani accountant caught up in matters beyond his comprehension. He needed only to say humbly as he always did, "I merely attempted, sir, as I always do, to give excellent service . . . I have no idea at all, sir, why Mr. Feiffer should have suddenly and inexplicably attempted to murder me . . . It was only by the sheerest chance that I happened to have the bank's revolver in my possession to hand in to the police for safekeeping that I was even able to defend myself . . ." And then, after he had recovered from his wound, in the same spirit of honest humility and unfailing cooperation, he would go back to the bank with the next investigator and find the memo that implicated Feiffer in the whole business from the beginning. And be shocked.

Perfect. Perfect.

He permitted himself what he thought looked like another smile.

He was almost done. He had only two more problems to solve and he solved them quickly and without effort.

The items were: *(1) Create appropriate scene of struggle to confirm all aspects of story.*

Mansor said softly, "*Action required: vandalize and destroy selected movable and fixed areas of bank to give appearance of struggle;*

(2) Utilize security guard as reinforcement of scenario and remove risk of security guard offering conflicting evidence of scenario."

Mansor said softly, "*Action required: lure security guard into bank on pretext of need for immediate medical assistance and dispose of with Feiffer's gun.*"

Mansor said softly, "Yes!"

He nodded.

He did not, this time, however, attempt to mimic a smile.

He had too many other more important things to do.

Putting his briefcase down carefully on the carpeted floor and placing both the revolvers on top of it, brushing away the drops of blood from his wrist as he bent down, he merely, only, for a final time, nodded and—knowing exactly what he had to do and the order in which he had to do it—went directly across the floor of the bank to the counter, took up the bank television sitting there in both hands, and, with careful aim, hurled it hard against the glass of the teller's cage directly above the dying man on the floor and brought the entire sheet down in an explosion of shattering, falling, razor-sharp glass spears and shards all around him.

The sound of the explosion of glass above him brought Feiffer back and he knew where he was. He was in the bank, dying on the floor where all the people from the bank had died, and, as he died, he thought somehow he had travelled back in time and was dying with them and heard their voices.

He thought he was lying in the exact same spot where the girl with the elephant chain had lain, and he thought he heard the sounds of her dying and then the sounds of all the people dying around her, and then as he himself died along with them, he thought he heard the whispers and sighs of all the ghosts and spirits of all the people who had died as they had fled from all the dying bodies and—

And then everything was silent and he could hear and feel nothing. And then, suddenly, he could feel his heart beating against the palm of his hand again and then there was a pounding in his ears, its pulse, and then, as he drifted away again, the pounding faded, and then, as something over his head smashed to pieces in the bank, he heard sounds so loud his ears rang with them.

And then he drifted away again and was somewhere dark and silent and sightless with only the sounds of the whispers and sighs of death around him, and he heard the faint tinkling sound of something like crystal breaking, or glass, and he thought it was the tinkling of the chain the dead pudgy twenty-year-old girl had worn around her neck, making the sound as she moved her head in a mirror to admire it and made her hair swirl, and he thought he heard—

As he drifted, he heard the voices of Tolliver and Shoemaker and the voices of the dead he had never heard in life, but the voices were all without meaning or sequence, voices and sounds without meaning. They were the voices and sounds happening in a dream—inconsequential, disembodied, without time or reference or space or reason, the voices of the dead.

They were the voices of George Shoemaker shouting, shrieking as he hit at the man on his knees in the laboratory on Aberdeen Road over and over and Tolliver's voice—not there in the scene with Shoemaker, but somewhere else—lost and hopeless and confused as the man shambled like a guide through the dusty rooms of his failed life and talked about what he had once been. And then there was a voice that sounded like Winter's voice, a voice drifting back from a black-garbed figure at the door to where Tolliver and Shoemaker were screaming back to the commander in the corridor to give him the order to go in and kill.

And then all the voices were gone and all Feiffer could hear was the sound of his heart beating against the palms of his hands and he could not understand why, shot through, it had not stopped and he was dead.

There was a terrible crash from somewhere above him, and then everywhere glass fell down around him, and he could not understand why all the voices and sounds kept coming to him in a dream and he could not force himself to awake from the dream and hear what they were saying.

He heard, as his mind kept losing the will and power to comprehend it, Mansor's voice, but he did not know what the voice said and he could not understand where Mansor was or why or when or to whom he even said it.

"*Item*—" He thought he heard it from a long way off in the past and, then, in the same instant so close it could only be the present. "*Item*—" He heard him listing something, doing something. "*Item*—" but he could not comprehend what it meant.

"*Item*—"

He could not understand why his body screamed at him in pain, and then ebbed away. He could not understand what had happened or why it had happened, and he got his hand flat under his heart and felt for the wound to count the moments he had left to endure before all the voices came for him and he could drift away and be with them.

"*Item*—" He heard it just above him. He heard it the way all the people in the bank must have heard it as they died.

He got his hand to his chest to feel the wound, but he could not feel it, and he could not understand why not.

"*Item*—"

He could not understand why all he could feel around where the wound should be was a softness like rotten fruit and the sharpness and jaggedness of dozens of tiny pieces of metal half embedded in the skin and why everything under the shattered and splintered bones in his chest was not shot through and bleeding his life away in heartbeats, and he could not understand what had happened or why the bullet was not burning hot inside him, and he could not—

He was caught at the edges of a dream, unable to force himself to wake from it, and as his mind tried to reach for the answer he heard all the voices come back and echo and re-echo in the dream.

He heard Mansor's voice from what seemed like an age ago, talking to him with a helpful tone in his voice in the vault, listing off to him that day all the things that were in the vault.

He heard him say in his helpful voice, glancing down at the piece of paper where he had written it on down, "One British Webley and Scott, Mark Four, .38–caliber six-shot revolver . . ." and then his mind could not cope with the pain and ebbed away and then, suddenly, came back with a start of alarm— ". . . with a three-inch barrel. Serial number . . ." and then he drifted away again and in his dreaming could not hear all the numbers that made up the number— ". . . loaded with six rounds . . . the weapon itself . . . the ammunition, although I did not attempt to unload it, old and heavily corroded and . . ."

And in that instant as his mind found something in the dream to save itself, the dream broke and he was out of it.

It was the bank's gun!

The gun Mansor had used to shoot him was the bank's gun! It was a weapon that had probably first seen life in the 1920s or 1930s almost eighty years ago and since then, like bank revolvers everywhere, lain untouched and passed on from one bank or commercial establishment to another without ever having once been used or looked at or cleaned or reloaded or—

And the jagged fragments of metal under his skin were the bullet! It was so old and corroded and frangible that when it had hit him it had instantly blown apart, and after it had hit the hard bones of his sternum and smashed them to splinters, the bullet had broken up into gravel and lodged in the skin like shotgun pellets!

And penetrated to his heart not at all.

And he was alive.

And he would not die there as all the other people in the bank had died there. And as all the voices fled and he heard everywhere in the bank only the sound of Mansor, he was out of the dream and—no longer one of the dead or dying— pressed his hand down hard against his chest and, one careful, agonizing inch at a time, began to crawl.

Once before, when Mansor had been present, people had crawled across the floor of that bank.

They had crawled away from him to die.

This time, however, as the man, with his back to him, knelt down carefully just inside the open door of the bank to call again to the guard to bring him in to die, Feiffer crawled, one terrible, painful inch at a time, towards him, to kill.

He had done everything required for success. Item *(1) Create appropriate scene to confirm all aspects of story* was complete, and, kneeling down a little inside the open door, he raised Feiffer's gun to check the line of fire to take the guard out with a single heart shot the moment he appeared there and complete the action required on Item *(2).*

Item:

(2) Action required: lure guard into bank on pretext of need for immediate medical assistance.

And dispose of with Feiffer's gun.

Mansor shrieked at the top of his voice in a tone he had practiced over and over in his head until he thought he had it right, *"For God's sake help me!* I'm bleeding to death! For God's sake, if you're there— *For God's sake, I need help now!"*

He listened hard. By now, the man would have called the police and moved beyond his initial decision to remain safe where he was on the ground floor to let them in, worked through the next question of whether it would look bad for him in the eyes of his employers if that was all he did, and, finally, nervously come to the conclusion that he should at least try to give the impression of doing his duty and come up the first flight of steps on the escalator to the second floor.

There, halfway up the flight, he would have thought, not of his employers, but of his family. And stopped, and then needed to know, before he proceeded, he was safe. And waited. And listened.

He thought people so pathetically predictable. Mansor shrieked, *"He's dead! Oh, God, I had to shoot him and he's dead!"*

He knew how, at that moment, the guard would stiffen and see suddenly how he could be a hero with no risk. He knew it with no doubt in his mind about it at all because, living among them, copying them, mimicking their every smallest expression and gesture and thought pattern to pass himself off as one of them, he knew how other people behaved.

He waited.

He knew just how long to wait.

He waited, exactly—counting it out in beats—eight seconds.

It was enough, exactly right—he knew it was.

Mansor, with his voice desperate and pathetic and alone, shouted, "Oh, *please!* Oh, *please!* Don't let me die here alone! Oh, please—*isn't there anyone out there to help me?*"

He had moved such a little way, and the pain from the shattered bones in his chest was so intense it made him gasp, and he thought for a moment as he felt himself go limp that he was going to pass out again.

But he did not pass out. With an effort of will that made his chest burn as if it were on fire, he got both his hands out from under his body and, reaching out with them, dug them hard into the carpet pile like a climber ascending a vertical mountain face and dragged himself forward another inch.

There were shards and splinters of broken and powdered glass everywhere under him, and as he hauled himself across them they cut into his chest and hips and legs, and as he made another single foot's distance, and then another and another, he left a bloody trail behind him like the track of a snail.

He had no weapon, nothing. He got his hands out in front of him and grasped at something hard on the carpet—a huge shard of shattered razor-sharp glass from one of the cages—and, using it as purchase, pulled himself forward another inch.

The glass was a perfect triangle, blasted out from the bottom of one of the cages, two feet long from base to tip, with the back edge still thick and blunt with putty, and, pulling it towards him, trying to focus on it as his eyes blurred out with the sudden pain in his chest from the movement, Feiffer got it under his chest like a fracture board and, reaching out, using the glass like a sled to cushion him as he went, got another single six inches forward.

*   *   *

From somewhere out on the gallery of the third floor, the
security guard yelled in English with his voice full of terror
and trepidation, "I'm not armed! I haven't got a gun! The police are on the way! I'm not *armed!*"

He was at the top third-floor step of the escalators—exactly where by now Mansor had calculated he would be.

Kneeling a little back from the open door with Feiffer's
gun out and ready in his hands, Mansor waited.

He counted the beats.

His plan was so perfect he thought he could almost hear
the man hesitating on the escalator stop breathing and clench
his fists to give himself courage.

He could almost hear his heart pounding in terror as he
took first one careful step out onto the gallery and then, un-
sure, trembling with fear, step back again.

He waited for what the guard would say next.

The guard, all his courage gone as quickly as it had come,
shrieked, "It's not my job to be up here! I'm the guard from
the first floor! I've called the police! I'm not even armed!
I'm just—"

He was what normal people probably thought of as a good
man, full of deep conscience and the even deeper stupidity
that attended it.

The guard shrieked, "Are you there? *Who are you?*"

Waiting a little back from the door, Mansor looked down
carefully at Feiffer's gun. The bullets in the cylinder looked
longer than the ones in the bank's Webley and he turned the
weapon over and read the manufacturer's die-stamping line
on the barrel.

The stamp read, COLT COBRA. .38 SPECIAL CTG., and although he was not sure, he thought when he had fired the
single shot into the lower bicep of his arm the report had
been a lot louder than the shot from the Webley he had used
to kill Feiffer.

The guard, on the point of fleeing, yelled desperately,
"Hello! *Are you still there?*"

There was no requirement at this point for a response, and,
kneeling back from the open doorway with still a few moments to wait, Mansor looked down again at the gun. When

the police came the last thing he needed was to have his ears ringing with the blast. Nodding to himself, he put the gun gently onto the floor for a moment and reached into his inside coat pocket for his calculator, flicked its leather case open, and took out the single neatly folded Kleenex tissue he always kept there to wipe the screen face and tore it carefully in two.

Hesitating at the very top of the escalator, the guard took a single wary step out onto the floor of the gallery and looked in the direction of the bank.

It was time. Mansor yelled at the top of his voice in extremis, *"Help! Help me! In the name of mercy, for pity's sake, please—! Please! Please! Please help me now!"*

Wadding the two pieces of Kleenex carefully into balls, he placed first one, then the other deep into his ears to protect them from the blast, then put his calculator back carefully into his pocket and, touching only once more at the wads to make sure they were secure and deep, took up the Colt in both hands and, ready, counting the beats, waited for the guard to come.

"I'm coming! Hold on! I'm coming now!"

It was the voice of the guard who had let him in the front door of the mall, a man he had not even looked at for more than an instant, a stranger. And in that moment as Feiffer, still twenty feet from the kneeling man at the door, got to his feet with every muscle and nerve ending in his body shrieking at him in protest, it came to him that he had never realized before how much people like the guard and all the dead people in the bank and Tolliver and Shoemaker meant to him.

Staggering, covering one single faltering step at a time, holding the blade of the glass hard in his hands as he went, his mind drifting back, it came to him that he had never realized before how much people meant to him and how he heard their voices and loved them and was amazed by them.

He had never realized how important each of them was in their own way, and unique, and valuable.

He had never realized before how irreplaceable each one of them was to him.

His mind was drifting, and as he fought to make his body go forward towards Mansor at the door, he heard all their voices as if they still lived. He heard the wonderful laughter of a pudgy, unattractive girl as she swirled her hair and thought with her new elephant-charm chain around her neck somehow she was pretty and slim and fresh.

He took a single step towards Mansor's back and heard, as if it emanated from him, the sound of the girl as she choked and burned and suffocated. He heard the sound as she died and was still. He heard the whirr of Macarthur's cranium saw as in the awful, dank, windowless Morgue, he took the top of her head off on the steel tray and matted all her hair with blood.

He heard them. He heard all the sounds at once.

He took another single faltering step forward towards Mansor and, with his eyes fixed on the man's back as he waited to kill again, it came to him that he had never realized how deeply and completely he was capable of hating.

From somewhere so close, the guard, full of good works and bravery and confidence, yelled, "*Hold on! Hold on!*"

He was almost there. The guard, running hard down the gallery to help, yelled to spur himself on, "*I'm coming! I'm coming!*"

He said nothing. He merely waited. With the wads of paper jammed deep in his ears to protect them from the sound of the shot, Mansor, counting the beats, raised the gun.

In the bank, in the place of all the dead, Feiffer took a single final step and he was behind Mansor, looming over him with the huge shard of glass held tightly in both hands against his knees like the blade of a shovel.

He heard the guard coming. The shard of glass was heavy, and as Feiffer raised it up, it glittered in the overhead ceiling lights like a guillotine.

Mansor called out for the final time to the guard, "Yes! *Help!*" and then in that instant Mansor turned and saw Feiffer's face and what was on it and as the guard reached the open door of the bank and screamed in horror at what he saw in there, Feiffer, saying nothing—having nothing to say to a man like that—drove the blade down into Mansor's neck and throat and, in a fountain of blood the guard would see in his nightmares for the rest of his life, killed the man with a single stroke that almost severed his neck from his shoulders, not like a man at all, but like a rabid dog, like vermin.

20.

Soon the Communists would come. A little at a time, piece by piece, Hong Kong was becoming a dying city, fading in light and brightness like a house bereft of occupants, sinking a little more each day back into its foundations and the soft, dark earth under those foundations.

There, in the dark, soft earth, there lived other forms of life not seen before, other forms that did not live in daylight or in the sounds and movement of life and families and brightness.

One by one, alien forms of existence, slowly and hesitantly at first, not only there in that city, but everywhere there was decay and loss and hopelessness of purpose, one by one, growing in number each day, they began to surface . . .